LIES
AND
DECEPTION

LIES
AND
DECEPTION

a reggie da costa mystery

laraine
stephens

First edition

ISBN: 978-1-68512-672-8

Cover art by Level Best Designs

This book was professionally typeset on Reedsy.
Find out more at reedsy.com

For my darling Bob

Praise for Lies and Deception

"Snake oil cures, confidence men, fortune telling and murder! Laraine Stephens is in fine form with her fourth novel about 1920s Melbourne crime reporter Reggie da Costa, *Lies and Deception*. Set in a well imagined historical Melbourne, *Lies and Deception* is a fast moving and highly entertaining mystery that contains just the right amount of fascinating side detail. Full of twists and surprises, it is a very engaging read that will appeal to fans of Kerry Greenwood's Phryne Fisher novels."—Jeff Popple, murdermayhemandlongdogs.com

"A fascinating journey into 1925 Melbourne, Australia, packed with snake oil remedies, con men and women, a tarot card reader and a cryptic clue left at two murder scenes! A real who-dunnit solved by suave investigative crime reporter Reggie da Costa. I confess I couldn't identify the killer...a real feat!"—Susan Waller Lehmann (true crime author, criminal defense investigator)

"I enjoyed the period flavor Stephens brings to *Lies and Deception*, her protagonist's attention to 1920's style, and other historic touches that drew me into one of my favorite eras. The clever plot and interesting characters make *Lies and Deception* an engaging read from beginning to end."—Skye Alexander, author of the Lizzie Crane Roaring Twenties mystery series

"Set in Melbourne in 1925, *Lies and Deception* offers an engaging glimpse into the racy world of crime reporter Reggie da Costa. This fast-paced and entertaining mystery will appeal to fans of Phryne Fisher as it paints a vivid picture of Melbourne and Sydney in the Jazz Age. We look forward to further adventures with the dashing Reggie da Costa."—Carol Bruce, author of the Gwen Armstrong Mysteries

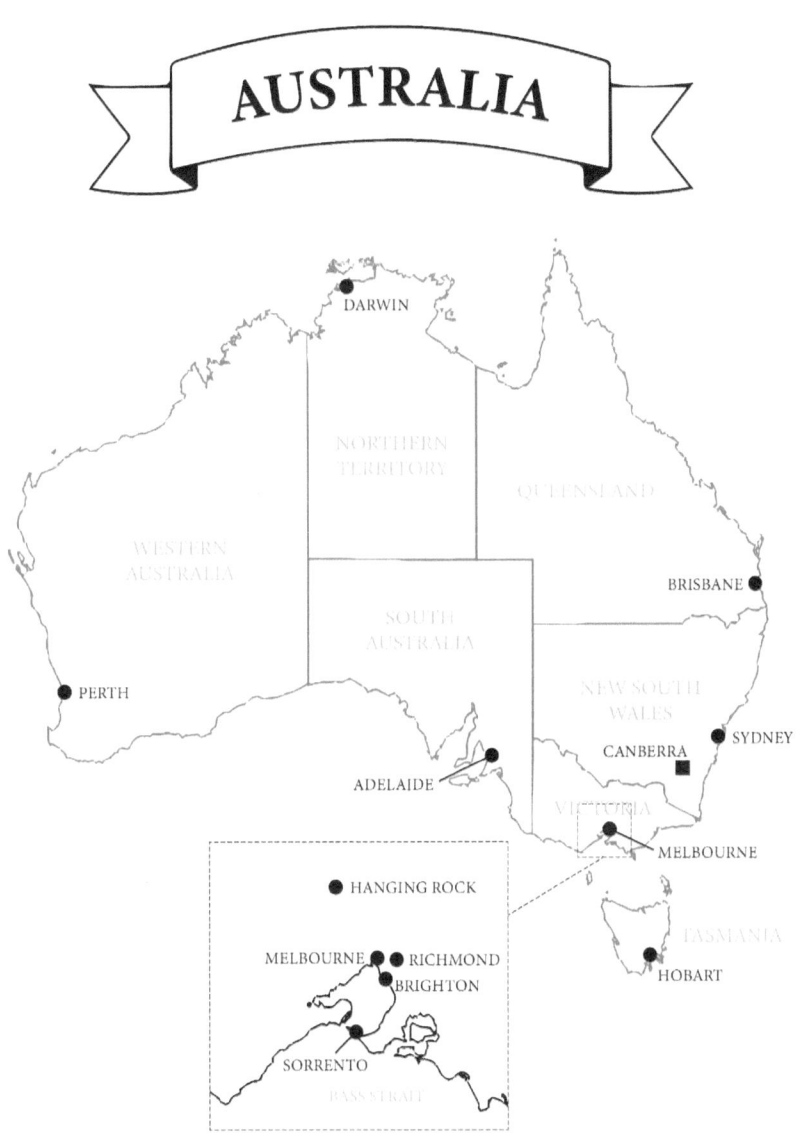

AUSTRALIA

DARWIN

NORTHERN TERRITORY

QUEENSLAND

WESTERN AUSTRALIA

SOUTH AUSTRALIA

PERTH

BRISBANE

NEW SOUTH WALES

SYDNEY

CANBERRA

ADELAIDE

VICTORIA

MELBOURNE

HANGING ROCK

TASMANIA

MELBOURNE RICHMOND

BRIGHTON

HOBART

SORRENTO

BASS STRAIT

July 1925

Off busy Bourke Street, a chill breeze wafted through the once-thriving Eastern Arcade. The residue of years of neglect cast a dusty shroud over the walkway, with refuse and uncollected mail piled up against shuttered shopfronts and 'to rent' signs lying forlorn and forgotten on the ground. A few resilient shopkeepers soldiered on, scraping a living, but they had departed for the day, heading out into the drizzle of a wintry Melbourne evening.

However, there was one who still remained. Behind the façade of shop number 6, with its heavy red door and curtained windows, lived Madame Esmeralda, fortune-teller and tarot card reader. Her exotic costume–golden earrings, a bright scarf tied around her dyed red hair, a billowing skirt and blouse in purples and reds, and garish makeup–belied her mood as she sat in silence, troubled and despondent. Now that her customers had gone for the day, it was she who needed answers, which only the Tarot could provide.

Heavy velvet curtains cloaked the windows, cutting out the light from the deserted arcade. A single candle flickered and smouldered, its feeble flame playing with the shadows that engulfed the room. Madame Esmeralda placed her hands on the edge of the table, her mind absorbing the darkness. It was time.

She reached for the pack of cards. After shuffling them, she cut them twice. Slowly, she dealt herself a hand, face down, in the shape of a horseshoe. Seven cards in all. The first three represented the past, present, and future, respectively. The next three would offer advice, suggest influences in her life, and obstacles to overcome in making her decisions. The final card would foresee the way forward.

Inwardly, she felt apprehensive as she considered what their message might be, in contrast to the sense of happy anticipation that she had experienced in the past when she had consulted the Tarot about the route that she should take in her life. This time was different. This time, there was a growing sense of bitterness and regret. But the reading could not be delayed any longer. She had to know.

Madame Esmeralda bent her head and deliberated, drawing on past experience and practice. The first question came easily.

'What should I take from my past life?'

She turned over the first card. It was The Moon. Such a strange card, difficult to interpret, she thought. Between two towers ran a river, overlooked by a full moon, a crescent within. In the foreground a lobster emerged from the sea, while on each side of the river two dogs howled, one wild, the other domesticated.

'The moon,' she whispered, 'is shadowy and mysterious. It is at the heart of both myth and magic. It is not rational; it is one of life's mysteries.' She paused; her face was sad. 'There is so much that has made me uncertain, that has confused me. And The Moon tells me that I must acknowledge that.'

She spoke haltingly. 'What challenges do I face now?'

The next card, the Two of Cups, represented the present. Two figures faced each other, holding cups, between which was drawn a figure eight of serpents. The card's position was reversed, facing away from her, meaning that the traditional interpretation, of the union of like-minded souls, did not apply. Madame Esmeralda shook her head in despair and understood. Her relationship with her lover was no longer a meeting of two minds, as it had been in the beginning. She was the needy one now, craving Jasper's affirmation and affection: a gentle touch, the brush of his lips, his gaze resting on her. But he had grown tired of her. She could see it in his face, hear it in the tone of his voice. That other woman occupied his thoughts. The letter proved it. The letter he had not wanted her to see.

She closed her eyes. 'What will be the consequences for me?'

Her eyes flicked open as she turned over the third card. It was the Wheel of Fortune, surrounded by a winged lion, an angel, an eagle, and a winged ox.

As with the second one, the card was reversed, facing away from her. The meaning was clear. After all the sacrifices she had made in following Jasper, she was being sent back to the beginning to start again. Alone, without him. Tears filled her eyes, angry tears. He had betrayed her, and she was the one who would pay the price.

The next three cards confirmed her reading. The Three of Swords depicted a red heart pierced by three swords, suspended in a stormy sky lit by flashes of lightning. An emotional rift was inevitable, it seemed. The fifth card, the Two of Wands, urged her to overcome her doubts and take action, but what that entailed eluded her. She felt helpless, unsure of herself, with no sense of what she would do.

She turned over the sixth card. Her eyes fixed on the Grim Reaper, clad in armour, riding a pale horse and bearing a scythe, a fiendish grin emanating from the skull beneath the helmet. Death stared her in the face: the death of the life she was living now.

Madame Esmeralda took a deep breath. The last card lay waiting, the one that would define her future. A deep sense of apprehension filled her.

'How do I make a new life for myself without him?'

She turned the final tarot card face up. The flame of the candle grew bright, almost blinding, picking out every aspect of the image. It was the Ten of Swords. A body lay face down with ten gleaming silver swords protruding from its back. She blinked; put her hand to her mouth; shook her head in despair. The Tarot had spoken. Treachery. Betrayal by the one she trusted and loved the most.

She snuffed out the flame and, in the darkness, a vision arose: of Jasper Howard, her lover, dead, with ten silver knives piercing his body.

Chapter One

Reggie da Costa was staring idly into space, twirling a pencil in his fingers. He was sitting at his desk on the second floor of the new offices of Melbourne's premier newspaper, *The Argus*, surrounded by the buzz of voices and the clatter of typewriters. Crime in Melbourne had plateaued, and that was bad news for a senior crime reporter. The other bad news was that Floyd Kramer, his sub-editor and immediate boss, was off sick, and had been replaced temporarily by Curtis Flange, who was editor of the social pages. How could a gossip columnist be put in charge of crime? And how could the powers that be have overlooked the experience and skills of the one and only Reggie da Costa?

He shifted in his chair, aware that the trousers of his new suit were a trifle tight around the waistline. More bad news. He shook his head, unable to decide which was the worst problem he was facing: another visit to the tailor, Curtis Flange's interference, or a lack of crime.

He sighed and turned his focus back to the story he was researching: patent medicines and the 'quacks' who sold them to unsuspecting victims. It was Ruby, his lady friend, who had supplied the impetus for the story. She had told him that one of the typists at work had been using a herbal remedy to help with her digestion. Within a week, she was admitted to hospital, badly dehydrated. It had been touch-and-go, but she had recovered.

'Why would she try something like that?' Ruby had asked him at the time.

'Because they don't trust doctors and can't afford the time and money to visit them,' he explained. 'It's easier to buy patent medicines from a grocer or a travelling salesman.'

'Can't someone do anything about it?'

'The government's planning to regulate the trade from the start of next year. Legislation has been passed, forcing the producers to list the ingredients on the label. But the makers of 'quack' cures are fighting back.'

It was likely that the tactics they'd used to discredit the law would be dirty, Reggie thought as he turned over the pages of his notes. They'd not give in without a fight. They had too much to lose. He heard footsteps and looked up. Dusty Rhodes, his assistant, sank into the chair in front of Reggie's desk.

'What are you working on? Still quack medicines?' he asked, stretching his legs out and running his fingers through his uncombed thatch of fair hair.

Reggie took a pile of newspaper clippings from an envelope and spread them across his desk.

'Look at these, Dusty. You'd never believe that people could be so gullible. Advertisements for "tried and true" remedies and secret formulas, claiming to cure everything from cancer to varicose veins, all approved by so-called eminent physicians and world-renowned scientists.'

Dusty picked up an advertisement for Lane's Emulsion. 'Two shillings and sixpence a bottle. It claims to cure coughs, colds, whooping cough, bronchitis, asthma, and bleeding.' He shook his head in disbelief, then examined another. 'Mother Seigel's Syrup. This one aids digestion by stimulating the liver and the bowels.'

'Don't forget Dr Williams' Pink Pills for Pale People,' said Reggie. 'You see them in every shop.' He read from the newspaper advertisement. '"Cures St Vitus' Dance, rheumatism, heart palpitations, pale and sallow complexions, and all forms of weakness in males or females."'

Dusty laughed. He studied the advertisement for a scientific vibrator. 'This one's recommended by 6,000 doctors! How's that? It says that it restores lost Nerve Force, whatever that is. It revives the healthy function of nerves, kidneys, stomach, liver, intestines, and heart by creating a continuous stream of 20,000 vibrations a minute, without using electricity.'

He guffawed, drawing raised eyebrows from the other reporters in the newsroom. Undeterred, he exclaimed, 'Goodness me! Is there anything it can't cure? What's your angle, boss? Find some patients who haven't experienced a miraculous cure?'

'That's one possibility. But I intend to show that these claims aren't backed by science. I've bought some pills and tonics and sent them off to a laboratory. Not at my expense, of course, but *The Argus*'s. They'll be analysed and once I know what's in them, I'll be writing up a report on the sham that is patent medicines. Some of them contain alcohol, morphine, opium, and cocaine.'

'It's a shame you're not with *The Truth*, Reggie,' said Dusty, grinning. He made a gesture with his hands, as if picturing it. 'I can see the headline now: "Quacks and quackery. Devious dodgy doctor's diagnosis. Parlour parties for pill-popping."'

Reggie chuckled and smoothed his thin 'Ronald Colman' moustache. 'I hope that you're not finding it too hard an adjustment, now that you're with *The Argus* and not *The Truth*. It's a different newspaper altogether, as you now know. No wild assertions. Only well-researched stories.'

'I'm learning so much,' said Dusty, his face growing unusually serious. 'You've helped me immeasurably.'

'I'm glad of that. But I confess that I could do with a dash of those *Truth* headlines right now. What I wouldn't give for a murder or an armed robbery. That would really brighten up my day.'

He gathered the advertisements together and filed them back in the folder, then leaned forward and looked at Dusty intently. 'I hope that you're keeping your ear to the ground for a good story. Your series on political corruption was a great start, but you can't afford to rest on your laurels. Crime stories don't land in your lap. Spend as much time as you can out of the office; mix with the riff-raff and your sources from the Coroner's Office, the police, the legal system, and politics.'

Dusty did a mock salute. 'Good advice, boss. I've been doing just that, and I think I might be onto something interesting.'

'Which is?'

'Another angle to your story about swindlers and tricksters. You're looking at the patent medicine trade and what's really in those bottles. It made me think about the people behind them. The people with aliases. The people who forge documents claiming to be someone they're not. I reckon that between the two of us, we could shine a light on confidence men.'

Reggie nodded his head. 'That certainly has potential. It would make for a great series of articles rather than one. Innocent people deceived. You're right, Dusty. Two heads are better than one, and we could cover twice the ground in our research. Tell me more.'

Dusty flushed and ran his hand through his unruly mop of hair. 'I haven't got much further than that.'

Reggie leaned back and propped his feet up on the edge of his desk, taking a moment to admire his new highly polished cream and olive-green shoes. 'You're too young to remember him, but there was a case before the war. Charles Edward Chadwick, his name was. One of many aliases. He was born in Redfern, New South Wales, and was arrested in countries all over the world. Chadwick posed as a doctor and a parson, swindled banks, and was a bigamist many times over. He had a big reputation with the ladies. He even defrauded the Queensland Government of nearly two thousand pounds. Then he headed to Canada, where he posed as a minister of religion. He was preaching at a church in Toronto when the authorities caught up with him, but he escaped arrest by the skin of his teeth. They called him a super-confidence man.'

'And you want me to write about him?'

'No, Dusty. He's past history. But I reckon there are confidence men running around Melbourne, like Charles Chadwick, changing their identities and swindling gullible investors.

'Get out in the streets. Listen at doorways. Talk to your snitches. If you can uncover just one of these blokes, it will really excite our readers. Go to work.'

Dusty picked up a battered hat from a hook on the wall. 'Thanks, Reggie. I'll get onto it.'

Reggie smiled. His protégé was coming along nicely. If only he'd dress better! There had been a brief moment in time when he had improved his appearance, but that seemed, regrettably, to have been a passing phase.

He took his pencil and doodled the initials 'RR.' Six months had passed since he had first laid eyes on Ruby Rhodes, Dusty's sister. His relationship with her had begun when she asked him for assistance in tracking down the killer of her identical twin sister. At first, she had struck him as conventional and reserved, her beauty hidden beneath an unflattering selection of clothing but, as time went on, Reggie was surprised to discover that he liked her, really liked her, despite her being neither wealthy nor socially connected. And he had decided that the time had come to introduce her to his mother, even though he knew that Mavis would not find her acceptable due to her lack of social status. In all likelihood, dinner with his mother and Ruby would not end well: the equivalent of pairing his new green shoes with a blue check suit.

Chapter Two

Doctor Hiram T Wishbone leaned against the railing of the P&O liner, *Chitral*, as it docked at Prince's Pier, Port Melbourne. It was early, seven o'clock in the morning, but the wharf was a hive of activity as the mooring lines were attached, and porters and dock workers waited below, ready to unload the ship and transfer cargo and luggage to the terminal. Most of the passengers had come up from their cabins, excited and eager to get their feet on dry land again, after the voyage from Plymouth.

Tall and angular, with steel framed glasses and an impressive pair of voluminous sideburns set off by a pointed goatee beard, Hiram T Wishbone looked every inch the Southern gentleman, even though he'd been born in New York City. His white linen frock coat and trousers, wing collar and black ribbon tie, and exaggerated South Carolina accent gave him a certain stature and distinction, he believed, particularly when he travelled abroad. Whether he was a qualified medical man was a mystery that only he knew, but he certainly made an impression on the impressionable.

Despite minor hiccoughs in his early career, one of which was a short stay in Sing Sing prison, he still regarded himself as the best in the business: the business of separating fools from their hard-earned cash. Fortuitously, whilst incarcerated, he had made the acquaintance of another inmate, William McCloundy, also known as 'I.O.U. O'Brien,' who was serving over two years for selling the Brooklyn Bridge to a tourist. It was a case of the master and the apprentice, McCloundy and Wishbone, respectively, with Hiram acquiring the necessary tricks of the trade to become a consummate and archetypal 'snake oil' salesman.

After his stint in prison, the good doctor met up with a herbalist and developed Dr Wishbone's Liver Pills, a concoction consisting of flowers, roots, and leaves, which was purported to relieve the symptoms of indigestion, depression, and rheumatism. Another of his potions was Dr Wishbone's Restorative Syrup, containing some undisclosed ingredients of a suspect nature, which would supposedly eliminate insomnia and stomach ailments. Advertisements were posted in the newspapers, and a mail-order business thrived. But, the ill-timed death of two of his patients and the unwanted interest of the authorities necessitated a speedy exit from his homeland.

London was a disappointment. The patent medicine trade was well-established there and Dr Wishbone found it hard to find his niche. And there was the unfortunate case of Miss Birdwhistle, who would rather see him in court than provide him with a testimonial. He shook his head as he recalled that particular unfortunate episode.

Miss Beryl Birdwhistle, resident of Walton-on-Thames in Surrey, was a needy woman plagued with insecurities. Dr Hiram T Wishbone regarded her as the snake oil salesman's gift because, not only was she a hypochondriac but, in her view, she was never good enough or pretty enough. However, she did have money, and lots of it, inhabiting a lovely cottage bequeathed to her by her parents. It transpired that the local reverend had come calling, offering more than the weekly sermon at the pulpit, with the result that Miss Birdwhistle was soon to become Mrs Black. With the nuptials fast approaching, she asked the good doctor if he could transform her into a beauty just for one day, or longer, if possible. Wishbone recommended the full treatment: an anti-ageing lotion, which would remove wrinkles and redness and transform the skin. The bride-to-be agreed.

His decision to go ahead with administering the treatment was ill-advised. The cure was in the planning stage and had not been tested, but the promise of fifty pounds up front was enough for him to put aside any misgivings or scruples (if he had any).

The lotion was applied. Immediately, Miss Birdwhistle complained of a burning sensation. Her face started to swell. Before she could view the results, Wishbone slapped sticky plaster all over her face. The next day, the plaster was removed, producing a countenance like a half-roasted beefsteak. A glutinous jelly was then applied, and left to work its magic for five days, whilst the patient stayed on a liquid diet of milk from a feeding cup. The mask was removed, and Dr Wishbone declared that, despite some redness, 'You resemble a young woman of eighteen years, such is the nature of your face. Full, clear, and fat; without a scar, wrinkle, or a blemish.'

Wishbone packed his suitcase, knowing full well that it would end badly. In one fell swoop, greed had put an end to his time in England, a country where he had hoped to put down roots and establish a lucrative market for his products.

Predictably, within days, the blotchiness and discolouration of Miss Birdwhistle's skin had reappeared, the wrinkles in her face resembling a collapsible concertina. The outraged bride and her groom showed little Christian compassion, sending the bailiffs to arrest the charlatan. However, they were too late because, by that stage, Dr Wishbone had boarded the *Chitral*, which was pulling out of Plymouth harbour *en route* to Australia.

A chance meeting, with a fellow travelling salesman, had convinced him that endless possibilities for the sale of his miraculous remedies lay in Australia. A young country offered scope to begin again, without the competition of well-established patent medicines and a plethora of travelling salesmen. And there would be no annoying references to lawsuits, or dead patients, such as he faced back home.

Dr Wishbone couldn't afford another failure. The fact was that he was running out of options, country-wise, taking into consideration those deaths back in Florida and that close call in England, which had cost him his nest egg.

Disembarking in Melbourne, after a productive period of spruiking his products to his fellow passengers and making useful connections onboard, Dr Wishbone found temporary lodgings in a hotel and, next morning, went in search of a pharmacist whose name he had been given. It seemed that this man had a good knowledge of the Australian market and could offer advice as to what patent medicines would be most successful.

In a laneway off Collins Street was a small laboratory hidden discreetly behind a clothing shop. Wishbone knocked and, after introducing himself, was admitted into the premises by the pharmacist, a little man with rheumy eyes and sparrow chest.

Wishbone looked around him and was impressed by the professional set-up of the place. 'Excellent, excellent,' he commented.

On one bench was a mortar and pestle, two sets of scales, a prescription book, and an extensive collection of reference books on diseases and pharmacology, which looked to be well-thumbed. In a cabinet were the ingredients for patent medicines, including small packets of borax, powdered lead, silver nitrate, arsenic, beef extract, cod liver oil, liniment, alcohol, mineral oil, turpentine, camphor, and rattlesnake venom, as well as vegetable leaves and roots, all clearly labelled.

'You come highly recommended, Mr Clegg,' he said in his South Carolina twang. 'I am a native of the United States of America, most recently come from a sales convention in Great Britain, and am planning to expand my markets into Australia. I would greatly appreciate your advice and expertise in my new endeavours.'

The pharmacist took out a large checked handkerchief, using it to muffle a hacking cough.

'I would certainly be willing to help you settle in,' Clegg wheezed. He took a sip of water from a glass on the counter and cleared his throat. 'There's a ready market for pills, tonics, powders, and syrups that can cure a wide range of maladies,' he continued. 'My advice is to diversify. Produce anything from hair tonics to remedies for children's coughs and colds. If your product can cure a wide range of illnesses—insomnia, tuberculosis, cholera, liver disease, stomach ailments, headaches, sciatica, rheumatism, and "women's problems"—you are likely to do well. One product to fix them all. The more maladies, the better.'

The doctor removed his spectacles and cleaned the lens with a pristine, white handkerchief. 'I have some well-established remedies that fit that description. It is, however, a long-held desire of mine to branch out into the field of rejuvenating products.' He placed his glasses back on his nose.

'For those who are seeking the fountain of youth, I assume?' asked Clegg. 'You'll do well in Melbourne, Dr Wishbone. Ladies wanting to recapture their lost youth and beauty. Gentlemen in their twilight years wanting to restore their vitality, if you know what I mean.' He winked lasciviously at his companion. 'You should have little competition.'

Wishbone rubbed his hands together. 'Excellent. And I will need the endorsements of other medical practitioners for these new products.'

'I can help you there. I have numerous testimonials and endorsements available for a small fee. It doesn't matter if these doctors are not identified; it doesn't matter if they even exist! You're a man of the world; you know what we're dealing with here.'

Wishbone nodded his head. 'I can see that we understand each other. I was, indeed, fortunate to be given your name. There is one problem I can foresee. Back in my country, they passed laws regulating patent medicines. What is the situation in Australia?'

The little man scowled and beat his sparrow chest in anger, bringing on another coughing fit. 'There's talk about it, but we're fighting hard against it. Our industry shouldn't be threatened by government intervention.'

'How right you are,' the doctor agreed. 'It's free enterprise and free will. It's not for governments to decide what goes into our remedies. These are trade secrets and traditional recipes developed over the centuries. It's what sets us apart from the rest. Our patients should have the freedom to make a decision as to whether they try them or not, not be dictated to by governments.'

'I agree,' said Clegg.

Wishbone walked over to the cabinet and eyed the bottles and jars of ingredients. 'These are, how shall I say, the traditional components of patent medicines. Do you have others? I think you understand what I mean?' He cocked his head at the pharmacist.

'Of course, Dr Wishbone. Those are kept in a locked cupboard, away from public gaze. One could not make efficacious remedies without them. Unfortunately, there are some who are misinformed or ignorant. They may make incorrect assumptions about their effects. A little bit of alcohol here;

a little bit of cocaine there. Alleviating pain and encouraging good sleeping habits, what's the harm in that?'

'Indeed, you are quite right. Many of us have spent years learning our trade and, by skilful observation, we can make minor adjustments to the remedies we sell, with excellent and far-reaching results. Our patients reap the benefits.'

'I can tell that you are a man of learning. Is there any way that I can be of further assistance, Dr Wishbone?'

The American stroked his goatee and eyed the little man. 'I need someone to compound my remedies. Can you help me?'

'I'm your man. I've been in business now for thirty years. And I have contacts in the trade.' Mr Clegg took out his handkerchief and blew his nose. 'I can organise the design and supply the packaging, if you require it.'

Wishbone smiled approvingly. 'I also wish to expand outside conventional patent medicines. In fact, I'm interested in developing an electrotherapy machine. Have you the name of a manufacturer who might assist me?'

'I know of a small engineering factory in Collingwood not far from here. Mr Higgs will make anything according to your requirements.' He wrote down the name and address on a card and handed it to Dr Wishbone.

'And advertising? What publications are the best in your fair city?'

'The daily Melbourne newspapers. *The Argus. The Age. The Australian Woman's Mirror. The Bulletin.* I can get your products into grocery shops and pharmacies. I have so much experience which I would happily share with you. For a price, of course.'

Wishbone was impressed. 'Of course. Let's get down to business.'

Shortly after, Dr Hiram T Wishbone, a map of Melbourne in his hand, was on a tram heading towards a factory in Collingwood, feeling highly optimistic and satisfied with his move to Melbourne. Once the manufacturing side of his business was agreed upon and he had found permanent lodgings, he would return to Mr Clegg's establishment within the week to organise the production of Dr Wishbone's Restorative Syrup, Dr Wishbone's Liver Pills, Dr Wishbone's Invigorating Tonic, Dr Wishbone's Skin Rejuvenator, Dr

Wishbone's Pills for Feeble People, and his *pièce de résistance*, Dr Wishbone's Elixir of Youth.

Chapter Three

Ruby Rhodes, Reggie's new lady friend, lived in a little weatherboard house in Tanner Street, Richmond, dating from the 1870s. It was painted white, with a pretty front porch trimmed with cast iron lacework. Her home was surrounded by a mix of workers' cottages and brick terraces, with small front yards and corrugated iron roofs. The neighbours' children used the street as a playground, kicking footballs in the winter and playing cricket in the summer, emulating their sporting heroes. In the time that she had lived there, nearly eight months, Ruby had come to appreciate the neighbourhood, despite it being the untimely death of her twin sister, Katherine, that had brought her there.

She remembered her first visit to the house like it was yesterday. Although she had been estranged from her identical twin for ten years, Ruby had inherited most of Katherine's estate: a house, expensive jewellery, and a dazzling collection of the finest fashions that money could buy. And, beneath the floorboards of the spare bedroom was stashed a wad of money, the final clue that Katherine had been engaged in criminal activities. Otherwise, how could Katherine, an administrative assistant at the Melbourne Museum, have been able to afford all this?

With the death of her sister, Ruby's life had been thrown into turmoil. She discovered that Katherine had been leading a double life: museum assistant during the day whilst, at night, she became 'Miss Kitty,' frequenting gambling dens and clubs run by gangsters, such as Horace Striker and Squizzy Taylor.

Faced with her sister's double life, Ruby became convinced that Katherine's death was no accident. Drawing on Reggie's advice and his contacts in the criminal world, Ruby made the decision to impersonate her vibrant, impetuous, and fashionable identical twin, which involved shrugging off her innately reserved and conventional disposition in order to expose a killer. But, in the process of taking on Miss Kitty's persona and infiltrating Melbourne's criminal underworld, Ruby had herself undergone a transformation in personality and was now coming to terms with finding a middle way between the excesses of Katherine and the conservatism of the old Ruby.

Not only had she been successful in discovering her sister's killer, but something equally as significant had happened as she cast off her inhibitions and started to enjoy life: she had come to enjoy the company of *The Argus*'s senior crime reporter and, indeed, had become fond of him. And now, she was to meet his mother that very night.

Ruby checked herself in the mirror. Her dress was of deep blue silk and wool morocain, with three-quarter sleeves and a flounced hemline. She wore a bandeau around her crimped bob of flame-coloured red hair, as well as pearl earrings and necklace. Quite presentable, she thought. But would it be enough to satisfy Reggie's mother?

Mavis da Costa was a handful, according to her son. 'Mother has no judgment, particularly when it comes to men,' he admitted. 'My father left with the maid when I was thirteen. He nearly ruined us. Used up all my mother's money and walked out. You'd think that she'd be more suspicious of men, but she's easily taken in by a handsome face and a persuasive tongue. I don't understand it, Ruby. I just don't.'

Despite the fact that her reputation and financial circumstances were almost destroyed by the actions of Mario, her absent husband, Reggie's mother still tended to view him through the lens of rose-coloured glasses.

But, judging by some of the comments that Reggie had let slip in recent weeks, Mavis da Costa's rose-coloured glasses were a distinct shade of grey when it came to a potential wife for her beloved son. Only a wealthy woman from the upper classes would do, according to Mavis and, on that basis, Ruby ruled herself out of contention. But, given her feelings for Reggie, Ruby was prepared to fight for him despite his mother's objections.

* * *

Mavis da Costa opened the front door and immediately ran her eyes over her son's new lady friend. She was quite pretty really, with her red hair and well-cut dress. But Mavis was well-versed in the drama accompanying the discovery of Katherine Rhodes' killer, and no amount of good taste or good looks could excuse Ruby's connection to a criminal.

'Mother, this is Ruby Rhodes,' said Reggie.

Mavis extended a plump little hand. 'Miss Rhodes.'

'Mrs da Costa. Thank you for inviting me to dinner.' Ruby handed over a small bouquet of roses.

Rather too small, Mavis thought. 'Please come in. We'll have drinks in the parlour.'

She led them into the front room, filled with overstuffed floral armchairs. Once Ruby and Reggie made themselves comfortable on the couch, she offered them sherries, then took a seat opposite the couple. Reggie was looking exceedingly handsome, she thought, in a navy pin-striped three-piece suit, with wide lapels and a gold and red tie. He really was the image of his father. Any woman would want to get her hooks into him, given half a chance. She noticed, with an element of concern, that his hand was straying in the direction of Miss Rhodes. What was it about this woman that had ensnared his attention? She couldn't see it.

Mavis sighed heavily and studied Ruby. 'Tell me about yourself, Miss Rhodes.'

'Please, call me Ruby,' she replied.

'I couldn't possibly. I hardly know you.'

Reggie leaned forward. 'Really, Mother? I've told you all about her.'

Mavis's big blue eyes widened. 'You told me that her sister was a criminal.'

Reggie went pale. 'But Ruby isn't responsible for what her sister did.'

'And this sister was mixed up with gangsters.' Mavis played with the lace collar on her fussy blouse, avoiding her son's gaze.

Ruby looked at her, her expression defiant. 'It's all true. I don't deny it. And it's also true that I pretended to be my sister so that I could find her killer. And I did.'

'That isn't the sort of thing a nice, respectable woman would do, Miss Rhodes. It's not proper.'

'I had Reggie to help me, Mrs da Costa. And I never engaged in any illegal behaviour myself.'

'We only have your word for that.' Mavis noticed the angry look on her son's face and fell silent. She didn't like this woman's attitude at all. Her confidence and assertiveness were unexpected and unwelcome. In Mavis's opinion, a woman should be deferential and obedient, the way she had been with her Mario.

'It's a shame that Reggie's father isn't here to meet you. Mario was so handsome, like his son,' she said, misty-eyed. 'Smouldering eyes, coal black hair, and white teeth. He could make that violin sing. He swept me off my feet, you know.'

'Mother. Really?' said Reggie.

'Where is Mr da Costa?' Ruby asked, narrowing her eyes.

Mavis gestured vaguely. 'Overseas.' She focused on Ruby again. 'Are you related to the Rhodes of Wirra Wirra Station in Western Victoria?'

'You know she's not, Mother,' said Reggie, casting a worried eye in Ruby's direction.

Ruby put down her glass and crossed her arms. 'As a matter of fact, I work as secretary to the managing director at Smith and Sons in Carlton. I have done for a few years now. But I own my own home in Richmond, not far from here, and I have enough to live an independent life.'

'You seem very sure of yourself, Miss Rhodes.'

'I've had to be that way. My mother died when I was young; my father died shortly after. I had to support my younger brother. Life was hard.'

At this, Mavis softened. 'You were left on your own?'

'I was. But I learned to stand on my own two feet, and for that, I have no regrets. I didn't feel so alone when your son came into my life. Reggie was a huge support when I decided to find my sister's killer. He was very brave, and he saved my life.' Her gaze moved to Reggie, who took her hand and squeezed it.

'Reggie is a good boy. He has been a good son to me.'

'Indeed, I'm sure he is and always will be.'

'A mother wants the best for her son.'

Ruby sat, stony-faced.

Reggie stood. 'Time for dinner, Mother? I'll open a bottle of wine.'

'Show Miss Rhodes to the dining room, then help me with the plates, please.'

Shortly after, mother and son faced each other in the kitchen.

'What's this all about?' said Reggie. 'You're determined not to like her, I can see.'

'Do you really think she's suitable, Reggie? She has no connections and no money. She's not in our class.'

'What class would that be, Mother? Before Dad ran off? Before we moved to Richmond?'

'Don't use that tone with me. How do you know that she wasn't mixed up with criminals like her sister was?'

'Don't be ridiculous. Ruby would never do that.'

'You could do much better.'

'Could I? I think that's for me to decide.' He softened and touched her on the arm. 'Try and get to know her. She understands me. We've both had difficult childhoods.'

'You did not,' Mavis retorted.

'But I did. Luckily, most children don't have a father who spends all his wife's money and runs off with the maid. I had to find work at thirteen, because of him.'

'And look at you now. *The Argus*'s senior crime reporter.'

'But with no thanks to Mario da Costa.' He took both her hands and looked her in the eye. 'Be nice to her. I like her.'

Mavis shook her froth of white curls. 'I'm always nice. It's because you mean so much to me that it matters who you bring home. And I want you to be happy.'

Reggie's eyes drifted in the direction of the dining room. 'I am happy.'

'If you think so.'

She put the plates on a tray and returned to the dining room, followed by Reggie, who was carrying the bottle of wine.

Ruby watched as Mavis placed dinner in front of her. 'This looks delicious, Mrs da Costa.'

'Oh, that's so sweet of you, Ruby. And I must say, I love your dress.'

Chapter Four

It was a Monday afternoon in the offices of *The Argus*. Reggie's eyes swept the newsroom. The other reporters were bent over their typewriters, stabbing away at the keys or calling for the office boy to take their stories down to the typesetter or sub-editor. He felt frustrated that a front-page story was eluding him. Surely somewhere there was an armed robbery going on, or a deserted wife had handed her last pound note to a dodgy salesman with a persuasive tongue, or a gang war was erupting on the streets of Collingwood? Where was crime when he wanted it?

Over the years, Detective Sergeant Clary Blain, from the Criminal Investigation Branch, had been Reggie's primary source of information on police matters, apart from a brief period when he'd been demoted for drinking on duty. Disciplinary action had not affected Clary's thirst for good Scotch and, with his return to active duty, he could often be found at the Duke of Wellington Hotel, imbibing at Reggie's expense in exchange for insider intelligence.

Over a glass of whisky the previous week, Clary had supplied him with a snippet of information that could lead to a story.

'Stolen motorcars,' Clary had offered, nodding sagely. He scratched a couple of the errant hairs that still sprouted from his skull, then wiped his bulbous nose with a spotted handkerchief. To an outsider, Clary had the appearance of an over-indulged but affable, distant uncle rather than a detective sergeant in the Victoria Police.

Reggie looked puzzled. 'Tell me more.'

'You've noticed that there are more vehicles on city streets, Reggie? Which means that more motorcars are being stolen by joy-riders and speedsters. They don't leave them intact once they've had their fun. We're fishing them out of creeks and rivers, damaged beyond repair. Or they burn them, and all that's left is a pile of ashes. It's out of control, my friend.'

Clary downed his Scotch in one gulp and waved the glass at the bartender. He pulled out his notebook as he watched the publican place a fresh whisky in front of him.

'Only last week, an average of three cars per day were taken. Three cars!' He referred to his notes. 'A double-seater Dodge, with black-rimmed windscreen, from Flinders Street in the city. Worth £495. A Morris Oxford single-seater, light grey with a black hood, driven away towards Frankston.'

Reggie interrupted him. 'My assistant, Dusty, used to work for *The Truth*. If he were here, listening to this, he'd be thinking up some headlines. Something like: "Joy-riding jaunt by juveniles" or "Let's apply the brakes to car thefts."'

Clary chuckled. 'This is one you won't like. A blue double-seater Hupmobile, stolen from Orlando Street, Hampton. Worth £375.'

Reggie shook his head. 'A Hupmobile? Not the Series R Special Roadster with wire wheels and whitewall tyres?'

The detective smirked. 'It wasn't yours, Reggie.'

'Mine's forest green, not blue.'

'That's true.' Clary paused. 'So, I'm thinking, there must be more to this. What if these thefts were more than random crimes, but the work of an organised gang? What if illegal gambling, sly-grog, and prostitution aren't enough to satisfy them anymore, and they're looking for new sources of wealth?'

'It's an interesting idea. But where does the money-making come in?'

'I haven't got any evidence to prove it yet, but I reckon they're re-birthing them.'

'Re-birthing?'

'That's right. They pick particular models, cut them up and weld them back together again. Or they paint them. Or they change the wheels.'

'So that the owner won't recognise his car?'

'Exactly. And they sell them as if they're brand new.' He checked his watch and frowned, then gulped down the rest of his whisky. 'I've got to go. I'll be in touch if I get any more on this.'

Reggie looked up from his notes and took in the chaos of the newsroom. Bluey Talbot, one of his colleagues, was on the telephone, taking notes as someone fed him information. He winked at Reggie as he caught his eye. A sub-editor was arguing with the reporter who wrote the entertainment column, pointing at the clock and waving his arms around in desperation. Curtis Flange, the gossip columnist and now Reggie's temporary boss, raced past, hurriedly putting on his jacket as he went out of the door. It was all about deadlines and stories and being first on the scene before the opposition got there.

Clary's snippet of information was the beginning of a story, but lacked the impact of a good, old-fashioned murder or armed robbery. Hopefully, he would come back with some information that would flesh out the details and add some drama to what was a fairly pedestrian report: perhaps the police raiding the premises of an illegal automobile re-birthing operation, or charges being laid against a gang leader overseeing the racket, or a little old lady tricked into buying a stolen car only to have it recognised by the original owner, an Anglican minister? At the moment, Clary's information wouldn't make headlines or sell many newspapers, but it could be useful as a filler, in case he needed a couple of paragraphs in his crime column.

He was startled by the arrival of the office boy, who dropped an envelope on his desk. 'Just in, Mr da Costa.'

Filled with expectation, Reggie ripped it open and read: 'Man's body found at The Windsor Hotel, Sunday morning. Stabbed to death. I'll be at The Duke for the next hour.' It was signed 'Blain.'

'You're worth every penny of the whisky I pour down your throat, Clary,' said Reggie, running his fingers through his thick black hair. He reached for his hat and jammed it on his head, then sped down the stairs to the foyer.

* * *

21

Detective Sergeant Clary Blain was leaning up against the bar of the Duke of Wellington Hotel, waiting for the arrival of Reggie da Costa. He was staring longingly at a bottle of Scotch whisky, which was sitting on the glass shelf behind the bartender's right shoulder. He looked towards the door. Where was Reggie? He must have received his note by now. Clary scratched his nose, which was hosting an ever-growing supply of spidery red veins, then hoisted up his trousers, which were in danger of losing traction on his expanding belly.

It was getting on to four o'clock, and the bar was filling up. 'The Duke,' as it was called, was a workingmen's pub, patronised by manual labourers, factory workers, tradesmen, and their apprentices. In keeping with its clientele, the hotel's interior was down at heel, with its well-worn furniture, the familiar smell of grog ingrained into the bare boards, and the slight odour of urine emanating from the toilets.

Clary breathed a sigh of relief as the crime reporter entered the public bar. Reggie was wearing the latest in stylish suits: a jacket with low pockets, wide-rounded lapels over a six-button vest, in brown and beige checked tweed, teamed with a cream homburg. His trousers were cut wide, known popularly as 'Oxford bags' to the fashionable set, but not to the clientele of The Duke. Hobnail boots, rough khaki trousers, and collarless shirts were the preferred mode of dress for the regular drinkers.

Reggie ordered a beer for himself and a whisky for the detective, then made a beeline for Clary. They found a quiet table away from the hubbub of the drinkers. Reggie lit a cigarette and sat back.

'What have you got for me on this murder?'

Clary took a slurp of his Scotch and smacked his lips, then put down the glass. 'Not a lot, unfortunately. Jasper Fitzalan Howard is new to Melbourne. He's only been here for two or three months.'

'Who was he?'

'Not sure. Information is scarce.' He swirled the amber liquid around in the glass. 'We can't find anyone who knew him well. According to the hotel manager, he's related to the Duke of Norfolk. Says he has an estate in England. Planned to invest in a sheep property in rural Victoria. That's really all we know.'

Clary drained the glass and beckoned to the bartender, who supplied him with a refill.

Reggie took out his notebook and a pen, jotting down the details. 'Tell me about the crime scene.'

'No sign of forced entry. We think Howard let the killer into the room. He stabbed him in the back, and then, in the chest. Howard fell back on the bed, and the perpetrator finished him off, going to the trouble of turning him face down. According to the preliminary report, there were ten stab wounds in all. Blood everywhere.'

'You said 'he'? The killer was male?'

'Force of habit, mate. Could be a woman.'

'Must have been a strong woman.'

'The stab wound in the back went deep. It was the fatal blow.'

'Anyone seen leaving The Windsor covered in blood?'

Clary chuckled. 'Now, that would raise some eyebrows. Unfortunately, not, mate.'

Reggie took a drag, then blew a smoke ring into the air. 'The killer came prepared. Must have had a change of clothes. A premeditated crime.'

'You're good, Reggie. You should join the police force.'

'The uniform has no style.'

Clary chuckled. 'But the pay's improved.'

Reggie ignored him. Crime was his bread and butter. And *The Argus*. 'Ten stab wounds. Someone was angry.'

The detective referred to his notebook. 'Long-bladed knife. Serrated edge. Like a kitchen knife.'

'Anything else?'

'Isn't that enough?'

'Suspects?'

'That's where it gets tricky. He mixed with the upper classes while he was in Melbourne.' He rubbed his chin, as if making up his mind. 'No real evidence against anyone in particular.'

'You do have someone in mind. Who is it?' Reggie asked, leaning forward.

Clary lowered his voice. 'Mrs Plumstead.'

Reggie tapped the ash off his cigarette. 'The wife of the Honourable Donald Plumstead? Member of the Legislative Council? Are you sure? There's never been a whiff of scandal around her. How do you know?'

'A letter amongst the deceased's possessions. From her.'

Reggie whistled softly. 'Incriminating?'

Clary nodded. 'She wrote that she'd meet him in his room at five o'clock on Saturday evening.'

'A rendezvous, perhaps?'

'Looks that way, but she's not the sort of sheila that you'd think would go in for that sort of thing. Conservative. Very respectable.'

'Can't say the same for her husband. He likes the ladies. What does she say about it?'

'Nothing, yet. We've said that we intend to interview her tomorrow. Reckon the lawyer will be there, too.'

'That's right,' agreed Reggie. 'Politicians don't like having their wives in court. Not a vote catcher.' He took another puff, then butted out his cigarette. 'You have Mrs Plumstead at the scene of the crime, but with no apparent motive. Howard checked in on his own at The Windsor?'

Clary nodded his head. 'No travelling companion that we know of.'

'A man of mystery.'

'Maybe. Maybe not. I'd like your help on this one. Put out some feelers for me, Reggie. Ask your readers to let the police know if they have any information. Here's a photograph that you can use.' Clary pushed it across the table towards him, then finished his whisky. 'But don't mention any names. We can't afford to get the councillor and his cronies in the Victorian Government upset. It's early days.'

Reggie glanced at the photograph and then tapped his nose. 'No worries, mate. I'll make some enquiries of my own on the sly. I'll keep you posted if I find anything. You can trust me.'

Clary chuckled. 'Keep the whisky flowing, mate, and we'll be right.'

As Reggie put a ten-shilling note on the bar and waited for his change, Clary Blain wandered over and leaned in towards him. 'I meant to tell you.

There was one really strange thing about the body. When we found Jasper Howard, dead on the bed, he was holding one of those big tarot cards.'

Reggie raised an eyebrow. 'Which one?'

'It's called the Ten of Swords. Pretty horrible, it was. A dead body with ten silver swords sticking out of it, like what happened to Jasper Howard. Fair gave me the creeps, it did.'

Chapter Five

That same day, sheltering from the rain beneath her umbrella, Mavis da Costa looked up at the exotic façade of the Eastern Arcade and sighed. Perhaps today, she would find answers to the questions that were troubling her, particularly concerning Reggie's interest in that woman, Ruby Rhodes. Of course, it would never do to tell her son that she was consulting a fortune-teller about his romantic liaisons. He would certainly not approve.

Bourke Street was quieter at the top end; not so many pedestrians and traffic in that part of the city, and that was bothering her, too. You never knew who might be hiding in a doorway, ready to attack, she thought. She held on to her handbag grimly, watching some of the undesirable types who were either entering or leaving the arcade.

It was at one of the afternoon teas hosted by her great friend Mildred Bardsley Smith, that Gladys Onions, a member of the wealthy Onions farming family of the Western District, had waxed lyrical about the amazing abilities of Madame Esmeralda, who had set up shop in the Eastern Arcade. According to Gladys, the fortune-teller, or 'character reader' as she preferred to be known, had shown an uncanny perception of the problems Gladys was facing in her marriage and seemed to have a sixth sense of what lay beyond for her. Mavis's friend had come away mightily impressed.

Spurred on by the memory of Gladys's glowing recommendation, Mavis entered the dilapidated interior of the Eastern Arcade. She looked around her, beleaguered with doubts. This was not the place for a nice middle-class lady to frequent, given its place in Melbourne's criminal history. 'Gun Alley,' the newspapers called it, no doubt because of its sullied reputation after the body of young Alma Tirtschke was found there back in 1921. Her killer, Colin Ross, had been hanged a year later.

Many of its shops were shuttered. The neglected and dirty promenade was almost empty of customers. Mavis walked slowly down the main walkway, occasionally looking up at the glass-paned roof which lit the interior. Passing the premises of J. Meyers Botanic Druggist, a barber shop, and a costume hire business, she finally stopped at a red wooden door, with '6' painted above it. Checking the number on the slip of paper that Gladys had given her, she turned the handle and stepped inside.

Within was a small waiting room, poorly lit by the bare bulb of an overhead light. Three sets of eyes watched her as she took an empty seat next to a small table on which lay some well-thumbed magazines. Mavis averted her gaze at first, until her eyes rested on the door leading to an adjacent room. Nailed to it was a sign: 'Madame Esmeralda. Character reader. Wait until you are called.'

She sighed, trying to collect her thoughts. What should she ask? Whether Reggie would marry this woman, Ruby Rhodes? Whether her husband, Mario, would come back to her? She shifted in her chair and was about to pick up a magazine when the inner door opened, and a well-dressed lady appeared in the gap. She was smiling and nodding her head, as she put a small bottle in her handbag.

'Wonderful, miraculous,' she muttered, her eyes shining. 'I would never have believed it.'

Catching the eye of one of the waiting women, she said, 'Madame Esmeralda will see you now.'

* * *

Forty minutes passed before Mavis was finally invited to enter the inner sanctum. The windows were blanketed with heavy crimson curtains, a couple of armchairs were decorated with tawdry cushions, and an array of cheap ornamental dragons and Indian gods decorated the mantelpiece.

A single candle burned, a feeble light revealing a woman in her thirties, wearing heavy makeup and clothed in oriental dress, a brightly coloured scarf wrapped around her head. She sat at a round table covered with a black velvet cloth, her hands with their red painted fingernails placed flat on the edge. The smell of incense filled the air.

Without saying a word, she motioned to Mavis to sit in the chair opposite.

Moments passed, during which the eyes of the fortune-teller never left Mavis's face, making her extremely nervous. At last, Madame Esmeralda pushed a document across the table towards her.

'Sign this,' she said in a thickly accented guttural voice.

Mavis was nonplussed. 'What is it?'

'It is a formality. You sign to say that you are having a character reading. Nothing else.'

Mavis signed and handed it back to Madame Esmeralda.

'You pay five shillings; we start.'

The money paid, the silence returned as the fortune-teller closed her eyes and reached out across the table. 'Take my hands.'

Mavis removed her gloves. Madame Esmeralda's hands were unexpectedly soft for someone who looked as if she had lived in some backward Eastern European country where people worked on farms and superstitions abounded and people didn't go outside at night, for fear that they might encounter the spirits of the dead.

'We will begin.'

Madame Esmeralda gave a low moan, seeming to come from somewhere deep inside her. She started to twitch, her tics growing in intensity. Mavis was unnerved, glancing around the room, unsure what she should do. Suddenly, the fortune-teller's eyes flicked open, transfixed and glazed. She fell silent. Her shoulders slumped, and her head dropped, as if she had fallen asleep.

But her voice was clear and pure. 'I see a beautiful man in a cloud. It is your father. He has white hair, and he is thinking of you.'

Mavis was shocked. She leaned forward. 'You can see Daddy? Is he alright?'

'He is worried about you. He knows that you are troubled.' She paused and raised her eyes to Mavis's face. 'I see a man with dark hair. He is close to you.'

Mavis's large, innocent eyes opened wide. 'Do you mean Mario or Reggie?'

'He made you unhappy.'

'You must mean Mario,' Mavis insisted. 'My money. He took my money. He went away with a woman. But how do you know this?'

'He is far away now. There is a dark cloud over him.'

Mavis looked bewildered. 'Poor Mario. Will he come back to me?'

'I cannot tell you. It is getting hazy. It is hard to see.' She closed her eyes and dropped her head. Her breathing became laboured. 'I see the number seven.'

'Seven?'

'Or three. Three will be very important to you.'

'Mildred lives at number three. She is a good friend.'

'She looked after you when others neglected you.'

'That is so true. It was terrible after Mario left. If it weren't for Mildred, I'd be all alone.'

'I see the letter "R."'

'Reggie. My son.'

'You are worried about him.'

'You know that?' Mavis shook her head in dismay. 'He's taken up with a young woman. She has no name to speak of. No connections. Her sister was a criminal. Reggie can't see it. He thinks that he likes her.' Mavis gripped Madame Esmeralda's hand. 'What should I do?'

'Your son is clever. Handsome.'

'You're right. You know everything.'

The fortune-teller stared into the candle flame. 'I see a dark time ahead for you. You will be in great danger. A woman will save you, someone you least expect.'

Mavis opened her eyes wide. 'In danger? Me? Which woman?'

'The candle is burning down. Our time together is drawing to a close.' She leaned forward, studying Mavis. 'There is one more thing. I see it in your face. You are tired. All your worries have worn you down. You find it hard to sleep.'

'So tired. So tired,' Mavis said, listlessly.

'I will give you a tonic that will cure your insomnia.'

She reached beneath the table and produced a small bottle filled with dark liquid.

'Take two teaspoons of this each night before you go to bed.' She held out her hand. 'That will be three shillings and sixpence.' Her voice had become business-like, the accent gone.

Mavis took out her purse and counted out the coins. 'I don't know how to thank you.'

'If you need more medicine, contact the doctor. The address is on the back. Tell him Madame Esmeralda sent you.'

She held out a card. On it was written: 'Doctor Hiram T Wishbone. Purveyor of fine tonics, pills, and syrups.'

Chapter Six

There was no time to be lost. Murder waited for no man. Outside the Duke of Wellington Hotel on Flinders Street, Reggie's beloved Hupmobile was waiting, the forest green of its paint dotted with raindrops. He paused briefly to admire its low-slung fashionable chassis, then jumped aboard and started the engine. The automobile roared into life. Reggie slammed it into second gear, released the brake, and planted his foot on the throttle. After executing an audacious U-turn in front of a horse-drawn buggy and three cyclists, the crime reporter headed for Spring Street, home of Melbourne's Hotel Windsor.

It was an incongruous location for a murder, he thought, as he parked his Hupmobile out on the street. The scene of the crime was an imposing Victorian hotel with over three hundred rooms, a grand ballroom, a magnificent, cantilevered staircase, twin cupola-capped towers that offered views all the way to Mount Macedon and the Dandenong Ranges, and a guest list that included royalty.

In a matter of minutes, he was inside the lobby, addressing the clerk at the reception desk.

'Reggie da Costa of *The Argus*,' he said, leaning in towards the young man behind the counter. 'I believe that a crime has been committed here.'

The desk clerk was unimpressed. 'I'm sorry, Mr da Costa, but I'm not at liberty to give out information. Perhaps you might like to talk to the manager? I'll get him, if you wish.'

Reggie watched as the clerk strolled to the other side of the hotel lobby and knocked on a door. No time to lose. He cast his eyes around, saw that the concierge was occupied with a guest, and took his opportunity. He ascended the grand staircase, two steps at a time.

The corridors on the first floor were empty. With hundreds of rooms in the hotel, it would be impossible for Reggie to locate the crime scene without assistance. Fortuitously, as he was about to ascend the staircase to the second floor, a young maid came out of a room, carrying a mop and bucket. She was dressed in a black uniform, with a white apron, starched collar, and cap.

'Excuse me, Miss...' he said, giving the girl the full wattage of his smile.

She looked up, startled. 'I'm Rose. Can I help you, sir?'

'I'm from the Coroner's Office, investigating the murder. Can you direct me to the crime scene, please? I'm running late; otherwise, I'd ask downstairs.'

'Of course, sir. Room 206. I'll take you.'

He followed her up the stairs and along a corridor until they came to a room, the door ajar. Two suitcases had been placed outside.

Reggie nodded at the bags. 'The deceased's possessions?'

'Yes, sir. The bellboy will be up later to take them away.'

'Where to?'

'The coppers said they didn't want them. We should put them out with the rubbish.'

Reggie raised an eyebrow, a glimmer of a smile on his lips.

'Were you on duty when the body was discovered?'

'I was, sir. Me and Molly was doing the rooms yesterday morning. She knocked on Mr Howard's door about eleven o'clock, and there was no answer, so she opened the door and went in. She screamed, and I came running upstairs. Terrible it was.'

'You saw him?'

'I did, sir. Lying on the bed, blood everywhere. Molly's new here, so I told her not to touch anything. I ran downstairs and got Mr Grimes, the concierge. He rang the coppers.'

'What can you tell me about Mr Howard?'

'Spoke really nice. Posh-like. English. Good-looking. Lovely black hair and brown eyes.'

'You fancied him?'

She blushed. 'I'm a maid, sir, but Mr Howard could turn heads.'

'How long has he stayed here?'

'About two months.'

'Did you see anyone suspicious on Saturday?'

'No, sir. I don't do this floor.'

'This man, Mr Howard. Did he check in alone?'

She nodded her head.

'Did he talk to anyone apart from the staff while he was here?'

'I wouldn't know, sir.' She frowned. 'But now that I come to think about it, I saw him talk to the lady in Room 101. They were going down into the lobby. Probably being friendly. But that was the sort of man he was.'

'This lady in 101. Is she still here?'

'No, sir. She left yesterday.'

'And her name?'

'Miss Smith.'

'Anything taken from Mr Howard's room?'

'I did hear that the safe was open.'

'I need to have a look in the dead man's room.'

'Certainly, sir. Is there anything else?'

'No, thank you.' He took out a shilling. 'For your assistance.'

The maid grinned and put the coin in the pocket of her apron. 'Thank you, sir.'

Reggie pushed open the door to Room 206 and stepped inside. The blind was up, but the dreary weather outside allowed little daylight to intrude. Reggie switched on the electric light. The room was spacious and opulent, the decoration in the style of the Edwardian era, with a substantial dressing-table in one corner, a couple of chairs covered in tapestry fabric, and a few potted palms. Above a marble fireplace was hung a large mirror in a gilt frame. An impressive mahogany bed dominated the room, its bedding stripped away, leaving the mattress exposed. A rug, covering dark polished boards, had been rolled up, ready to be removed.

Standing over the bed, Reggie looked down at the mattress. It was soaked in dried blood. The bedding had been bundled up and left next to the rug. His eyes took in the embossed lavender and red floral wallpaper above the headboard. He thought the colour scheme strange until it dawned on him that the red was actually blood splatter from the attack. He shook his head, in no doubt now as to the severity of the assault. Given his long experience as a crime reporter, he knew a crime of passion when he saw one. This one was personal.

Someone had opened the window, a gentle breeze disturbing the lace curtains, but Reggie knew the smell of death would linger. He moved away from the bed and opened the wardrobe. It was empty, as was the chest of drawers, apart from two clean towels, neatly folded on the top. It was clear that the police had searched the room, removing any evidence. Howard's remaining possessions had been removed, presumably packed into the two suitcases outside the door.

Reggie went to the open window and looked out. It was a typical August day, bleak and cold, the leaves swirling like little whirlwinds around Spring Street. In the distance, he could see the spires of St Patrick's Cathedral, whilst, to his left, the grand sandstone colonnaded façade of Australia's parliament house dominated the scene.

He took one last look at the room before scooping up the suitcases. He'd send a note to Clary Blain, letting him know that he had the luggage. It wouldn't do to upset his primary source of information on Melbourne's criminal underworld.

As he placed the cases in the boot of the Hupmobile, he glanced back at the impressive exterior of The Hotel Windsor. It was an incongruous location for a murder. Not the usual seedy laneway, boarding house, drug or gambling den. Not usual, not at all.

* * *

Back in the newsroom, Reggie placed a fresh sheet of paper in his typewriter and began the report that would appear in the next day's *Argus*:

GRUESOME DISCOVERY
BODY FOUND AT THE HOTEL WINDSOR

By REGGIE DA COSTA, Senior Crime Reporter

Since its beginnings in 1887, The Hotel Windsor has welcomed the rich and famous through its doors. It has been the preferred residence for visiting prime ministers, politicians, actors, and performers. Only two years ago, the Grand Hotel, as it was known then, played host to His Royal Highness, The Prince of Wales. In honour of the Royal Family, the hotel was renamed The Windsor.

Today, it is a crime scene, its glorious reputation sullied by the discovery of the body of a man who died in a frenzied knife attack on Saturday. The victim was stabbed ten times and was found dead on his bed by the maid on Sunday morning.

Bizarre touch!

A tarot card, the Ten of Swords, was clutched in the right hand of the corpse, presumably placed there by the perpetrator. The significance of the card is not known, but police are following leads to see if there is a connection between the deceased and fortune-tellers or sideshow folk.

Police have identified the murdered man as Mr Jasper Fitzalan Howard, who was visiting from England. He is believed to be a wealthy landowner, seeking to purchase a property in Victoria's rich farming community, the Western District. Mr Howard is a member of the wealthy Fitzalan Howard family, and is related to the Duke of Norfolk. In his time in Melbourne, he has been seen at many social events, dining and mixing with some of Victoria's best-connected families.

A photograph of the deceased man is printed below. If

you have any information that may assist the police in their investigation, please contact either *The Argus* or Detective Sergeant Blain of the Criminal Investigation Branch.

[The Argus September 1, 1925]*

Reggie re-read the report and placed it in the tray, ready for the office boy to take down to the typesetters. Taking his hat and coat from the stand behind his desk, he strode out of the office feeling refreshed at the thought that crime was once again stalking the streets of Melbourne. What a relief!

Chapter Seven

One week had passed since the body of Jasper Howard had been found. Early enquiries as to his identity had revealed little new information. The police had not been able to find any documents amongst his personal possessions to prove or disprove that Howard was an Englishman. No passport. No letters from home in England.

With this information now in his possession, courtesy of Clary Blain, Reggie dug deeper, intrigued by the mystery of the man who had created such an impression on the well-to-do in Melbourne. Acquaintances confirmed Blain's statement that Howard was in the process of buying a property in the Western District but, when Reggie contacted his colleagues at the rural newspapers, they could find no trace of the man approaching any of the land or stock agents in country Victoria.

The plot thickened when Reggie wired his contacts in London. Not one of the reporters who commented on Vice Regal matters or who wrote for the social pages had any knowledge of a Jasper Fitzalan Howard, cousin of the Duke of Norfolk. He had never attended the round of debutante balls and other society gatherings that consumed the interest of the aristocracy.

It appeared that he was a mystery man, a man whose background could not be authenticated and who had claimed to be involved in property deals that didn't exist. And yet, there was no evidence to suggest that Howard was involved in wrongdoing. Was it all talk on his part, designed to impress?

The first blot on Howard's reputation came a day after the publication of Reggie's report. It was from an unlikely source, an automobile salesman, who had seen the photograph of the murdered man in *The Argus*. His telephone conversation was revealing:

'When I saw that photograph, I was shocked. That bloke in the paper told me that he was Mr Waters, not Mr Howard. He showed me identification, too. He told me that he wanted to take the Buick for a test drive. I thought he was a legitimate buyer. To my never-ending shame, I let him take the motorcar and didn't see it again until the police contacted me. They found it parked in the street outside a greengrocer's shop in a back street of Melbourne. He'd clocked up about four hundred miles in the time he had it. To think I fell for his spiel. Never again.'

The automobile salesman was only the beginning. The floodgates opened. Soon there was a veritable queue of tailors, jewellers, and hat-makers, all waiting for payment for goods received that would never come. And there was also the red-faced admission from the manager of The Hotel Windsor:

'Mr Howard paid for the first two weeks of his accommodation. When that time passed, he told me that he was waiting for money to be wired from his parents in Norfolk. By the end of six weeks, I asked him for payment, and he handed over two hundred pounds with the promise that the balance would be paid by the end of the month. It wasn't only for the room, you know, but also the meals that he had in the dining room and room service as well. French champagne. Laundry. It adds up. The Windsor is very much out of pocket, and we will be forwarding the bill to his parents once the amount has been tallied.'

Reggie decided that it was not his job to tell the manager the bad news, that there didn't appear to be any cashed-up relatives in England who could pay Jasper Howard's bills. He'd leave that unpleasant task to Clary Blain.

'A lady checked out the day Mr Howard's body was found. Did she pay her bill?' asked Reggie.

'Miss Dulcie Smith? She was a nice lady, the sort The Windsor likes to have as a guest. Paid cash, she did. No problems there.'

'Any forwarding address?'

The manager shook his head.

Reggie was disappointed. If there were a link between Mr Howard and Miss Smith there was only a slim chance of finding and interviewing her now.

The questions remained: Who was Jasper Howard? More importantly, who had a grievance against the man, one which would drive them to murder? And a vicious one at that.

Chapter Eight

Despite Clary Blain's best efforts to keep the Plumstead name out of the newspapers, Melbourne society was soon buzzing with the news that a politician's wife had been interviewed by the police. Speculation was rife, but the woman's lawyers resisted any requests from *The Argus* for an interview. However, her friends and associates were not reluctant to discuss the murder of the charming and well-connected English gentleman they knew as Jasper Howard.

Amongst them was Mrs Beatrice Van Cooth, who presented herself at the offices of *The Argus* after being asked for comment by Reggie da Costa. She was shown to a small interview room where the crime reporter was waiting. He shook her hand and beckoned for her to take a seat while he poured them both a cup of tea.

'Thank you for coming, Mrs Van Cooth. If you can help us with any information about Mr Howard, we would be most grateful.'

'When you rang me, I had to come. Simply shocking,' she said, between sips of tea. 'Mr Howard was such a nice man. So polite. A classic English gentleman.'

Reggie looked over the edge of his teacup at the woman's outfit. It was like nothing he had ever seen before. Her dress was an insipid yellow, with a cherry red trim. Its oversized collar almost swallowed her neck whilst the belt strained to encircle her substantial hips. What took his eye most was the sight of her stockings, rolled up below the knee.

Oblivious to his reaction, she smiled and simpered as she spoke. 'Mr Fitzalan Howard has an estate in England, near his cousin, the Duke of

Norfolk. They're the cream of English aristocracy, you know. He told me that he was visiting Melbourne for a couple of months with an eye to buying a property in the Western District. A few thousand acres for grazing sheep.'

'Did he ask you if you were interested in investing in his scheme?'

'He did speak to my husband. Something about wool production, I believe. Mr Van Cooth was not keen.'

'Why was that?'

'James is a cautious man.' She sighed. 'Sometimes too cautious. He likes a "sure thing", rather than promises of future earnings. Sir Ambrose Beauchamp Kiddle and Mr Bentinck Jones, I believe, were prepared to invest in the venture. Whether it will go ahead, now that Mr Howard is dead, is another matter.'

'Mr Howard had a background in sheep farming?'

Mrs Van Cooth nodded. 'He had a large farm in South Africa. A ranch, he called it. Very successful. Such an interesting man, Mr Howard. He had an engineering degree from Oxford, you know. He told James that he spent a good amount of time in the United States, building a dam, or something.'

'What else did he tell you?'

'He'd been part of a syndicate that raised funds to renovate the Theatre Royal, in Drury Lane. He was a supporter of the Arts, you know, and was an actor at some stage. It was a hobby, nothing more.'

Reggie nodded. 'A man of substance and good taste, I take it?'

'Indeed,' she replied. 'Such a loss.' She leaned forward, putting down her cup. 'I've heard that my friend, Mrs Plumstead, has been questioned by the police. Is that true?'

'I couldn't possibly say,' replied Reggie, knowing that anything he did say would immediately embark on a trip around the social grapevine and would find its way back to Clary Blain, who would not be amused. 'Do you think that she might have had something to do with Mr Howard's death?'

'Mrs Plumstead–Peggy–has a spotless reputation. Her husband is a member of the Legislative Council. I'll never hear one word against her.' She paused. 'However–'

'Yes?'

'Her behaviour at the Mayoral Ball was extraordinary, to say the least. Did you go?'

'Alas, no.'

'Such a shame you weren't invited. I met the guest of honour, Admiral Coontz, from the United States fleet. The cream of Melbourne society was there: the Lord and Lady Mayoress of Melbourne, city councillors, representatives of the Australian military, consular officials, State and Federal politicians, dignitaries by the dozen. Mr and Mrs Bentinck Jones, the Beauchamp Kiddles. Extraordinary occasion. And the Exhibition Buildings had been transformed into an exquisitely decorated garden. It was wonderful.'

Mrs Van Cooth was quite carried away. It was up to Reggie to bring her back.

'You were saying about Mrs Plumstead?'

'Oh yes, Peggy.' Her gaze shifted back to Reggie. 'We were chatting to Mr Howard. He was keen to take a day trip outside of Melbourne before he left Australia. I suggested a visit to Hanging Rock. He thought that sounded wonderful. We decided on the following Sunday, and he was going to collect me from my home in Brighton.' Her eyes narrowed. 'But Peggy insisted that she wanted to come, even though she knew that Mr Howard was mine.'

Reggie was perplexed. 'What do you mean by *mine*?'

'He was mine. I'd told her what the fortune-teller said, but she ignored it completely.'

'I don't understand.'

Mrs Van Cooth frowned. 'It was at Mrs Bentinck Jones' soirée a week before. There was a fortune-teller, Madame Something. She was telling fortunes using those big cards.'

'Tarot?' suggested Reggie.

'That's right. She told me that I would meet a tall, dark stranger with an accent. He would make all my dreams come true. And, minutes later, there he was on the other side of the room, being introduced to the hostess herself. Poor Mrs Bentinck Jones was taken ill shortly after. Deathly pale. Terrible. Mr Howard and I were introduced, and I could tell he was the man the fortune-teller was talking about. I told him that I would be at the Mayoral Ball in a week's time, and he said he would make a point of seeing me there.'

'Did that happen?'

'It did. That's when he suggested a day trip, and I mentioned Hanging Rock. But Peggy ruined everything. She said that she'd come, too, even though I told her that I liked him. I mean, the Fitzalan Howards are the cream of English aristocracy, and he was such an attractive man.'

'The three of you went to Hanging Rock?'

'That's right.'

'Tell me about it.'

'We went in his Buick. Brand new it was. A beautiful car. Peggy wanted to sit in the front with Mr Howard, but he insisted that I should be his guest of honour. She had to sit in the back, but that didn't stop her from trying to be the centre of attention. Throughout the drive, she kept up this commentary about the Australian countryside and the birds and animals, as if anyone would be interested in that.

'We arrived at Hanging Rock and went for a stroll. The weather was perfect. Mr Howard was a true gentleman, but you could see that he was getting sick of Peggy. I think she liked the attention, seeing that she lives in her husband's shadow, him being a politician and a member of the Legislative Council.'

'Was there anything that Mr Howard said that you thought was noteworthy?'

She paused, tapping her finger against her cheek. 'I asked him if he had broken any hearts.'

'And how did he react?'

'He said that he had broken up with a woman who took it badly. Such a sensitive man. I wouldn't have expected less.'

She flapped her eyelashes at Reggie. 'Although if I took a lover and then dumped him, I'm sure that he would be suicidal.'

Reggie ignored the innuendo. 'And after your walk, what happened?'

'Mr Howard had brought a picnic lunch, made up by The Hotel Windsor's kitchens. Such elegant and exquisite food. We ate, and then we left. But not before Peggy talked herself into accompanying us on another day trip, this time for lunch at the Hotel Continental in Sorrento. The nerve of the woman!'

'And was it enjoyable?'

Her eyes flashed, and her lip curled in distaste. 'I wouldn't know. I received a telephone call that morning from Jasper, telling me that he was unwell. He'd have to cancel our day out. I told him that we could go the following weekend, but he said that he would be busy packing. I spent the day most upset and finally rang Peggy. She wasn't there. The maid said that she'd gone out with Mr Howard. My friend, my best friend, had deceived me. She wanted Mr Howard for herself.'

'Did you speak to her about it?'

'Why would I bother? It was obvious what she'd done.'

'Do you think she was planning an affair?'

'I never would have thought so six months ago, but you never really know someone, do you.'

'Is her marriage a good one?'

'She's married to the Honourable Donald Plumstead, a member of the Legislative Council. She's done well.'

'That's not what I mean. If Mrs Plumstead did plan to be alone with Mr Howard, doesn't that mean that her marriage was not...ideal?'

Mrs Van Cooth smoothed her dress down over her knees and gave Reggie a knowing look. 'He does spend a lot of time away. On business.'

'Do you believe she was, shall we say, unfaithful?'

The lady was outraged. 'I would never ever spread gossip about one of my closest friends.' She paused. 'However–'

'Yes?'

'Peggy has not been herself lately.'

'In what way?'

'I don't know. Just not herself. Secretive.' She paused, considering her words. 'I heard that there might be a few money troubles, if you know what I mean. That sort of thing can make a woman act out of character.'

'In what regard?'

'I couldn't say. I'm not in that situation, obviously. But I think that the facts speak for themselves.' Mrs Van Cooth shifted in her chair. 'Do the police have any other suspects?'

Reggie shrugged. 'They're carrying out enquiries. Interviewing witnesses. Why do you ask?'

'I don't know. I was interested, that's all.'

Reggie looked at his watch. 'Is there anything else you can tell me?'

'I think I've said it all, don't you?'

'Indeed, I think you have.' He rose and opened the door. They stepped out into the newsroom. 'Thank you so much, Mrs Van Cooth. You've been very helpful,' he said, shaking her hand.

She beamed at him, holding onto his hand for a few seconds longer than necessary, whilst running her eyes over his fashionable chalk-striped tan suit and bold copper-coloured tie. 'Mr da Costa. If there's anything, anything at all that I can help you with, you know where to find me.' She batted her eyelashes at him and smiled coquettishly.

Reggie sighed as he watched her leave. One of his colleagues, Bluey Talbot, nodded his head at her departing figure. 'What did she want?'

'To find out what we had on the Howard murder.' His eyes narrowed. 'I think there's more to Mrs Van Cooth than meets the eye. She's either the consummate performer, or I'm not senior crime reporter for *The Argus*.'

Chapter Nine

Mildred Bardsley Smith was seated in the drawing room of Glenrothes, her home in Grosvenor Street, Brighton, hosting a group of her closest friends, including Mavis da Costa, Reggie's mother. The origins of the group dated from 1916 when the founding member, Mrs Florence Darrow, now deceased, had rallied the ladies of Brighton in response to a newspaper article outlining the problems experienced by soldiers on the Western Front. Heavy November rains had flooded the trenches, resulting in the men suffering from frostbite and trench foot. From that point on, a group of women met in Mrs Darrow's home each week to knit socks, balaclavas, and scarves for the boys at the Front. Nearly ten years later, the group now gathered at the 1890s Italianate Victorian mansion of the Bardsley Smiths, after the demise of the redoubtable Mrs Darrow, with the purpose of assisting in charitable ways those who were facing personal tragedy or financial difficulty.

The hostess pushed a stray lock of wispy white hair back into her chignon and waited for the maid to pour the tea from an ornate silver teapot. A petite woman, Mrs Bardsley Smith was dressed in a gown that could have been worn by the widowed Queen Victoria herself, of thick black satin, her figure defined and restrained by a whale-bone corset. Once the tea was poured and the ladies had helped themselves to the first of two or three cream cakes, Mildred opened the proceedings.

'As we remember so vividly, a parcels van hit a motorcar at the Wickham Road railway crossing back in March, killing eight people. Such a tragedy. Unfortunately, the financial circumstances of the families involved have been severely affected. I suggest that we hold a fund-raising event to help with the educational costs of the orphans.'

'So sad,' agreed Mavis. 'I support it wholeheartedly.'

There was an enthusiastic nodding of heads, and, for the next half hour, there was a subsequent discussion of the venue, the date, and who might be called on to assist.

With plans in place, the formal part of the meeting drew to a close and the ladies relaxed, ready to share the latest gossip.

'Have you heard about the murder at The Windsor?' asked Gladys Onions.

'Of course, I have,' said Mavis. 'My son is senior crime reporter at *The Argus*.'

'They say Mr Howard was found dead, with thirty knives sticking out of his body.'

Mavis leaned forward. 'That's not what my Reggie says. The man was stabbed, that's true, but only one knife was used. There was a lot of blood.' She lowered her voice. 'Reggie said it was a crime of passion.'

'There's talk about Peggy Plumstead being involved,' Gladys said, her eyes darting around the group, waiting for a reaction.

Mildred Bardsley Smith drew herself up to her full height of five feet and glared at Gladys. 'Mrs Plumstead's mother is a good friend of mine. There is absolutely no possibility that Peggy is involved in murder.'

'Of course not,' replied Gladys, her voice quavering. 'I would never suggest that Mrs Plumstead–'

'In fact,' Mildred continued, 'I was going to ask Mavis if Reggie might assist in the investigation.'

'Reggie? I'm sure he would be honoured,' replied Mavis, her cheeks flushed with happiness. 'But I'm not quite sure what you mean, Mildred.'

'It's very simple, my dear. Your son is an experienced investigator as well as a reporter. My suggestion is that Reggie helps clear Mrs Plumstead's name.'

Gladys rallied. 'But I don't understand. Why would the Plumsteads want to talk to the press?'

'It's a delicate matter,' replied Mrs Bardsley Smith, giving the woman a stern look. 'I can't say anymore.'

'Perhaps the Plumsteads could drop in to *The Argus* for a chat?' ventured Mavis.

'I think not. People would talk.' Mildred glanced again at Gladys Onions, who knew better than to comment. 'On second thoughts, say nothing to your son, Mavis. We should leave it up to the Plumsteads to contact Reggie. Now, what is happening, ladies? Apart from crime and gossip?'

The ladies were lost for words.

Edith McGillicutty had been studying Mavis and was moved to comment. 'My dear Mavis, the dark rings around your eyes are fading. You don't look as poorly as you normally do.'

The ladies' attention was now focused on Reggie's mother, scrutinising her for signs of near collapse.

Mavis touched her face. 'Was it that obvious? That I've not been sleeping?'

'Oh yes, you've looked exhausted. In fact, last month, I thought you looked awful.'

Mavis reached into her bag and pulled out a bottle of Dr Wishbone's Restorative Syrup.

'It's amazing,' she said. 'Works miracles. I sleep like a newborn baby once I've taken two teaspoons of this before bedtime.'

Mildred took the bottle from her and peered at the label. 'It says that it cures insomnia and stomach ailments. According to this, it's recommended by eminent physicians and thousands of satisfied patients.' She passed the bottle to Edith.

'Dr Hiram T Wishbone. He's probably some quack,' said Edith, her thick dark eyebrows knitting together.

'Not at all,' insisted Mavis. 'He studied medicine at the University of South Carolina.'

'How would you know? Have you met him?' asked Mildred.

'Oh, yes. I needed another bottle of tonic. It was so efficacious; I couldn't do without it.'

Edith smirked. '*Efficacious?*'

'Dr Wishbone's own words,' said Mavis smugly. 'He's so well-educated.'

Edith snorted. 'Gullible woman.'

'I disagree, Edith,' said Gladys Onions, shaking her head vigorously. 'There's a lot to be said for herbal remedies. I've been suffering from indigestion for months, so I thought, why not? I bought a box of Dr William's Pink Pills for Pale People from a door-to-door salesman. Such a nice man.' Gladys took a card from her handbag and handed it to her. 'Read this.'

Edith adjusted her glasses and peered at the card. '"Dr. Williams' Pink Pills do more than help the nerves. Their main function is to enrich the blood, and as the blood supplies the whole body, new life and vigour are given to the entire system."'

'I'm a new woman,' asserted Gladys. 'My indigestion is gone.'

Edith sniffed. 'Ridiculous.'

A glare from Mildred Bardsley Smith restored order. 'Now, now, ladies,' she said, 'time for one last cup of tea?'

As Gladys's hand reached out to grasp another cream cake, Edith said, 'If you suffer from indigestion, Gladys, dear, perhaps you should forego too much afternoon tea. Remember what the Bible says: "Be not among winebibbers; among riotous eaters of flesh: For the drunkard and the glutton shall come to poverty: and drowsiness shall clothe a man with rags." Proverbs 23:20-21.'

The poor woman looked properly chastened. She put the cake back on the plate, reluctantly. 'If you think so, Edith.'

Chapter Ten

The last thing Reggie da Costa wanted was to meet with Curtis Flange, his temporary boss whilst Floyd Kramer was away sick. The murder of Jasper Howard was uppermost in his mind and there were witnesses to interview and reports to be written. However, he had been summoned to Flange's office and there he sat, waiting for the meeting to begin. He tapped his foot impatiently and shifted in his chair.

Curtis Flange sat opposite Reggie, shuffling some papers on his desk, trying to look busy. Flange's face was round and rosy-cheeked, his brown hair parted down the middle and slicked with oil, rather like a schoolboy who was on holiday from boarding school. Reggie fiddled with his tie as he waited, unhappy that he was being treated in such a cavalier fashion by this temporary sub-editor who knew absolutely nothing about crime and Melbourne's underworld. It would be a happy day when the ailing Floyd Kramer walked back through the door and resumed his role in charge of the crime desk. Reggie would even welcome Kramer peering at him through the magnified lenses of his horn-rimmed glasses again, unsettling though it might be.

'Mr Flange, I'm a busy man. I'm investigating a murder, you know?'

Flange ignored him, giving a little squeak of pleasure as he found the document he was seeking. It was a cutting from the newspaper. Reggie could see that it was his report on the Howard killing.

'This is what I was after. I wanted to discuss this with you.' Flange's voice was high, thin, and reedy, which Reggie found particularly irritating.

'Indeed?' Reggie sized up his temporary boss. Plain white shirt, black braces, and red bow tie. Not to mention the straw boater, which was propped on the hatstand behind him. It was not a look that should grace the drawing rooms of the rich and famous, Reggie thought, and yet Curtis Flange was a fixture there. The social pages were filled with his observations of Melbourne society: who was marrying whom; who was holidaying on the Italian Amalfi coast; who was hosting the best soirées of the season; who was attending the opening night of the ballet or the opera.

'I think that you could enliven your reports a little more, Reginald. Inject some spice, if you like?'

Reggie glowered at the use of his proper name. 'What did you have in mind?'

Flange sat back and put his hands behind his head. 'Our readers want to know more about the people who appear in our pages. What they looked like. What they wore. The exotic places they visit. That sort of thing.' He leaned forward and tapped the newspaper. 'Now, your article is excellent. Excellent.'

'But–?'

'You lack the detail.'

'Ten stab wounds and the Ten of Swords isn't enough for you?'

Flange missed the sarcasm. 'Exactly. You've hit the nail on the head. Our readers want to know more. What was this Howard character wearing when he died? Was he sharply dressed in a three-piece suit from Savile Row? What did his hotel room look like? You understand that many of our readers have no idea how The Windsor is furnished. The colour of the drapes. The rugs. The fine porcelain china of the bathrooms. The mahogany beds. And, of course, there's the ballroom. Dining room. The magnificent staircase. High tea.

'This is exactly the sort of information that appears in my social column. And our readers love it. Coincidentally, I was attending a charitable event at the same hotel the night of the murder. You should read my account if you want some clues as to what should be included.'

Reggie's ears pricked up. 'Did you notice anything that might relate to the murder?'

'Don't be ridiculous. Of course not.' He tapped the article again for emphasis. 'This link to the Duke of Norfolk. Perhaps you could explore this further? Our readers would like to know more about London society. The debutante balls. The theatre. The English aristocracy and how they live their lives. There's a wealth of material here that you could research.'

Reggie's thick black eyebrows knitted together. 'Indeed?'

The sub-editor beamed. 'I can see that you understand me.'

It seemed premature to reveal that Jasper Howard appeared to have no familial ties to the Duke of Norfolk. Indeed, it was clear to Reggie that this salient fact might encourage Flange to take him off the case, or at least give it minimal attention. The only reason why Flange was interested in the murder was because of Howard's social connections. Still, in the interests of his standing as a crime reporter, Melbourne's finest, Reggie needed to assert his superiority over his boss when it came to expertise in the field of crime.

'I do understand you, Mr Flange, but there's one problem.'

'And what would that be?'

'I'm a crime reporter. I deal in crime, not the gossip columns. Robbery, murder, fraud. Who, where, when, why, and how? That's what my readers want to know.'

Flange reddened. 'I'm adding a new touch to the crime reports, Reginald. My own distinctive touch. I want to marry the social pages with crime. Give it an extra dimension. Widen the audience.'

'Crime and gossip columns, Mr Flange. That's an original angle.'

'I'm pleased that you're so open to new ideas. Otherwise, I might have to discuss your position with Dr Cunningham.' It was rumoured that the gossip columnist had a family connection with the editor-in-chief of *The Argus*, but no one had been able to discover whether that was true. Suffice it to say, Flange did nothing to dissuade any of the staff otherwise.

'You can go now, Reginald.' He waved a hand dismissively and turned his attention back to the pile of papers on his desk.

Back in his office, Reggie took out a flask of brandy that he kept for emergencies. He unscrewed the lid and took a swig.

'To Floyd Kramer. Make a speedy recovery, my friend.'

He replaced the flask and turned his attention to the intricacies of the murder at The Hotel Windsor. Shrugging off Curtis Flange's suggestions, Reggie opened the file on Jasper Fitzalan Howard. He had the distinct feeling that there was more to Howard than a man who didn't pay his bills. He had all the hallmarks of an experienced confidence man, the type who attempted to inveigle himself into Melbourne society by means of phony letters of introduction, in order to swindle unwary investors and blackmail naïve and disaffected wives.

If Mrs Van Cooth were right, the dead man had convinced Sir Ambrose Beauchamp Kiddle, and possibly other members of Melbourne's moneyed classes, to invest in his ventures, promising rich returns. Reggie had no firm proof of this, but years of experience in watching shysters at work, separating gullible folk from their money, told him it was true.

And if Howard were a confidence man, it was likely that he had a partner in crime, most likely a woman. The scenario was a familiar one. The confidence trickster would gain the trust of a wealthy man or woman, preferably married, and, by means of flattery and professions of love, lure them into a compromising situation. At this point, they would be interrupted by the wronged 'wife' or 'husband' who would accuse them of committing adultery, threatening the victim with being named as a co-respondent in a divorce case. The victim would pay up in the hope that the whole dastardly situation would disappear and that their spouse would never know of their indiscretion, preferring to submit to blackmail rather than being shamed in the scandal rags.

Reggie wondered whether the woman in Room 101 was Howard's associate, given that she had been seen in conversation with the deceased and had checked out of the hotel on the same morning that Jasper Howard's body was discovered. Or was it merely a coincidence? Miss Smith. An alias? Reggie needed to find out more. The problem was that the clerks at the reception desk were specifically chosen for their discretion and were drilled into protecting the reputation of the exclusive Hotel Windsor despite any 'incentives' that might come their way. Such as a ten-shilling note.

However, those who filled the role of maids or kitchen staff were in a different league. The work was long and hard, and often underpaid, so breaching their defences was so much easier. A kind word and a silver coin could elicit information that might never have seen the light of day. And Reggie was just the man to do that.

Chapter Eleven

I t was ten o'clock the next morning when Reggie parked the Hupmobile outside The Hotel Windsor and strolled into the lobby. It was busy. Guests were checking out, while porters carried luggage down the stairs and out to waiting taxis. The desk clerks were accepting cheques and cash, writing receipts, and giving change. The concierge was engaged in an altercation with an unhappy guest who had had his wallet stolen.

Taking advantage of the situation, Reggie slipped past him and took the stairs to the first floor. It was the time when the maids would be cleaning out rooms, changing sheets and tidying up.

As he strode down the corridor, he was delighted to see the young woman whom he had interviewed a few days earlier, emerging from a room with a mop and bucket. She looked up at him and smiled.

'Hello, sir. Back from the Coroner's Office again? You must be very busy.'

He tipped his hat. 'Indeed, I am, Rose. And I want to thank you again for your assistance.'

The young woman blushed. 'You are very kind, sir. Can I help you again?'

'The maid, Molly. Is she here today?'

She pointed to the stairs. 'Molly does the second floor. You'll find her up there.'

Reggie tipped his hat again and gave her a winning smile. He took the stairs and soon was walking along the corridor. Most of the doors were shut, but he could hear noises coming from a room further up, the door ajar. He stood on the threshold, then stepped into the room.

'Molly?'

The woman turned around, startled. She was older than he expected, with thick brown curly hair barely contained by a frilly white cap. She stared up at him questioningly.

'Sir?'

'I'm from the Coroner's Office. I'm investigating the murder of Mr Howard two weeks ago. Could you answer some questions for me?'

'Me, sir?' She'd gone pale.

'You have nothing to be concerned about. It will only take a minute.'

She put the dust cloth and polish down.

Reggie spoke kindly, trying to put her at her ease. 'I understand that it was a dreadful situation to find yourself in. A dead body in a hotel room.'

She shook her head. 'It's horrible to even think about it, sir. But I'll help you if I can.'

'That's good of you. Now, did you speak to Mr Howard prior to his death?'

'I never really spoke to him. He was an early riser, sir. Down to breakfast and out before I made up his room.'

'Did you gain any impressions of him?'

'He was a gentleman. From England, you know. The room was neat and tidy when I'd go in. Nothing out of place.'

'The day of his death. It was a Saturday. Were you on duty?'

'I was, sir. I made up his room in the morning. I was supposed to turn down his bed around five o'clock that night.'

'But you didn't?'

'I knocked on the door. I could hear voices coming from inside. Then he called out not to bother so I went away.'

'Was he with a man or a woman?'

'It was a woman's voice.'

'Did you hear anything of their conversation?'

The maid frowned. 'I didn't listen at the door, if that's what you mean. But they were arguing. Their voices were raised.'

'And did you see her leave?'

'No sir, I did not.'

'You didn't see Mr Howard that night?'

Molly shook her head.

'When you went into the room the next morning, what did you see?'

'The door was locked, so I knocked. There was no answer, so I used my master key and went inside. I thought he'd gone out for the day, like he usually did. It was dark in there. The curtains were drawn. I called out to be sure, but there was no answer, so I switched on the light.' Tears formed in her eyes. 'He was lying there on the bed, not moving. I walked over to see if he was asleep, and there was all this blood. It was terrible. Blood. Everywhere.'

She shook her head, overcome, and wiped her eyes with the hem of her apron.

'I still see him when I go to sleep, sir. I don't think I'll ever forget it.'

'Did you notice anything out of place?'

'There was one thing. The safe was open.'

'Was it empty?'

'I couldn't say for sure. I didn't look inside.'

'Did you notice anything special about the body?'

'I didn't get up close, sir. I was terribly upset seeing him like that. A gentleman, murdered. I screamed, and Rose came running.'

Reggie patted her on the shoulder. 'Thank you. You've been very helpful.' He pressed a shilling into her hand.

She smiled bleakly through her tears. 'Thank you, sir.'

As he walked away, Reggie considered yet another aspect to this murder. Was it a robbery gone wrong, after all?

Chapter Twelve

In the Melbourne suburb of Toorak, home to the rich and famous, a chill wind was blowing through the streets, almost as chilly as the mood gripping the two inhabitants of the breakfast room in the Plumstead mansion.

The man of the house, Councillor Plumstead, stared across the dining table at his wife, his breakfast growing cold on the plate in front of him. He was gripping his knife and fork.

'Tell me again. What were you doing with that man, Howard?'

Peggy Plumstead returned his stare. 'And I'll tell you again, Donald, absolutely nothing. I'm sick of the subject. First the police, now you.'

'Why did you go to Sorrento, alone, with him?'

Peggy sighed. 'I never wanted to go, but I had no choice. It was Beatrice Van Cooth's idea to go to Hanging Rock and then she suggested Sorrento. And he insisted that I come as well, rather than compromise Beatrice's reputation. She was supposed to come. But when Mr Howard arrived, he told me that she was ill. He was so friendly and polite that I didn't know what else I could do, but go with him. It would have been bad manners to refuse.'

Donald exploded. 'You're a married woman. A politician's wife. If I weren't in public office, I'd be considering a divorce.'

'You'd what–?'

'What does it look like when you go out for lunch alone with a handsome Englishman? I'll tell you, Peggy, it looks like you're engaged in a sordid little affair. That's what it looks like.'

'And I'll tell you something, Donald. Your fine words in parliament are just that: fine words. You speak about the importance of family and marriage, but your deeds tell a different story. Don't judge me by what you do. I would never, ever embark on an affair, unlike someone else I could name.' She glared at him. 'I don't know why I married you. I thought that you and I had similar values, but it appears I was wrong.'

'What does that mean?' he said, licking his lips.

'You know exactly what that means. What about that young woman who pretends to be your secretary? She can't even type.'

Donald spluttered. 'Don't be ridiculous. I would never–'

'Don't lie to me. And now you've taken up with that fancy woman. I saw you at the Mayoral Ball. You were fawning over her. It's me who should be divorcing you, not the other way round. I dare you. You take me to court, and I'll spill the beans on your nasty little interstate trips and your dalliances. That will fix you.'

Plumstead went pale. His voice lost its edge. 'Now, now, Peggy, calm down. I know you would never do that to me. And I would never divorce you. The problem is that once the newspapers get onto this, they'll drag my name through the mud.'

'Then help me, Donald,' she pleaded. 'You know me. It was an innocent mistake going with him. You were fooled by Howard, too. You invested with him.'

'To my eternal chagrin. The bastard.' He threw down his knife and fork.

'Have you employed a private detective yet? Someone who can verify my story?'

Plumstead shook his head. 'Howard cleaned us out. All our savings, gone.'

'You mean all *my* savings.'

He pushed his plate away. 'I've lost my appetite over this.'

She glowered at him. 'And you think that this business doesn't affect me?'

The councillor stared out the window, then focused his eyes back on his wife. 'I have to ask the question. Why did you go to The Windsor that evening?'

'Not for the reason you're thinking.'

'Why then?'

'He wrote me a letter. He said that we needed to talk. I went. He told me that we were being blackmailed by a man who saw us together at Sorrento. I told him that I wasn't going to pay when I'd done nothing wrong. He protested. That's when I knew the truth. He was behind the blackmail attempt.'

'Why didn't you tell me this in the first place?'

'Because I didn't think that you'd believe me.'

'When you left Howard on Saturday evening, he was alive?'

'I've told you that. We argued, and I walked out.' She stared hard at her husband. 'We need someone to investigate his death. Mildred Bardsley Smith says that Reggie da Costa solved the Death Mask Murders case back in 1918. And that Body in the Basement murder two years ago.'

'Da Costa is the crime reporter with *The Argus*?'

'That's right. Mildred is one of my mother's oldest friends, and I trust her opinion. She knows Reggie da Costa's mother, too.'

'But can you trust a member of the press?'

Peggy shrugged her shoulders. 'What choice do we have?'

* * *

That night, Reggie was standing at the window of his flat above the grocer's shop, overlooking Swan Street, holding a letter which had been hand-delivered that very day. He was wearing his favourite smoking jacket, made of crimson velvet, and had poured himself a Scotch. On the table close by, the remnants of his dinner were waiting to be cleared away, but he ignored that, his attention taken by the hustle and bustle of life on the street below. It was a clear night, nearly eight o'clock. In the light of the street lamp, a newsboy was spruiking the last of the day's papers while factory and office workers scurried past the lad, eager to get home. He smiled and sipped from his glass. Those people below were his readers. His public. And soon, they would be feasting their eyes on the story of the year.

Jasper Howard had been found stabbed to death in The Hotel Windsor, and the woman who was suspected of doing the dirty deed had written to him, asking him to visit her and her husband in the privacy of their Toorak mansion. He put down the letter and shook his head in wonder. An exclusive interview. With the woman suspected of killing Jasper Howard at one of Melbourne's most exclusive hotels. And her husband would be there, too. Councillor Donald Plumstead. The rest of Melbourne's press pack would be green with envy when they read his report in the paper.

He finished his Scotch and walked over to the large wardrobe that occupied almost one wall of the landing next to his bedroom. He threw open the doors and feasted his eyes on his extensive collection of suits. Which one should he wear? The navy one with the fine grey pinstripe and the half belt at the back? The brown houndstooth three-piece suit with the wide lapels and high waist? Or the sedate dark grey, which suggested that the wearer was a sober gent, trustworthy, and reliable? Which one would instil confidence and engender respect from the moneyed Plumsteads? With such a plethora of possibilities before him, he was in a quandary.

Every aspect of this visit had to be thought out: the questions he would ask to prise information from Mrs Plumstead regarding the exact nature of her relationship with Jasper Howard, whether he should reveal that Beatrice Van Cooth suspected that her friend had contrived to be alone with the Englishman; the degree to which the Plumsteads were aware that Jasper Howard was not whom he claimed to be. It would be an intriguing interview and one that would test his superior skills as an interrogator. The presence of the husband might, however, prove an impediment to arriving at the truth.

These thoughts played on his mind as he finally settled on his choice of clothing, a decision which would have a massive bearing on the success of the interview. Not the navy, brown, or dark grey. It would be the three-piece grey pin-striped suit, featuring the latest wide-cut trousers, teamed with a cream shirt and red and blue tie. Perfect.

Chapter Thirteen

The next morning, dressed to impress, his hair Brilliantined and his moustache trimmed, Reggie headed out into the lane behind his house, where his beloved Hupmobile Series R Special Roadster was waiting for him. He took a moment to admire it: its low-slung chassis, flamboyant and dramatic, its 'forest green' paint job with black fenders, top and interior, and white-wall tyres, complete with a four cylinder, three-speed transmission, capable of a top speed of thirty-five miles per hour. Classy yet stylish, much like himself.

He settled behind the steering wheel, threw the gear stick into second, and soon was crossing the new Church Street bridge. As he turned into Alexandra Avenue, with the Yarra River to his left, he took in the view as he drove. It was a lovely day in Spring, and people were out enjoying the hint of the summer to come. Through the screen of trees on the river's edge, Reggie caught a glimpse of the occasional rowboat or canoe, while on the other side of the Yarra, the slums and factories of industrial Richmond could be seen. He was about to visit another world: a world of wealth and privilege, merely three miles away from the gritty alleyways and the criminal classes who called Richmond home, as did he. Surprisingly, he had come to see it as a distinct advantage in his line of work, because the suburb seemed to be the appropriate place of habitation for a crime reporter who wanted to keep his finger on the pulse. He was so close to so many stories, stories that kept his readers glued to the pages of *The Argus*. And he would continue to live there, as long as no one stole his Hupmobile or his classy collection of suits!

In the past, it had been Reggie's ambition to buy himself a house amongst the elite of Melbourne, to travel abroad, and to surround himself with those little luxuries that made life so enjoyable. Unfortunately, this scenario had never eventuated, because the woman who could provide this lifestyle had remained elusive. There had been moments when he thought he had met her, but some minor detail had put up a barrier to romance: the fact that the woman in question had not been attracted to him, which defied belief, or that a woman had a different agenda in seeking his attentions, and had been intent on using him for her own selfish ends, which was unforgivable, in his view.

And, when unwanted grey hairs had started to appear, and his waistline had seemed to take on a life of its own, he had met Ruby, the sister of his assistant at *The Argus*. She seemed to offer nothing that he wanted. She was neither wealthy nor socially connected and could only be described as dowdy when they first met, but she had needed his help, and he had given it, not foreseeing where that would lead. Before his eyes, as they tracked down her sister's killer, she had transformed herself, shedding her shyness and conservatism and becoming a woman who was confident, self-assured, and very attractive. For the first time in his life, with Ruby by his side, Reggie was experiencing a measure of contentment that he had never known before.

* * *

The Plumstead mansion soon came into view. It was an architectural masterpiece, red brick in the Queen Anne Revivalist style, featuring a unique conical tower with terracotta shingles and decorative mouldings. The front gable over the entrance was intricately carved and timber-framed. An impressive oak door was inset with stained glass lead lighting. The extensive house occupied about an acre of prime Toorak land and, it was said, had been gifted to the couple on the occasion of their marriage by the bride's parents.

Reggie parked his motorcar in the driveway and knocked on the front door. It was opened by none other than Councillor Plumstead himself, who frowned when he saw the crime reporter on his doorstep.

'I suppose you can come in, Mr da Costa,' he said, appraising him coldly, 'although I want to make it clear from the beginning that this was not my idea.' He reluctantly stepped aside to let him pass.

Not a promising start, thought Reggie, but understandable given that he was a politician whose wife was a suspect in a murder case.

'Thank you, sir,' he responded, hanging his homburg on the hatstand near the front door. He had time to examine his host, having not had the opportunity to be close to him before.

Donald Plumstead was a portly gent, not much over five feet in height, and in his early fifties. His intention, it appeared, was to remain aloof throughout the interview, relying on his status as a Victorian politician and his wealth to discourage familiarity. But Reggie was not taken in, for he had caught a whisper that all was not well with the councillor's finances; there were rumblings of bills not paid and credit extended.

He led Reggie through into a formal sitting room, extravagantly furnished, with high ceilings and decorative cornices, dominated by a massive fireplace, above which hung a very flattering portrait of the honourable member himself.

Mrs Plumstead was waiting for them there, seated in an armchair in a semi-circular bay window. She was wearing a navy dress, calf length, embroidered with ivory flowers. She stood immediately and advanced towards him, a hesitant smile on her face. It was clear that there were at least two decades' difference in the ages of husband and wife. Close up, she was much more attractive than the photographs in the social pages suggested. Her long blonde hair was tied in a twisted knot at the back of her neck; her deep blue eyes, with their thick pale eyelashes, watched him intently. Reggie realised with a start that the woman's flawless complexion and rosebud lips were devoid of makeup, surprising for a woman of her class and style. And yet it made her even more beautiful, because she was unadorned and didn't need it.

'Tea, Mr da Costa?' She rang a bell, and a maid seemed to materialise out of thin air. She gave instructions, and then beckoned for Reggie to take a seat. Her husband sank into an armchair, a look of grudging acceptance on his face.

'Do you mind if I take notes, Mrs Plumstead?' asked Reggie, removing a notebook and pen from his pocket.

'Definitely not,' growled her husband. 'No notes.'

'Only if you think that there is something you can use,' she said calmly, ignoring her husband. 'You see, I need your help. I have asked you here to investigate the murder of Mr Jasper Howard, and I need you to prove my innocence.'

Reggie raised his eyebrows. 'That is the purpose of your invitation?'

'It is. If we talk to you, you must agree not to repeat this conversation until the case is closed and the culprit is discovered. Can we rely on you?'

'I'm not sure that this is a fair trade.'

'If that's the case, you may as well leave now.'

Reggie weighed up the pros and cons. Access to a suspect in the Jasper Howard killing was not something he could pass up, particularly someone of Mrs Plumstead's social status, and her account might give him a clue to crack the case. But, on the negative side, he rebelled against the idea that their conversation would be in confidence. The Plumsteads would have to understand that he was a journalist first and foremost. Whatever Mrs Plumstead told him would be in the public domain. He was a man with scruples, but sometimes, it was necessary to sacrifice them for the greater good. And his readers were the greater good.

'And if I agree?' he asked.

'You'll get a story to rival the Death Mask Murders case and the murder of Cornelius Stout.'

'You've been researching me, I see.'

'My mother's friend is Mrs Bardsley Smith, who, I believe, is close to your mother.'

Reggie sighed. This was, indeed, a stumbling block. He might actually have to keep his promise. Where her friends were involved, Mavis did not take well to Reggie breaking a confidence or reporting on conversations that were meant to remain private. And Mildred Bardsley Smith was a *very* close friend of Mavis da Costa. Reggie admitted defeat.

'Let's continue with the interview, Mrs Plumstead. I give you my word.'

However, her husband was not convinced. He stood up and pointed at Reggie. 'He's a reporter, Peggy. The enemy. He's not going to keep anyone's confidences. He can't be trusted.'

'Don't be rude, Donald. Mr da Costa is a guest in our home.'

Reggie looked from husband to wife. This was not what he had expected. The couple were evenly matched it appeared, with both sticking to their guns. But while Donald Plumstead was a lot of bluster and hot air, his wife was cool, calm, and confident. If nothing else, it would be an entertaining morning.

The politician subsided back into his armchair, rather like a deflated balloon.

Reggie addressed Mrs Plumstead. 'Perhaps you could tell me how you met Mr Howard?'

'It was at the Mayoral Ball through Mrs Van Cooth. I thought he was charming. It was apparent that Beatrice–Mrs Van Cooth–had met Mr Howard before and that she enjoyed his company. It was she who suggested a trip to Hanging Rock, but I had no intention of accompanying them. I was surprised when she insisted that I come with them, but I seem to remember that he was concerned about her reputation. Not that I think Beatrice cared.'

Reggie raised an eyebrow. 'Not a happy marriage?'

She shrugged her shoulders. 'They go their own way. It's no secret. However, I absolutely insist that you don't quote me. I have no wish to contribute to the gossip columns. Or lose my friends. Do you understand?'

Reggie could see no reason to disagree. This did not come under the heading of 'Crime,' and he kept a wide berth from the social pages despite Curtis Flange's insistence that he should mix the two. His was serious journalism, even if the peccadilloes of the upper classes sometimes impacted on the Melbourne crime scene. He nodded his head. 'Agreed.'

With Reggie's encouragement, Peggy Plumstead gave him a brief account of the day trip to Hanging Rock and the suggestion from the Englishman that they visit the Mornington Peninsula the following Sunday.

'It was Mr Howard who suggested it, not Mrs Van Cooth?'

Peggy Plumstead frowned. 'Actually, it *was* Beatrice who suggested Sorrento. Mr Howard was planning to be back on board a ship to England within a few weeks. He wanted to tie up some loose ends with the purchase of a farm in the Western District.'

Councillor Plumstead went into a coughing fit, distracting her. 'There, there, Donald. Do you want a drink of water?'

He said nothing, the look of contempt on his face saying it all.

She ignored him, then resumed her account of the proposed day trip. 'Beatrice said that she would book the Continental Hotel for lunch. Mr Howard insisted that I come, too. I thought he was being the perfect gentleman, not wanting to jeopardise a married woman's reputation. Beatrice's, that is. It appears that I was wrong.'

'What happened?'

'Let's have some tea first, and I'll tell you.'

Chapter Fourteen

D r Hiram T Wishbone was settling into Melbourne very nicely. In a few short weeks, he had established himself as a purveyor of patent medicines par excellence. His business was growing, thanks in part to the assistance of his new partner, the pharmacist Mr Aldous Clegg. Already boxes of Dr Wishbone's Liver Pills and his Pills for Feeble People were filling the shelves of pharmacies and marketplaces throughout the city, courtesy of his advertisements in Melbourne's daily newspapers, while salesmen going door-to-door hawked bottles of Dr Wishbone's Invigorating Tonic, Dr Wishbone's Restorative Syrup, and jars of his Skin Rejuvenator.

The doctor only had to look at sales of Dr Wishbone's Radium Water to bring a smile to his face. Bottles were flying off the shelves after he had advertised the therapeutic value of radioactive energy, which would reverse the ageing process if taken on a daily basis. In his advertising material he cited experiments from a French veterinary school, which had found that horses were rejuvenated after they had been injected with radium. And who could argue with science?

There was one product that he insisted was his and his alone to sell, and that was his celebrated Elixir of Youth. Only Dr Wishbone himself could speak for the miraculous curative effects that his remedy could have on wrinkles, hair loss, energy levels, and muscle tone.

Never one to let the grass grow beneath his feet, Wishbone was always on the lookout for new advances in the field of medicine. He had noticed that electrotherapy machines with medical applications were starting to appear in shop windows, some powered by batteries, some by plugging into a wall socket.

Taking a back room at a workshop in the engineering factory recommended by Clegg, Wishbone was unrecognisable without his white linen suit. He was dressed appropriately in the overalls favoured by workingmen, covered in grease and iron filings, as he worked on an experimental device that would come to be known as Dr Wishbone's Violet Ray Cure-All Miracle Machine. The advertisement outlining its benefits had already been printed; all he needed was the device itself, which would be produced in numbers to sell to customers for use in the home. The one problem was the nasty tendency of his machine to short out, sending sparks everywhere.

Over his time in Melbourne, he had found a useful ally in the form of Madame Esmeralda, a fortune-teller in the Eastern Arcade. For each sale of one of his remedies, she received a commission. And every time she recommended him to her clients, he paid her a bonus. This arrangement gave him access to patients in their own homes, who often spread the word amongst their friends and family. There was nothing like the grapevine and personal recommendation to build a market for his patent medicines. And Madame Esmeralda had been instrumental in bringing Mavis da Costa into his orbit.

The woman had been a godsend. Not only was she easily persuaded as to the efficacy of his remedies, but she was part of a network of wealthy matrons who met regularly in the home of Mrs Mildred Bardsley Smith, a rich and influential resident of Grosvenor Street, Brighton. Word had spread quickly amongst her ladies of the benefits of his tonics and pills, and from that one particular group, his reputation had grown, like tentacles from an octopus.

* * *

It was a day in mid-September when he parked next to the stables of Glenrothes and stepped out of his Ford Model T delivery van. He was proud of his purchase. Thirty-five pounds had procured him the means by which he could transport his patent medicines and devices around the city of Melbourne and promote his business at the same time. On the sides of the shiny black van were emblazoned the words: 'Dr Hiram T Wishbone's Patent Remedies and Devices. Miracle cures for all ailments. Direct from administering to the Crowned Heads of Europe.' On the back door of the van, the artist had also painted a fair representation of the doctor himself, with his goatee beard and wearing his trademark white linen suit. It had been an extra ten pounds for the advertising, but it was worth it.

Wishbone opened the back of the van and took out his suitcase, then turned to admire the beautiful 1890s Italianate Victorian mansion. It was a privilege to be invited to one of Mrs Bardsley Smith's afternoon teas, with the express purpose of discussing the benefits of natural remedies in healing common ailments.

He was shown into a large drawing room to be greeted by the hostess, herself. A petite woman with wispy white hair pulled back into a chignon, she was squeezed into a corset beneath a dress of fine grey silk embellished with a lace collar. Around her was gathered her intimate circle of friends, who had attended in the excited expectation of hearing the latest developments in medicine.

As an afterthought, Dr Wishbone had taken along half a dozen examples of his latest device: a massaging fat remover with a handle on each end and with four rotating rollers covered in small suction cups, the design reminiscent of a rolling pin. Once the introductions were made and he had given a preamble on the efficacy of his patent remedies, his decision to demonstrate the fat remover was a *tour de force*, judging by the reaction of the ladies. They shrieked in laughter as each massaged a section of thigh or arm or back using Dr Wishbone's Fat Remover, losing most of their inhibitions in the process. To be honest, the good doctor didn't know where to look! Only Mildred Bardsley Smith remained detached from the general air of hilarity, watching on with a mixture of dismay and disapproval on her face.

'Ladies, ladies,' she said above the laughter. 'Let's behave with some restraint, if you please.'

With order restored and the giggles subsiding, afternoon tea was taken, and the conversation returned to the more sober subject at hand: the advantages of patent medicines over traditional remedies.

'It's so much nicer chatting to you, Dr Wishbone,' said Mavis, her cheeks still rosy from the excitement of trying out the fat remover. 'My doctor is so dour. And he charges for a visit and dispensing the medicine. It's so convenient when you come to our houses.'

Gladys Onions nodded her head. 'And you get to try before you buy. All those little suckers on the fat remover. I could feel that fat dissolving away. I mean, it makes sense, doesn't it? You can roll the excess flesh away,' she said, her double chin quivering at the thought.

Even Edith, normally sober and disapproving, had been unable to resist the hilarity. 'It did feel good, but I'd need proof before I buy.'

Dr Wishbone leaned forward. 'Of course, dear lady,' he drawled, laying on his Southern accent so thick that it made his speech almost indecipherable. 'All my remedies come with an iron-clad guarantee. If you don't lose weight, sleep better, eat better, feel better, in fourteen days, your money is cheerfully refunded to you. And the same goes for my devices. There's also a free trial period.'

'What other devices do you have, Dr Wishbone?' asked Mavis, her eyes wide with interest.

'Well, ma'am, I'm working on an electromagnetic belt.'

'And what is it for?' asked Mildred.

'It's still in the developmental stage, but there are promising signs. It's in the magnets, ma'am. They will cure back pain, kidney and bladder disorders, muscle ache, tendonitis, gout, and, with regular use, cancer.'

'That's amazing, Dr Wishbone,' said Mildred. 'Forgive my scepticism, but can you prove this?'

'I have patients back in South Carolina who are trialling the preliminary incarnation of this technological and medical wonder, and, I have to say, the results are extremely encouraging. Of the fifty or so participating, almost all report that they feel energised and more youthful. The doctors presiding over the trial have been ecstatic.'

Gladys Onions was impressed. 'My husband suffers something terrible from backache, and nothing seems to make him better. When will it be available here, Dr Wishbone?'

'In a little while. We must ensure that our products are safe and effective.'

'Of course,' she concurred. 'How much will it cost?'

The doctor stroked his beard. 'I never talk money with my patients. When you think about it, a cure is priceless. Who can put a value on good health?'

He was pleased to see Mrs Onions nodding her head. He opened his suitcase and rummaged through it, then placed six bottles of Dr Wishbone's Elixir of Youth on the table.

The light from the chandelier glinted off his glasses. 'I know that you little ladies don't need it,' he said, 'but would anyone like to sample my elixir of youth?'

Chapter Fifteen

The tea things had been removed and now Reggie sat back in his armchair, his notebook and pen poised, waiting for Mrs Plumstead to begin her account of the trip to Sorrento. He tried to ignore the glowering look on the face of her husband, who was obviously uncomfortable with the prospect of forthcoming revelations.

'It was after ten o'clock in the morning when Mr Howard arrived,' commenced Mrs Plumstead, looking intently at her guest. 'Immediately he apologised for the fact that Beatrice would be unable to accompany us. He claimed that she had rung him only minutes before he was about to leave, complaining of a terrible headache and saying that she could hardly rise from her bed, much less go on a day trip to Sorrento. He was so full of regret that she couldn't come. It would be, in his words, a great loss without her. But he disliked the thought that I would be disappointed if the trip were called off, and he emphasised that he had been looking forward to the company of both of us before his visit to Australia ended. That was meant to reassure me of his good intentions, which it did. I could hardly refuse after that, so, to my everlasting regret, I agreed to go with him.

'He was the perfect gentleman on the drive down to the Mornington Peninsula. The conversation flowed, and he never ventured into any territory that I would have considered questionable. I had no reason to suspect that he was anything but respectful and well-bred.'

Her husband grunted. 'More fool, you.'

Mrs Plumstead's eyes flashed.

'When we arrived at the Continental Hotel, it was around midday. Mr

Howard had the top down on the Buick, and, although it wasn't a windy day, I'd had to remove my hat rather than have it blow off. Unfortunately, I'd forgotten to bring a scarf. As you can imagine, I needed to fix my hair before we had luncheon in the restaurant there. It seemed unnecessary to me, but Mr Howard had taken a room at the hotel in case I needed to freshen up after the drive, so I took the key and went up to the room. After about five minutes, there was a knock on the door. It was Mr Howard. He'd come to tell me that our table was ready. Before I knew it, he'd walked into the room and shut the door behind him. He spent the next couple of minutes admiring the view of Port Phillip Bay from the windows.'

Reggie raised his eyebrows. 'You thought nothing was amiss?'

'I did feel uneasy, I admit. I said that we should go, and he seemed quite relaxed about that. There was never any indication that he had any intentions of forcing himself on me. And I felt that I had kept a strong rein on my feelings and hadn't given him any indication that I wanted to be alone with him.'

Mr Plumstead sniffed and pulled a face. 'My wife has never let her feelings run away with her. At any time.'

'Donald,' she said coldly. 'Remember yourself. We have company.'

'Company? A reporter isn't company.'

Reggie shifted in his chair, uncomfortable with the direction that the politician's comments were going. He wanted to stay and hear the rest.

'Councillor Plumstead, I assure you–' he began.

'No newspaperman can be trusted with his assurances,' he replied.

'Donald. We need Mr da Costa.' She offered Reggie a weak smile and looked him in the eyes. 'We do need you. Please don't go.'

Reggie nodded and decided that silence would work in his favour more than commenting on his integrity, which, he had to admit, was in short supply when a story was brewing. He decided to get the conversation back on track.

'Mr Howard was in your room. What then?' he asked.

'I went out into the corridor, Mr Howard behind me. There was a man there. He turned around and looked at me. I was sure that I'd seen him

74

before at the Mayoral Ball. I think that he recognised me. He lifted his hat. He saw Mr Howard was with me and he smirked. I shrank inside at the thought that he was drawing conclusions about our relationship.' She turned to her husband, who was shaking his head. 'Which was completely platonic, Donald.'

'Go on, Mrs Plumstead,' said Reggie.

'We went down to lunch. I was feeling very uneasy by that stage. Very uneasy. The thought that someone I didn't know, but who knew me, might be making assumptions about my behaviour was very disconcerting. I confess that I hardly touched my lunch, and I was in a hurry to leave.'

'And did Mr Howard touch on this area of concern, for want of another word?'

'He did not. It was as if he didn't notice it. Anyway, he paid the bill, and we left the restaurant. When we went down to where the automobile was parked, I noticed the same man was standing a few feet away from the Buick. As if he were waiting for us. He came up close to me. Too close. He leered at me and winked. Said "Mrs Plumstead" in the most suggestive way. I glared at him, and he threw his head back and laughed. When I turned to Mr Howard, he acted as if nothing was happening. As if he didn't register what was going on. I asked him what he was going to do about the man, and he said, "What do you want me to do?" Just like that. The man said something to Mr Howard that I didn't catch. Next thing we were in the motorcar heading back to Toorak.'

'Did this man contact you?'

'Not directly. I avoided Mr Howard as best I could, but two weeks later, I received a hand-delivered letter. It was from Mr Howard, asking me to come to Room 206 at The Hotel Windsor at five o'clock on Saturday evening. He said that it was an urgent matter. We needed to talk.'

'Did he say why?'

She shook her head. 'The letter was brief. I was in a bind. Should I go, or should I stay away, as I'd promised myself? Curiosity got the better of me. I went.'

'What happened?'

'Mr Howard answered the door. He was alone. He showed me a letter from the man demanding £500 to keep our "affair" quiet. I was horrified and told him that we should go to the police. He said that my reputation would be ruined if I did that. He suggested that it would be better to pay up. I asked him what he was going to contribute and he said that it was my reputation at stake, not his. I said that I wouldn't pay a blackmail demand because it wouldn't end there. He assured me that it would. That he knew of this man and he would only ask for money once. I asked him how he knew that, and he was evasive. That's when I knew he was involved. He threatened me. He said that no politician would want their wife accused of adultery. Donald would never be re-elected, and it would destroy his career.'

'Hear, hear,' said Mr Plumstead, looking glum.

'I refused, and he got angry. We argued. I accused him of being in on the scheme. That he'd set it up. That he'd lied to me that Beatrice was sick so that I would be alone with him. That he'd rented the room at the Continental so that we'd be caught coming out of it together. It all fell into place.'

'Did he deny it?'

'He told me that I'd be a fool to resist paying the blackmailer. I told him I'd be that fool. And I left.'

'Have you spoken to Mrs Van Cooth so that she can support your story?'

'She won't take my calls or answer my letters.'

'When you left The Hotel Windsor, was Mr Howard still alive?'

'As I told my husband earlier, he was. Angry, but alive.'

'Have the police questioned you?'

'They have. I refused to answer most of their questions on the advice of my solicitor.'

'Do you know of anyone who might have a reason to kill Mr Howard?'

'There are rumours of other blackmail attempts. Some questionable investment schemes—'

Mr Plumstead interrupted. 'But nothing can be proven. They are rumours, nothing more.'

Reggie turned on him. 'Including your investment in one of Mr Howard's get-rich-quick schemes? Wool, I believe?'

The politician went red. 'I think you should leave, Mr da Costa.'

Mrs Plumstead stood. 'I think that's enough for today.' She gave her husband a quick look, but he had turned away. 'Perhaps we could meet again. I would be most appreciative of your help.'

Reggie closed his notebook and put his pen back inside his coat pocket. 'It appears that you have been set up, Mrs Plumstead. As you have gathered, Mr Howard isn't who he appears to be. There are others with a motive to kill him. In my wide experience of human nature, including the basest kind, I believe that the motivation for murder comes down to four main things: love, hate, revenge, and money.'

He cast his eyes in the direction of her husband, who looked away.

'Good afternoon, Mrs Plumstead. Councillor Plumstead.'

As he reached the front door, he glanced back in the direction of the drawing room. The couple were standing face to face, arguing. The councillor saw Reggie watching and scowled.

It was obvious that theirs was not a happy marriage, and Reggie suspected that the death of Jasper Howard had been the tipping point for an open declaration of war. It also occurred to him that Mrs Plumstead was not the only person in the family who had a motive for murder.

Chapter Sixteen

I n another part of town, feelings were running hot, too. In the back room of Mr Clegg's establishment, a like-minded group of about a dozen chemists, grocers, manufacturers, and travelling salesmen were holding a meeting.

'We must stop Regulation 79 becoming law!' cried Mr Clegg, his sparrow chest rising in indignation. 'If we don't act now, we'll be forced to list the ingredients of our tonics, syrups, and pills on their packaging. The government has no right to do this!'

'Hear. Hear.' Came the reply.

'Our once-secret formulas will be broadcast to the world,' he continued. 'Others will swamp the market with copies of our products. We'll lose business to cheap imitations. We will lose our livelihoods. It's an insult, that's what it is. If we don't win this fight, it will affect the economy. Advertisers and newspapers will lose business and profits if patent medicines are withdrawn from the market.'

A grocer, still wearing his striped apron, shook his head in disgust. 'What does the government know about patent remedies? Nothing, that's what. Members of the public, our patients, don't need governments to meddle in their business. Patients decide what works for them, not politicians.'

'And what about our customers in country areas?' asked one of the salesmen, who was wearing a loud checked suit, a spotted bow tie, and a bowler hat. 'Far away from hospitals and doctors, with no one to rely on for medical advice but their reputable and trusted purveyors of medicinal remedies.'

Mr Clegg stepped forward, mopping his brow with a large handkerchief. 'It's fair enough to ban any harmful drugs that come on the market, but not our "tried and true" cures. We help people. We treat their problems. We care about what happens to our patients. If we didn't, there'd be no customers. Why would we want to harm people? Patent medicines are essential to public health and welfare. This assault on our reputations must stop!'

The mood of the meeting was growing dangerous. Red, angry faces. Loud, impassioned voices. An exchange of increasingly heated and inflammatory viewpoints on what the government was doing to the average business owner and salesman.

'I'll go broke if they regulate my business!'

'Vote them out! Make them work for a living!'

'Burn down Parliament House!'

Mr Clegg raised his hands, calling for calm. 'Gentlemen. I appreciate your outrage. I share that with you. But why don't we consider a more *indirect* way to convince these men to repeal that law? Burning down Parliament House will not achieve our aims. And voting them out won't work. May I remind you that the next election is not until 1927. By that stage, many of us will have lost our livelihoods.'

The room had gone quiet, the assembled company waiting for the suggestion that would make this terrible situation go away.

'We need to convince our elected representatives that they have plenty to lose if this legislation is not repealed,' he argued. 'We already have politicians in the Legislative Assembly who will propose a law to override Regulation 79. But we need a majority in both Houses if it is to be passed. If we can pressure representatives to vote in its favour, we will win. I've prepared a list of members who need to be persuaded. Take a copy when you leave.'

The salesman in the bowler hat nodded. 'Good work, Clegg.'

'What else can we do?' cried the grocer.

'Write to the newspapers,' said Clegg. 'Use your influence in the business community. Talk to your customers. Put notices in your shop windows. We need a groundswell of citizens asking–demanding–for this unfair law to be removed.'

The grocer was not convinced. 'What do we do about the politicians who refuse to support it?'

Mr Clegg nodded his head slowly. 'Think of something that will convince them.'

There was a murmur amongst the group. The salesman shook his fist. 'He's right, you know. Those politicians live the easy life. And they enjoy being powerful. They say that power corrupts, so let's dig around and see what these men are hiding. Adultery. Taking bribes. Doing favours for their powerful friends using our money. Let's use their secrets to convince them to think our way. Pressure them into repealing Regulation 79.'

Mr Clegg smiled and rubbed his hands together. 'Why not? They threaten our lives. Let's threaten theirs.'

There was a nodding of heads and smiles as the idea spread.

He held up his hands to ask for silence. 'You know what to do. Spread the word. Use every means that you can think of. And when that's exhausted, think again. What can you do to convince our lawmakers that supporting public health is their primary purpose in life? Ask yourselves: What have they got that they can't afford to lose? This is our survival that we are talking about, so let's find out where their vulnerabilities lie.

'One thing is important. If you do venture down that path, be careful. If you write a threatening letter or make a telephone call, stay anonymous and out of sight. Whatever you do, make sure they don't know it was you who found out about their dirty little secrets.'

Chapter Seventeen

The weeks had passed quickly since Dr Wishbone's arrival in Melbourne. Great progress was being made. No accusations of dodgy practices. No dissatisfied customers clamouring for the police to intervene. His Electromagnetic Belt was selling fast through word of mouth, mail-order advertisements, and door-to-door sales. Dr Wishbone's reputation was spreading, aided, and abetted by the Bardsley Smiths' standing in Brighton society, where he was referred to as the miracle man from the Deep South. He was often to be seen in the best salons of Melbourne, spruiking his wares, but in a 'refined' way. His trademark pitch was that no money should pass hands until the patient was convinced of the efficacy of his mechanical devices. And it appeared that most of his clientele wanted to believe that they were benefitting from his treatment, a result of Wishbone's powers of persuasion and assurances that mental and physical improvement were just around the corner.

One of the images that would live in Wishbone's memory was the sight of Alfred Bardsley Smith sitting in a chair in the parlour of Glenrothes. An imposing gent, Smith was around six feet tall and almost as wide, with grey hair parted down the middle. Luxuriant side whiskers hung below his jawline, the two joined together by a well-waxed moustache. His vast bulk was encircled by the extra-large version of the Electromagnetic Belt. At the front was a metal box from which a power cord protruded, the end plugged into an electrical socket in the wall. As Bardsley Smith's wife watched on, Wishbone flicked the switch, generating a weak magnetic current through the insulated wires enclosed by the leather belt.

'Can you feel it, dear?' asked Mildred Bardsley Smith.

'I think so,' replied her husband. 'Are you sure this will help me, Dr Wishbone?'

It was the good doctor's mission to pour oil on troubled waters and to calm the fears of his patients. His powers of persuasion and the patient's desire to believe that he was being cured had worked miracles in the past, short-lived though they may be.

'The concept is based on Otto Heinrich Warburg's work on iron in the blood,' he explained patiently. 'My device will increase the body's absorption of oxygen to free the body from toxic diseases. Cancer, diabetes, tuberculosis, arthritis, neuritis, and insomnia have been cured by the restorative effects of the Electromagnetic Belt. In your case, Mr Bardsley Smith, your nervous disposition will be mightily reduced with frequent use of this miraculous device. The small sum of twenty-five pounds will secure your future as a man of robust health, confidence, and vigour.'

Mrs Bardsley Smith seemed uncertain, but there was no doubt in the mind of her husband. His friend, Oswald Onions, swore by the restorative powers of Dr Wishbone's Electromagnetic Belt in curing his bad back, and that was good enough for Alfred. The sum paid, the doctor departed, content in the knowledge that Mr Bardsley Smith would be instrumental in assuring his wife that the device was relieving his shattered nerves. And if Alfred Bardsley Smith was convinced, his wife's doubts would fade away, and she would become a powerful voice in spreading the word about the regenerative and therapeutic benefits of Dr Wishbone's products.

His next invention was coming along nicely, with the facilities and equipment provided by the engineering firm in whose building he was now lodged. Dr Wishbone's Violet Ray Cure-All Miracle Machine would make his fortune, he believed, and would command the princely sum of seventy pounds once it was put into production.

He opened the Violet Ray's velour-lined carrying case and studied the contents with pride in his achievement. Inside were a set of tubes or electrodes, an ozone generator with an inhaling mask, an electrical cord and plug, and a hand-held wand. Electrotherapy was the new frontier for medicine, and this device would apply a high voltage, high-frequency, low current to the human body. The miraculous Violet Ray Cure-All, according to the accompanying manual which he had plagiarised from that of a similar machine, stimulated the patient and massaged the cells, producing a pleasant warmth. The selling point, in Wishbone's view, was the violet colour that flowed through the tube when the machine was operational. That purple glow and the faint sparks that were emitted from the electrode looked so impressive, suggesting to the patient that a cure for his ailment was imminent.

Dr Wishbone opened the small safe that he had hidden beneath his workbench and counted the thick wad of notes that he had accumulated since his arrival in the state of Victoria nearly two months earlier. Eight hundred and fifty-two pounds. His speedy exit from the United States of America, with the authorities breathing down his neck, had convinced him of the need to have on hand an emergency fund for times such as those. No banks for Hiram T Wishbone. If one of his patients had a bad experience with one of his patent medicines, or there was an unfortunate surge in the electrical supply when one of his devices was in use, he would be on the first ship out of Port Melbourne, money in hand.

Time for bed. He pulled the curtain back from an alcove to reveal his sleeping arrangements: a mattress on the floor, with two thin woollen blankets and a lumpy pillow. A second white linen suit was hanging from a hook, whilst a small collection of shirts and underwear was folded neatly in a wooden cabinet. His suitcase sat close by, ready to be packed in a hurry, because travelling light was the first principle of the successful 'snake oil' salesman. And that was Dr Wishbone to a 'T.'

Chapter Eighteen

R uby strolled back up the hallway from the kitchen and stopped in front of the grandfather clock, where she cranked the weights into position and set the pendulum in motion. Six o'clock. Soon, Reggie would be arriving for dinner. The pot of beef stew was simmering on the stove and she'd spent a few minutes fixing her make-up and doing her hair. All was in readiness.

She sank into an armchair and sipped a cup of tea. Her eyes rested on the photographs on the sideboard. Katherine's picture took pride of place while, next to it, was a recent photograph of herself and Reggie in Ancient Egyptian costume, celebrating her birthday at Horace Striker's club, The Stockade. Ruby smiled as she looked at the picture. It had been a lovely night, and from the expression on Reggie's face, he had enjoyed it, too. That night had signalled the beginning of a new life for her.

Although she was still employed as secretary to the manager of Smith and Sons, she was now financially independent, courtesy of her sister. And Dusty, her brother, was forging ahead as a crime reporter with Reggie as his mentor. Life was good.

* * *

An hour later, with dinner finished and the dishes soaking in the sink, Reggie and Ruby relaxed on the couch, chatting about the Howard case.

'I was reading your latest report in *The Argus*,' said Ruby. 'Tell me, is there any conclusive evidence against Mrs Plumstead?'

'Not so far, except for her being at the crime scene on the same day as the murder.'

'I find it hard to imagine that she'd stab someone to death.'

'Even the unlikeliest people can be driven to kill. Fear of exposure. The shame of your indiscretions being made public. The possibility of divorce.'

'That's true, but if she did it, she'd have blood all over her. Someone would notice.'

Reggie smirked and shook his head slowly. 'Really, Ruby, you're finding crime far more interesting than you probably should. I'm not sure it's healthy.'

'It's a darn sight more interesting than typing up the minutes of the Smith and Sons board meeting.'

'I won't argue with you there. However, yours is a valid point. The amount of blood splatter over the floors and walls indicated that the perpetrator would be covered in it.'

'Did anyone see Mrs Plumstead leave?'

'Apparently not. But the maid heard raised voices coming from the room around five o'clock. A male and a female, so he was certainly entertaining a woman in there and it appears that it was Mrs Plumstead. She doesn't deny it. But she said that he was alive when she left.'

'The maid didn't go in later?'

'Howard told her to go away. Hotel policy is to do what the guests want.'

'Unless the maid got her times wrong,' ventured Ruby. 'Or Mrs Plumstead went back to The Windsor later and killed him.'

'Both are possible. I have the chance to interview Mrs Plumstead again in a few days' time. Without her husband. Perhaps she'll have more information for me.'

'Are there any other suspects?'

'Plenty, from what I've heard. It's clear that Howard kept himself busy while he was in Melbourne. There are rumours of liaisons with other women. I also know that a few investors had their fingers burned, Councillor Plumstead amongst them.'

'What happened with the councillor?'

'I had a chat with one of his golfing mates. Apparently, Plumstead was boasting that there was money to be made from importing British and Spanish sheep and experimenting with particular breeds to produce top-grade wool. It was to do with some Western District property that Howard was buying. There were plans to put a manager in charge when Howard went back to England. From all accounts, Plumstead put in a heap of cash. This golfing mate of his said that the councillor was hounding Howard for feedback on his investment. It's possible that, like me, Plumstead contacted property and stock agents around Horsham and Hamilton and found out that no one had heard of Jasper Howard in that region.'

'You think that Mr Plumstead might have been angry enough to kill him?'

'It depends on how much he's lost. From all accounts, he married money. And a politician's wage is good, but it won't fund the sort of lifestyle that the Plumsteads lead. He certainly didn't want me involved or sniffing around. He made that perfectly clear when I went to his home. It makes you wonder if he has something to hide.'

'Did anyone else invest in this wool business?'

'Sir Ambrose Beauchamp Kiddle, from what I've heard, although he's not going to admit it because it makes him look stupid.'

'More than the rest of them?'

Reggie chuckled. 'How true. And there's history with regard to Kiddle's financial mistakes. You know that he made his fortune out of scrap metal?'

Ruby shook her head. 'Tell me about it.'

'You know Sandridge Bridge, the one that crosses the Yarra River?' Reggie continued.

'The rail bridge from the city to Port Melbourne and St Kilda?'

'That's the one. Apparently, about ten years ago, a confidence man put out a story saying that the State Government wanted to demolish it and replace it with a better-designed bridge to take rail and street traffic. He told Kiddle that he would act as an intermediary if any scrap metal dealers wanted to get in early on the demolition. It's made of steel girders, you see. Kiddle jumped at the chance. The proposal was that the steel would be purchased from the State Government at bargain basement prices, then Kiddle would sell it on at a hefty profit. But first, he would have to pay a deposit up front to show "good faith.'"

'And Sir Ambrose paid the deposit to the confidence man?'

'He did, more fool him. The bloke told Kiddle that the deal had to remain strictly confidential until the Government made the official announcement. Kiddle waited and waited. By the time he realised that he'd been played for a fool, the confidence man had left town.'

'How much did he lose?'

'Thousands, according to my source. And it took Kiddle years to make up his losses.'

'You'd think Sir Ambrose would be more cautious before he invested in another get-rich-quick scheme.'

'It's called greed, Ruby. And some people are gullible and stupid. They never learn. And now we come to Howard's so-called investment opportunity. By the time that Sir Ambrose and Councillor Plumstead realised that it was a fraud, Howard would have left town, taking their money with him. But, in this case, someone killed Howard first, and the money that Kiddle and Plumstead paid is missing. The safe was empty.'

'I'm amazed that you know all this.'

'Contacts, Ruby. In my business, you need contacts.'

'Did you find any proof of skulduggery when you checked his hotel room?'

'As I said, the safe had been cleared out by persons unknown. The police had removed anything that could be used as evidence. I did, however, take Howard's two suitcases.'

Ruby flushed. 'Reggie, you can't do that.'

'The police know about it. In fact, Detective Sergeant Blain said that he didn't want to spend department money sending the luggage back to England.'

'That's not likely anyway, if Mr Howard really was a confidence man. You said yourself that no one knows him in England. He may not even be English.' She looked at him slyly. 'You might find something to wear in his suitcases. I hear he was a fashionable dresser.'

Reggie smirked. 'A dead man's clothes? I don't think so.'

'What's in the cases?'

'Nothing much.' Reggie checked his cufflinks and turned them so that the 'RDC' was visible. 'Some suits. Shirts. Ties. Nothing that one could call evidence.'

'Where are they now?'

'In the boot of the Hupmobile.'

'You've made me curious about Mr Howard. Can I see what's in those suitcases?'

Reggie raised his eyebrows but didn't argue. If the truth be told, he'd only given the luggage a cursory glance and had been intending to have a better look at some stage. He went out into the street and returned with two brown leather suitcases.

The first one was quite plain. It had silver latches, a leather handle, and straps with buckles to keep it securely closed. Inside was a selection of suits, shirts, nightwear, and underwear that had been packed quickly, probably by the staff of The Windsor, so that the wardrobes and drawers in the hotel room would be cleared ready for the next guest.

The second case was more elaborate. It had the same silver latches and leather straps, but the inside was expensively fitted out, with large pockets for documents and personal possessions. Inside, there was a woollen dressing gown, a coat with a thick, black fur collar, a pair of slippers, and two pairs of black shoes.

'Let's have a better look at the second one,' suggested Ruby. She removed the contents and watched while Reggie opened each of the pockets inside the lid.

'Empty,' he said, shrugging his shoulders.

'What's that?' She pointed at the edge of a piece of paper that could just be seen at the join, between the base and back of the suitcase. She leaned forward and picked at it, then noticed that the base had a protruding tag. She tugged at it, and a large piece of cardboard, covered in the same material as the lining, lifted out.

'What's this?' declared Reggie. 'A false bottom?' He smiled broadly as a cache of letters, photographs, and cards were revealed. 'I didn't see that slip of paper when I looked last time. The base must have dislodged when I threw the cases in the boot. Well done, Ruby. You're an asset to any investigation. Let's see what you've found.'

Chapter Nineteen

Dusty Rhodes was working back late at the offices of *The Argus* while Reggie was off having dinner with his sister, Ruby. He was reading about a case of blackmail and murder from 1857, brought to his attention by one of the older reporters at the newspaper, who thought it might have relevance to his present-day enquiries. It concerned a Scottish girl called Margaret McIvor, who had poisoned her former lover, a Frenchman by the name of Pierre Emile L'Angelier. When Margaret had told him the relationship was over, he had unsuccessfully tried to blackmail her by threatening to publicise the letters that she had written to him. She had responded by putting arsenic in his cocoa. The Frenchman had died shortly after.

In the dock, Miss McIvor had remained calm throughout the nine-day trial, impressing the jury. She had smiled as her letters were read and didn't seem fazed at the thought of a prison sentence, telling the prison matron later that she could endure the hardship if she had a piano in the cell. It was said that when the jury pronounced the charges 'Not proven,' the defendant had stepped down gracefully from the dock and smiled radiantly, murmuring, 'Well, they won't catch me with arsenic again.' Her counsel, invited to call on her sometime later, had said, 'Thank you, Miss McIvor, but please don't forget, I never touch cocoa.'

Dusty chuckled to himself as he read that last remark. However, Miss McIvor's story was ultimately a sad one. Despite being found not guilty, the young Scottish woman was not welcomed back into her family. In an effort to escape the rumours and gossip that circulated around her, she married an eccentric medical man, who suggested that they start a new life in Perth, Western Australia.

Some years later, after her husband's death, Margaret McIvor remarried and returned to London as the wife of a merchant. At one of her many parties, a guest commented on the McIvor case, unaware that his hostess was none other than the poisoner herself.

'She ought to have been hanged. Her beauty should not have saved her from the scaffold,' he was heard to say.

Her past was subsequently exposed, and Margaret McIvor's social life crumbled to dust. She sought solace in music and died in London thirty-four years after her acquittal, having failed to escape her notoriety.

Dusty put the report down and stared off into the distance. A case from 1857 still held relevance in 1925: the blackmail of a woman who had compromised herself by writing passionate letters to her lover. This was a woman who had not succumbed, as so many did, and given her former lover what he wanted. She had allegedly killed him, been sent to trial, and been acquitted. But she paid the price for the rest of her life. Although she had been declared not guilty and had been the innocent victim of a blackmailer, she had been haunted by the stigma of being accused of murder. Her lover's reputation was never an issue. No one talked about him and how he had driven her to it. Her acquittal was attributed to her beauty and its effect upon the judge, rather than to a lack of evidence.

What if the murderer of Jasper Fitzalan Howard had been in a similar situation to Margaret McIvor? If Howard had attempted to blackmail his victim, was his killer justified in taking action against him, even to the point of murder? Howard had put reputations and livelihoods at stake, so did he deserve to die? It was a moral dilemma, and Dusty wasn't sure where he stood.

The more time he spent working on the crime desk, the more he was coming to believe that people's motivations and actions didn't fit neatly into categories of black and white, good or bad. There were so many shades of grey. The unique circumstances of each case required consideration.

Dusty shook his head. He could almost hear Reggie's voice telling him that he was overthinking things. He was here to report on crime, state the facts, not deal with the moral dilemmas that might lie behind a felony. Readers were not interested in ethical issues; they wanted to be entertained with stories about those who flouted the Law and those who went to prison. It was as simple as that, Reggie had told him.

He looked at his watch. It was eight o'clock, time to head home. He was putting on his coat when the telephone rang.

'I didn't know if you'd still be here, Dusty,' said the operator on the switchboard. 'There's a woman on the line. She wants to talk to Reggie. She won't give a name.'

Another anonymous tip, hopefully with information that would lead to a good story.

'Put her through.' He heard the click and said, 'Crime desk. Dusty Rhodes speaking.'

'Is Reggie da Costa there?'

'Unfortunately, no, but can I help you? I'm his assistant.'

There was silence at the other end.

'Madam, are you there?'

'I really wanted to speak to Reggie.'

'I promise you that I will pass on any information that you give me.'

He waited patiently, then she spoke. 'Very well. The fact is that I saw the photograph of that murdered man in the newspaper, and I know him. His name isn't Jasper Howard. And he isn't English. I knew him as Jasper Waters.'

Dusty grabbed a pencil and paper. 'When did you meet him?'

'About six months ago.'

'Where was this?'

'Adelaide.'

'Tell me what happened.'

She sighed. 'I'm not sure I can do this, Mr Rhodes. I feel like such a fool.'

'I can assure you that Mr Howard, or Mr Waters as he was to you, fooled many people, including intelligent, trusting people who thought only the best of their fellow human beings. There is no shame, miss. He is the one to blame, not you.'

'Thank you for that.' She paused. 'I met him in Adelaide at an art exhibition. Jasper said that he was an art dealer from Melbourne. He even showed me his business card. He seemed to know all the galleries and art dealers in Adelaide. When I went to leave the exhibition, he asked me if I'd like to go out for dinner. I thought, why not? He was handsome, polite, the perfect gentleman. He took me to one of Adelaide's most exclusive restaurants. I admit that I was completely taken in by him.'

'Did he ever ask you for money?'

'Not at first, but eventually he did.'

'What happened?'

'I was such a fool. Sometimes I find it hard to believe how foolish I was.' She paused, and he could hear her sigh. 'We were visiting an art gallery and planned to have afternoon tea in the city. He claimed to have left his wallet at home. He asked me if I had some spare cash on me. A couple of pounds would do. Of course, I gave it to him, and he repaid me the next day. But it happened again and again, and the amount grew that he owed me.'

'He didn't repay you.'

'He didn't. I admit I was naïve. And inexperienced. Jasper was so handsome and charming. He said that his family was rich. He told me that he was expecting a large endowment from a trust fund.'

'Which never arrived.'

'That's right.' She paused, her voice catching with emotion. 'Life was so good. He told me that he loved me. We started planning a life together. He suggested that I sell my house and we'd buy one together. A home for the two of us. I can't believe that I was so gullible.'

'You sold the house and gave him the money?'

'I did.'

'What happened after that?'

'It was awful. I'd moved into a guest house. One evening, a woman came to the door. She accused me of seeing her husband on the sly. I told her that Jasper wasn't married. She said that I was a liar. She asked for money; otherwise, she'd go to the newspapers. I couldn't afford a scandal so I gave her fifty pounds, and she left. You can understand how I felt about that. I was so confused and angry that I went around to Jasper's hotel to confront him. He was gone. No forwarding address. And my money, gone with him. Luckily, I still had my job, but the whole experience ruined me. I'd lost my home, my money, and my self-respect.

'It took me a while to realise that he'd planned the whole thing. It's so hard to accept something like that.'

Dusty frowned. 'That's terrible. And, from what you've said, it sounds like he had a partner: the woman who pretended to be his wife.'

'That's right. She would have been in on it, too.'

'Do you mind giving me your name?'

'I can't do that. My reputation would be ruined if you wrote about me. At the time, I couldn't even go to the police. If they caught him and it went to court, I'd have to recount what I'd been through. It would have been in all the newspapers. My family would have been identified. I would have lost my job. And I'd be a laughing stock.'

'You still live in Adelaide?'

'I do. I was visiting my sister in Melbourne when I saw the report in *The Argus* about the murder.' She was breathing heavily, the emotion getting the better of her. 'He deserved everything he got. I wish I'd had one of those knives. I would have stabbed him right through the heart, like he did to me.'

Dusty waited, but she offered nothing more. 'Why did you want to speak to Reggie?'

'I don't know.' She sounded tired now that she'd got it off her chest. 'I suppose it was the shock of seeing Waters' photograph in the paper. And I wanted to set the record straight: that he wasn't the man people thought he was. He was a cruel, heartless, shyster who used women for his own material gain. I'm glad he's dead.'

'Do you mind if I use your story? I don't know your name and there's no way that anyone can identify you from what you've told me.'

There was silence, then she spoke. 'I suppose so. Maybe it might warn other women to be careful about whom they trust.'

Dusty heard the click of the telephone as she hung up.

Chapter Twenty

Back at Ruby's house, Reggie had emptied the contents of Jasper Howard's suitcase onto the table. In front of them lay a pile of letters and photographs and a pouch full of business and calling cards.

'Where do we start?' asked Ruby.

'With the photographs,' suggested Reggie.

He took up the first one. It was of a woman, in her twenties holding two large lilies. She was expensively dressed, wearing a thick fur coat and a large, brimmed hat.

The second photograph featured a man and a woman posing for the camera. It was the same woman, but this time she was standing next to a well-dressed man who was seated in a wicker chair. While the fingers of her left hand were curled around a long strand of pearls, her right hand rested on her companion's shoulder. The man was instantly recognisable with his handsome features, intense dark eyes, and high cheekbones.

'Jasper Howard,' said Reggie. He turned it over and smiled. 'Look at this. It says "Jasper and Dulcie 1920." If I'm not wrong, this would be Miss Dulcie Smith from Room 101 at The Hotel Windsor. I'll confirm it with the concierge to be sure.' He nodded slowly. 'I'll bet my last shilling that they were partners in crime.'

The third and last photograph was of a woman in her thirties, wearing a frilled satin dress and a cloche hat. A fox fur was draped around her shoulders. She was looking off to the right of the camera, a thoughtful expression on her face.

'Someone's written on the back of this one,' commented Ruby.

'That's interesting,' said Reggie, looking over her shoulder. 'It says "Love, Lottie. January 1923."' He held the picture up close. 'She looks familiar.'

'You recognise her?'

'I saw a report last week in *The Sydney Morning Herald*. I'm almost certain that she's Lottie O'Leary. She's going on trial for fraud and blackmail.'

'What do you know about her?'

'She goes by the name of Odette de la Tours, Marchioness de Montignac. She was supposedly a relative of the French actress, Renée Adorée, and was a darling of Sydney society. The truth's come out now. Behind the scenes, she worked with Louie "The Dodger" Hayes. Lottie seduced her blackmail targets, then Louie would contact the men and demand money in exchange for keeping quiet. Unfortunately, Lottie finally picked the wrong man. Louie got a beating, and their target bravely took the matter to the coppers. Both are facing charges.'

'That photograph suggests that Mr Howard lived in Sydney at some stage.'

'I'd say so,' agreed Reggie. 'As far as I know, Lottie confined her activities to the New South Wales' capital. If I'm right, and this is Lottie O'Leary, it looks like he knew her better than most. I have some contacts up there who might know more about our Mr Howard. He would have been active up there, just as he's been in Melbourne.'

'You're convinced he's a confidence man?' asked Ruby.

'Undoubtedly. Look at these.' He took some of the business and calling cards from the pouch. 'They confirm it.'

He recited what was written on them. '"Jasper Fitzalan Howard. Property Investment." "Redmond P. Waters. Investment Broker. The Atlantic Investment Co." "Howard Redmond. Importer." "Howard J. Waters. President. Waters & Son. Mergers and Acquisitions." "Jasper Waters. Appraiser of Fine Arts." That last one was the name Jasper Howard used when he stole the Buick from the car salesman. Certainly, a man of many talents. And names.'

Each card was professionally printed, some with the trademark of the company that he supposedly represented. In the case of the Jasper Fitzalan

Howard calling card, the Duke of Norfolk's coat of arms was emblazoned in the top left corner.

'That's brazen,' remarked Ruby, pointing at the shield. 'No wonder he had everyone fooled.'

'Someone saw through it. Someone who was angry enough to kill him.'

'Look at this one. "Madame Esmeralda. Character reader. Eastern Arcade, Melbourne." I wonder if the fortune-teller told him what was in store for him? She should have warned him to be careful.'

Reggie chuckled. 'Mrs Van Cooth mentioned a fortune-teller. She had her fortune told at a soirée at the Bentinck Joneses'. It might be the same person. When I get a chance, I'll follow that up. It might be the link with the tarot card found next to Howard's body.'

'Who do you think Mr Howard really was?'

'We may never know. Probably some nobody. These men and women have the gift of the gab and can persuade people into believing anything. That they're related to the Duke of Norfolk. That they can guarantee that you'll make thousands of pounds if you invest in such and such a scheme. And when the truth comes out, that it was all a tissue of lies, they'll be far away. Their cheques will bounce. The money, that you gave them to pay for that investment opportunity, is gone.'

'That's immoral.'

'Undoubtedly. The trouble is that there are a lot of greedy and gullible people out there who are prepared to place their trust in someone they hardly know. Consequently, they're surprised that they've lost everything: their reputation, their self-respect, their marriage, and their money.'

Ruby shook her head. 'That's terrible.'

'I agree. Let's have a look at what else is here.

'Here's a letter of introduction from the Vice President of J.P. Morgan Bank in New York. And here's another from the Board of Customs and Excise in London. There's even one from the manager of the Theatre Royal, Drury Lane.'

Ruby picked up a couple of letters and skimmed through them. 'You think they're fakes?'

'Definitely.' He examined a few others, which had been tied together with a piece of ribbon. Reggie's eyes sparkled as he flipped through them. 'Now, these are different. Letters from his victims. If these got into the wrong hands, their reputations would be ruined.'

He stroked his moustache as his eyes greedily consumed the contents of the first one. 'Well, well, well. Someone has been very naughty. And they'd pay anything to keep their secrets safe.'

'Let me look, Reggie.'

Ruby went pale as she read the letter. 'My goodness, me. This is dreadful. She's pleading with him to leave her alone. She says that she's already paid him what he wanted, and now he's demanding another two hundred pounds. She says that her husband will divorce her if he finds out.' She looked at the bottom. 'You know who this is, don't you? She's the wife of–'

Reggie nodded slowly. 'Yes, she is.'

'We can't let these be made public. It would ruin their lives.'

'You're right. Although Curtis Flange, my new boss, would love them, being a gossip columnist himself. They would be his bread and butter.'

'Look at this next letter, Reggie. See the name of the writer?' She handed the letter to Reggie and waited. 'Wasn't he found dead a year ago? Up in Sydney? I'm sure I read about him.'

'That's right. Took his own life. They say that he lost all his money in some shady scheme.'

'Howard was behind it?'

'Judging by this letter, it would seem so. And now, Howard's dead, but not by his own hand.'

'Mr Howard must have had a lot of enemies.'

'He moved around to avoid getting caught. But someone found him in the end.'

'What are you going to do with these letters?'

'Keep them somewhere safe. Until I work out the best way to deal with them.'

'You don't think that we should burn them? Or hand them over to the police? Surely, that's the right thing to do?'

'I will, eventually, but I'll need them if I'm going to track down a killer.'

'Reggie, are you sure about that? Shouldn't the police have that task?'

'Most victims won't talk to the coppers. That's why confidence men are so successful. They know their targets would choose to pay up rather than have their private affairs made public in court. Even if they're innocent, they're afraid of being gossiped about or written about in the newspapers. They wouldn't talk to the coppers, but they might talk to me, if I guarantee that they remain anonymous.'

'You could give them back their letters.'

'A bargaining tool to get their cooperation? That's a good idea.'

Ruby frowned. 'I didn't mean that at all. Really, Reggie, I wonder about your ethics sometimes.'

Reggie chucked her under the chin. 'I was making a joke.'

'Really?' Ruby raised an eyebrow. 'Give the letters back to Howard's victims so that they can feel better about the future. It will assure them that their mistakes will stay in the past.'

'I'll think about it. The important thing is that these letters might lead to Howard's killer.'

'Isn't that dangerous?'

He smiled at her. 'Don't worry, Ruby. I'm experienced at this sort of thing.' Reggie pointed at the letters. 'Each of these people had a motive for murder. Each one would have wanted him dead. But only one of them carried it out.'

Ruby placed her hand on Reggie's arm. 'So many lives ruined, by one man.'

The crime reporter looked into her eyes. 'Ruined by more than one person, Ruby. Howard had a partner and, if I'm not wrong, her name was Dulcie Smith. And she's still alive.'

Chapter Twenty-One

Twilight had fallen. On the corner of Elizabeth and Bourke Streets, the Melbourne General Post Office clock chimed six. The footpaths were filled with city workers and weary shoppers making their way home. Drinkers spilled from the pubs onto the streets. Blinds were drawn on shop windows, doors were padlocked, lights were extinguished in office buildings, and the street lights were switched on as trams laden with passengers lumbered down the tracks of Swanston Street towards Flinders Street station. It was the end to yet another working day.

At the top end of Bourke Street, the Eastern Arcade was deserted. Waste paper and leaves swirled around in the dirt, caught up by a chill breeze that blew in from the street. The few shopkeepers who still ran their businesses there had left for the day, except for Madame Esmeralda.

In the light of the candle, she sat at a table spread with a black velvet tablecloth, staring into space. She felt so tired. Each day was the same, putting on performances for people who wanted solutions to their problems, their questions answered, or their anxieties soothed. Sometimes, she wanted to scream at them to fix their own lives when she had so many worries of her own. She unwrapped the scarf from her head and hung up the fringed shawl that she had draped around her shoulders to keep out the chill. No longer Esmeralda, just plain old Essie, that's who she really was. She blew out the candle and switched on the electric light.

She sighed and rubbed her eyes, wondering if she would sleep that night. There was so much to think about; her thoughts disturbed her more than she could express. Jasper dead. The Ten of Swords. Knife wounds in the flesh. Betrayal. It had come true. The Tarot had spoken.

A knock at the door startled her. Surely, no one else wanted her services that day. She'd had enough. They could go away. But the knock came again, and the hinges squeaked as the door was pushed open.

'I thought you'd still be here.'

In the inner doorway stood a dark-haired woman. She was wearing a black satin coat, cloche hat, and black gloves, a fox fur draped over the collar. Her face was pale against the sombre outfit. In the electric light, the dark rings around her eyes were plain to see.

Essie looked startled. 'Hello, Dulcie. I wasn't expecting to see you. Come in and sit down.'

They faced each other across the table. The silence stretched between them until Essie spoke. 'I'm sorry about what happened to Jasper.'

'Are you? Are you sure of that? You see, I've been wondering who killed him. And I thought you might know.'

The fortune-teller flushed. 'I don't know anything.'

'The Ten of Swords. It was in the newspaper.' Dulcie stared at Essie, her eyes accusing her.

'I showed it to him when he came here last,' Essie explained, her eyes drifting in the direction of the tarot pack on the sideboard.

'Why would you do that?'

'I did a reading before he died. The Tarot predicted that we were going to part ways, that the life we'd been living in Melbourne was coming to an end. The Ten of Swords made that message perfectly clear. I told him about it. He must have taken the card with him.'

'When was this?'

'The day before he died. He came here in the late afternoon. He knew that he needed to leave Melbourne and start afresh in Sydney. He said that it would be safer for us if we split up. I told him that my business was going well, so I was happy to stay in Melbourne.'

'Jasper told me that he was tired of you; that's why he was going.'

Essie shook her head. 'I don't believe you. Jasper wasn't tired of me. He said that it was getting dangerous in Melbourne. He felt that someone knew who he really was and was going to turn him in to the police.'

'Is that true?' Dulcie asked sharply. 'He never told me that.'

'He didn't want to scare you. He was your brother, and he wanted to protect you.' She met Dulcie's gaze. 'I'm telling you the truth.'

'I don't know what to believe,' Dulcie replied. 'I thought you might be angry with him. I know that you were in love with him. And what about the tarot card in his hand? Everything pointed to you. But now the newspapers are saying that Mrs Plumstead is a suspect. The fact is that Jasper's hurt a lot of people in his time.'

'So have you,' said Essie, contempt in her voice. 'You should share the blame. Playing the part of the outraged wife. Or the irresistible *femme fatale* luring men on, only to trap them. If someone had a grudge against your brother, they might have one against you, too.'

'How do I know it wasn't you?' cried Dulcie. 'You were in love with him, and he was going to leave you. And that tarot card. Your tarot card. Ten swords sticking out of a body. Jasper's body.'

'How dare you come here accusing me of killing him. I can't believe that you'd think I was capable of that. You're being hysterical.'

Dulcie rubbed her eyes. 'Sorry, sorry. I can't sleep. Every time I close my eyes, I see him ... dead.' She stifled a sob. 'Everything is topsy turvy now that he's gone.'

'Of course, you feel bad. You were his sister. Leave Melbourne. Start afresh.'

Dulcie sighed heavily. 'I don't want to. I've met someone.'

Essie stared at her. 'Surely not Councillor Plumstead? I've seen you with him, staring at him with lovesick eyes. Be realistic. He's married, and he wouldn't contemplate a divorce. His career wouldn't allow that. And that wife of his would make a fuss.'

Dulcie rallied. 'But he promised me that we'd marry. And he buys me lovely presents.' She touched the pearls around her neck.

Essie laughed. 'You're falling for the same lies that you used on your male victims. And does the councillor know that you're the sister of Jasper Howard, the man who was blackmailing his wife?'

'Of course not.'

'Won't he be angry when he finds out who you really are?'

'Why should he find out? I'm not telling him. I'm Dulcie Smith to him, not Dulcie Howard.'

'Can't you see how you're complicating the situation? Having an affair with Councillor Plumstead when his wife is a suspect in Jasper's murder?'

'I understand that, but I need to have a future, and Donald can give me one. And if Mrs Plumstead goes to prison for murder, that leaves me in a better situation. No one will quibble about him divorcing her and marrying me.'

Essie shook her head in despair. 'You're a fool. And you're putting us in a dangerous situation. If your relationship with Plumstead is made public, the newspapers will want to know who you are and where you've come from. They'll find the connection between you, me, and Jasper. You would never have considered this if Jasper were still alive. He would have talked you out of it.'

'That's where you're wrong,' Dulcie retorted. 'I was going to stay in Melbourne rather than follow him to Sydney. Jasper knew about that. Besides, he was getting difficult to work with. He'd changed so much. It was all a bit of a game to him at first: get a bit of cash from those who had plenty, live the good life. I was happy with that. But, over the last few months, it's become more personal. As if he were taking revenge on a world that had treated him badly when we were young. He was making money at the expense of innocent men and women. Not necessarily those who deserved to be swindled. And nothing was ever enough. It was always "find another sucker, another victim and squeeze them dry." Jasper ruined so many people.'

Essie stared at her, incredulous. 'And you didn't? I never heard you complain.'

'I wanted to stop and find another life. An ordinary life. And now, my brother's dead.' Dulcie looked around her, her eyes wide with fear. 'Someone took their revenge on him. Now I've reached the stage where I see strangers and wonder if we've met before, in another city or town. They stare at me, and I wonder–'

'What?'

'If they know who I am. What I've done. If they're going to kill me, too.'

Essie laid a hand on her arm. 'Calm down. You know that you can trust me. We can look after each other, if that's what you want. Tell me where you're staying now, so that I can get in touch with you.'

'I've taken a room at the Menzies Hotel, on the corner of Bourke and William Streets.'

'Still the best of everything.'

'I deserve a good life.'

'Jasper thought so, too.'

Dulcie was silent, tears forming in her eyes. 'I miss him. I look in the mirror, and I see him.'

'You are very much like him, I agree.' Essie had been surprised by the resemblance between the siblings when she first met them. Their dark hair, high cheekbones, and brown eyes. 'Do you remember when we first met?'

'I do,' replied Dulcie, calmer now. 'It was at a house party. Mount Lofty House, in the Adelaide foothills. I remember saying to Jasper that they had a fortune-teller in the gardens, providing a bit of entertainment for the guests.'

Essie nodded. 'It was in the afternoon. I was sitting alone at the table doing a reading for myself. I'd turned over a tarot card showing the Fool. Jasper came and stood next to me. He asked me who the Fool was. I told him that it didn't mean that; the Fool represented new opportunities, the beginning of a new journey, a new venture, filled with hope and enthusiasm. He asked me if I was open to that. I looked up at him and I knew someone special had come into my life.'

Dulcie nodded. 'We were lucky to find you. You were so clever at directing people our way. Your ability to sum up personalities. Recognise those who would be willing to invest in Jasper's schemes. And those who were gullible and weak-minded looking for love.'

Essie frowned. 'I wish I'd stayed in Adelaide. I wish I'd never met you. I've never been as calculating as you and Jasper. The Tarot is the only thing

I've ever been able to rely on.' She studied Dulcie. 'Do you really think that Plumstead is the answer for you?'

'Hopefully, I can make a new future for myself with this man. He might buy a house for the two of us. Somewhere quiet. That would make me happy. I'd change my ways. Stay out of the limelight. Stay out of the newspapers.'

'That might be harder than you think. If people see your photograph now, they might recognise you.' Her eyes narrowed. 'And you might end up like Jasper.'

Dulcie leaned forward, fear etched into her face. 'Why did you say that? What should I do, Essie?' Her eyes moved to the pack of tarot cards lying on the table. 'What do the cards say?'

Essie covered her hair with the scarf and wrapped the shawl around her. She lit the candle and turned off the electric light.

'Let's see what the Tarot has in store for you.'

* * *

The reading was almost over. Dulcie had found little comfort from the fall of the first six cards. Now, there was only one card left, one that might offer her a future. Madame Esmeralda turned up the seventh card. She smiled grimly. How fitting. It was the Tower, built on a rock precipice, struck by lightning, with flames licking the structure. Two bodies and a crown were falling into the abyss below.

Dulcie went pale. 'What does it mean?'

Madame Esmeralda's voice remained steady. 'The Tower represents chaos and destruction, sudden upheaval and unexpected change.'

'Jasper's death,' whispered Dulcie.

Madame Esmeralda nodded. 'The tower is built on shaky foundations, just as your life with Jasper was based on lies and deception. It has been struck by lightning, and flames threaten to destroy it.'

'What does this mean for me?'

'It means that life will be very difficult for you for a while. You must be careful. Because if you're not–'

The words died on her lips as the flame from the candle flickered briefly and died, leaving them in darkness.

Chapter Twenty-Two

It was Friday morning. Reggie was sitting at his desk contemplating the chain of events in the Howard murder. He was eager to fill in some of the gaps about the man known as Jasper Howard. The murdered man remained an enigma, and that rankled with the crime reporter. By now, he should have had an accurate picture of the dead man, but all he had were impressions from his victims, which didn't add up to much. Who he really was and where he came from remained a mystery, and Reggie didn't like mysteries. Added to this was that Jasper Howard had dual roles in this case: that of predator and also that of murder victim. There were letters, there were photographs, but the man himself remained out of reach, elusive, like a reflection in a mirror.

He checked his watch and saw that it was ten o'clock. He was due at the Plumstead mansion at eleven.

Over three weeks had passed since his interview with the Plumsteads, as his mother had pointedly reminded him over dinner the previous Wednesday.

'Peggy Plumstead is the daughter of one of Mildred Bardsley Smith's greatest friends. You mustn't let her down, Reggie. I gave her my solemn promise that you would help her.'

Bowing to her wishes and by skilful organisation, Reggie had engineered another meeting with the lady that day, while her husband was sitting in parliament. Hopefully, Mrs Plumstead might be more forthcoming without her antagonistic husband present. Perhaps there was some detail that she had forgotten? Perhaps there was something she wanted to confess? He also thought that it would help his cause if they met away from the Plumstead mansion in neutral territory. She certainly could not be seen with him in the offices of *The Argus* and she had the advantage over him if they met at her Toorak address. They had agreed on a picnic lunch at the Melbourne Botanic Gardens, given the favourable weather forecast.

He was about to pack up the file on the Howard murder when the telephone rang.

'A lady for you, Reggie,' said the telephone operator. 'She won't give her name.'

'Put her through, thanks.' He waited until he heard the click. 'Reggie da Costa. Crime desk.'

'Mr da Costa. I have some information for you regarding the murder at The Windsor.'

The voice was that of a woman, well-spoken and cultured.

'Can I have your name?' asked Reggie, reaching for pen and paper.

'I think not. It would not do if it became known that I had incriminated someone within my social circles.'

'What can you tell me?'

'I was attending a soirée at Mrs Bentinck Jones' home in July. It was a large affair. A guest list of the finest, in fact. Mr Jasper Howard was there. So were the Kiddles. I might add that I had not been introduced to Mr Howard, but his face appears on the front page of every newspaper these days, so I recognised him.'

'Go on.'

'I took myself out into the garden; I was wanting a bit of fresh air. I sat next to the fountain in the fernery. Who should come out but Mr Howard and Sir Ambrose, and they were talking quite loudly; in fact, they were arguing over some investment scheme.

'I was about to leave, but the argument was getting heated, so I stayed hidden in the shadows, not wanting to embarrass either man. Besides, to tell the truth, it was fascinating. Who would have thought?'

'What did they say exactly?'

'Sir Ambrose was very agitated. He accused Mr Howard of being a swindler, a confidence man. That the property purchase was a fake. That there wasn't any plan to improve wool production. That he feared that his money was gone.'

'And what did Mr Howard say to that?'

'Mr Howard was unfazed by the accusations. He kept reassuring Sir Ambrose that the money was safe and that the sale of the property was in the process of being completed.'

'Sir Ambrose swore at him. He said that he wanted his money back. That he wanted to renege on the deal. Mr Howard wasn't happy with that and he told him so. Withdrawing was not an option, he said.'

The woman's voice grew softer, but there was an intensity in her speech. 'Sir Ambrose said, "Give me back my money or I'll kill you."'

'He said that, did he?'

'He did, and he sounded like he meant it.'

'What was Howard's reaction?'

'He laughed at him. And then, he walked back inside. Very nonchalant about it all.'

'What did Sir Ambrose do?'

'I could see him from the light on the back patio. He had gone red in the face, and he was swearing and clenching his fists.

'I followed him inside a minute or two later, just in time to see he and his wife leaving. She was none too happy, I might add. Mr Howard was still there, chatting to some of the other guests.'

'It's October. Why didn't you ring me a month ago?'

'I've been weighing up whether I should say anything. Sir Ambrose is a friend, you see.'

'Is that all you can tell me?'

'Sir Ambrose Beauchamp Kiddle threatened to kill Jasper Howard. And now, Mr Howard is dead. Isn't that enough?'

There was a click as the woman hung up the telephone. Reggie sat on for a few minutes, making notes of the conversation and digesting the information that he had received. This case was becoming too complicated. Blackmail and swindles, and now, another suspect. And there was still the question of Mrs Plumstead's guilt or innocence. He looked at his watch. Half-past ten. Time to get changed and freshen up before his meeting with the main suspect in the case.

Chapter Twenty-Three

At eleven o'clock, the Hupmobile, polished and gleaming, purred up the circular driveway of the Plumstead mansion and stopped in front of the entrance. Reggie was dressed in what he termed his 'sports suit,' in olive green wool tweed, with a half-belt across the back and four flap pockets. It was his preferred choice for informal race meetings or picnics. It didn't crease, and it always sprang back into shape.

Standing beneath the intricately carved and timber-framed front gable was Mrs Plumstead, a picnic hamper at her feet. Reggie walked over, shook her hand, and, after helping her into the motorcar, went back to collect the basket.

Driving along Alexandra Avenue, Reggie stole the occasional glance at his passenger. She looked very attractive in a heavy-weight crepe de chine blouse, in vintage rose. The top was pin-tucked with embroidery around the neckline over a matching box-pleated skirt. Her hair was pulled back into a twisted knot at the neck, beneath a wide brimmed straw hat trimmed with a single rose.

'This is a lovely automobile, Mr da Costa,' she commented. 'Lovely colour, too.'

'It's a Hupmobile. In forest green,' Reggie replied. He smiled. A good first impression often paved the way for a more revealing interview.

They motored along, the Yarra River to their right, which could occasionally be seen between the screen of trees at its edge. Soon, they were driving along Birdwood Avenue, which bordered the Melbourne Botanic Gardens. Reggie parked the car near the entrance and together they took a leisurely stroll through the English-style gardens, with their sweeping lawns, meandering paths, and exotic collection of tropical and temperate plants. Beautifully tended traditional garden beds contrasted with Fern Gully, a shady haven of ferns, shrubs, palms, and a bubbling brook crossed by small bridges. The Gardens attracted a range of birdlife, from graceful swans gliding across the ornamental lake, to the musical 'tink tink' of bell birds, the riotous laughter of kookaburras, and the raucous squawking of cockatoos.

After admiring their surroundings and making casual conversation for a while, Reggie and his companion found a spot to eat near the Temple of Winds, a portico built in the classical style. The sun came out from behind the clouds, and there was a slight breeze, making it an excellent day for a picnic. Reggie spread a rug on the grass and invited Mrs Plumstead to make herself comfortable. She unpacked the picnic hamper and handed Reggie cutlery, crockery, and a white napkin. He uncorked a bottle of ginger beer and poured two glasses.

'What a wonderful place for a picnic, Mr da Costa. And the weather is divine.' She smiled. 'It's good to be away from home and unpleasantness. Let's toast an end to this murder investigation.'

'Do you want to discuss it now?' Reggie asked tentatively.

'Let's eat first.'

She laid out the food, delicacies prepared by the Plumstead kitchen staff. There was roast duck, slices of cold roast beef and ham, and sandwiches filled with grated cheese, cream, and watercress. For dessert, there were small sweet plum puddings and jam puffs, washed down with more ginger beer and lemonade, followed by a thermos of tea.

When they had finished, Mrs Plumstead packed the remains of the lunch away.

She looked at him intently. 'You have questions to ask, I believe.'

Reggie took his opportunity.

'Tell me again how you met Mr Howard.'

She was silent for a time, and then, after gathering her thoughts, she began. 'It was at the Mayoral Ball, held to celebrate the arrival of the American

Fleet. The 29th of July. I was chatting to Beatrice–Mrs Van Cooth–when she noticed Mr Howard talking to Lady Beauchamp Kiddle. Beatrice pointed him out to me. She was very excited. She told me that a fortune-teller had predicted that she'd meet a handsome stranger with a foreign accent, and she had, at a soirée only a week or so before. It was Jasper. English, cultured, very good-looking, impeccable manners. And there he was again. At the Mayoral Ball. One of the waitresses offered him some food and then, he came over to us.

'He flattered Beatrice. He told her that she was looking radiant. She liked that. I must say that he knew how to make the best of himself. Jet-black hair lightly oiled with Brilliantine. Fashionable suit, cut to accentuate his height and his broad shoulders. Crisp white shirt, silk waistcoat, highly polished shoes.'

'You notice these things?'

'I do.' She stared at Reggie, holding his gaze. 'You, Mr da Costa, appreciate the need for a well-cut suit and the importance of making a good impression. I can see that. But the difference between you and Mr Howard is that he would have been described as a ladies' man.'

'You realised that at the time? That he was a *ladies' man*?'

'Hindsight is a wonderful thing. I should have seen the signs that he was interested in me rather than Mrs Van Cooth. But he didn't deliberately direct any overt flattery my way.' She shrugged. 'We were introduced. We made easy conversation. He asked where my husband was. I said that Donald was at the ball, but I didn't know exactly where he was.

'Mr Howard said, "I can't imagine why a husband would leave such a lovely wife alone." I took that on face value, nothing more. Men often say things like that. But I don't think Beatrice liked it. He asked if I was enjoying myself. I told him that I was a bit of a homebody, but that the ball was an important occasion for the people of Melbourne, so I had come.

'We chatted for a bit. Mr Howard asked Beatrice to recommend a day trip for him. He was going back to England, to his estate, and wanted to see some of the Victorian countryside before he left. Beatrice suggested Hanging Rock. She offered to be his guide. He agreed immediately but insisted that she would be put in a compromising situation if they went alone, she being a married woman and such an attractive one, as he put it. He gave her no option. She was none too happy having to ask me to come. I was feeling uncomfortable, knowing that I was going to be a chaperone. I didn't have much choice. She wanted to go, and I was the only person who could give her what she wanted. We agreed on the following Sunday.'

'Tell me about the trip to Hanging Rock.'

Mrs Plumstead shifted position, leaning back on the picnic basket.

'It was actually very nice. He picked us up about ten o'clock in his Buick. Although now I know it wasn't his automobile at all. He'd had a picnic basket made up by the kitchens of The Hotel Windsor. I sat in the back seat while Beatrice was in the front passenger seat. He chatted away. Occasionally, he'd direct a comment my way, but he gave most of his attention to Mrs Van Cooth.'

'Designed to put you off guard?'

'In retrospect, yes.

'We travelled out towards Mount Macedon along the North Western Highway. During the trip, Beatrice chatted about the delights of the Australian countryside while I watched the scenery. By the time we reached the turnoff to Hanging Rock, after the road to Woodend, I was feeling quite comfortable in his company. He had behaved impeccably.

'Mount Diogenes, Hanging Rock that is, is an awesome sight, Mr da Costa. I don't know if you've ever been there.' Reggie shook his head. 'It's an ancient volcanic plug shaped into a conglomeration of the most bizarre and wonderful formations. We were talking about its history. One of the rock formations resembles a woman. It reminded me of a Greek myth I'd read about, so I recounted it for them. It goes something like this: A man is driven to suicide when the woman he loves rejects him. When Aphrodite asks her about it, the woman reacts coldly, saying that she doesn't care if he's dead. Then, Aphrodite turns her to stone.

'When I finished, Beatrice asked Mr Howard whether he'd broken many hearts. He went quiet, then said that there was one woman who had taken the end of their relationship badly.'

CHAPTER TWENTY-THREE

'What did Mrs Van Cooth say to that?'

'She didn't say anything, which was unusual for her.'

'Then what happened?'

'Mr Howard changed the subject, and it was forgotten. At the time, I didn't think too much about it, but later on it struck me as strange because he never spoke about his personal life. His conversation was all very superficial, if you know what I mean. Flattering us, showing interest no matter what we said, agreeing with us. I wonder now who that woman was, and if she were involved in his murder.'

'When it was suggested that the three of you go to Sorrento, how did Mrs Van Cooth react?'

'She was angry. There was no doubt in my mind that she wanted him to herself.'

'Her marriage is not a happy one?' asked Reggie.

'A marriage of convenience, Mr da Costa. But who am I to judge?'

Chapter Twenty-Four

The murder of Jasper Howard was not the only subject occupying Reggie's mind. Soon, Regulation 79 would become law, and opposition to it was unfortunately gathering pace, fuelled by those who benefitted from lax governmental supervision of patent medicines. Not only travelling salesmen and grocers who sold remedies concocted by fake doctors, but also anyone who had a vested interest in overturning the legislation, had joined together to call for its repeal, insisting that the status quo should continue. Whispers had reached Reggie that politicians were being pressured to oppose the passing of the law.

Now that he'd received the laboratory report that he'd commissioned, Reggie had positive proof that the public was being hoodwinked. Patent medicines could be dangerous and were unregulated. It was up to him to enlighten his readers as to the true state of play. People had to recognise that confidence men, like Jasper Howard, existed in different forms, whether it be leading husbands and wives astray, then blackmailing them, or convincing individuals to invest their hard-earned money in non-existent get-rich-quick schemes, or persuading the public to purchase medicinal remedies based on ridiculous claims about their efficacy.

As he sat in his office, Reggie re-read the report that had appeared in that day's *Argus*:

THE GREAT DECEPTION
PATENT MEDICINE HOAX

By REGGIE DA COSTA, Senior Crime Reporter

Victoria is in the grip of an influx of patent medicines, whose producers and salesmen make outrageous claims that they cure a wide range of illnesses. From the 1st of January 1926, the Victorian Government will introduce laws to require that the ingredients of pills, potions, and powders are listed on their packaging, so that the general public is no longer being deceived into believing that patent medicines are harmless.

Recent tests, carried out by independent laboratories, have shown that some pills and tonics are brimming with opium, cocaine, tar, heroin, and alcohol. Is it any wonder that these remedies prove addictive, or worse, fatal?

'Snake Oil' Salesmen

Purveyors of these products are often known as 'snake oil' salesmen. In the past, snake oil was peddled as a cure for rheumatism and arthritis, although its effectiveness was untested. Since then, ridiculous claims have been made that syrups, tonics, pills, and salves can cure everything from rashes, insomnia, indigestion, and toothache, to major ailments such as blood diseases, mental illness, tuberculosis, and cancer. Lies and deception are the bait that 'snake oil' salesmen use to hook gullible and innocent members of the public in order to sell their fraudulent and dangerous remedies. Many of these 'quacks' are criminals, engaged in deceptive behaviour.

Two recent cases illustrate the dangers that lie with taking patent medicines. Recently, in court, Lucius C Clutterbuck was fined £12 for falsely claiming that his 'Clutterbuck's Household Panacea' could cure cancer, consumption, hernia, pneumonia, pleurisy, diphtheria, scarlet fever, typhoid fever, appendicitis, cholera, and septic poisoning. The Government Analyst found that Clutterbuck's Household Panacea contained 96.5 per cent of methylated alcohol. Clutterbuck gave evidence that he had tried it on birds, cats, and dogs before he put it on the market! This is hardly scientific proof that his 'Panacea' works.

The second case shows the disastrous effects that some of these so-called remedies can have on the health of unsuspecting patients. Some believe that the radioactive element Radium is a cure-all. It has been found in mineral springs and well water, and has been bottled for personal use as an elixir. Radithor is advertised widely as 'A Cure for the Living Dead' or 'Perpetual Sunshine.' Stories are coming out of the United States of America about one user who has died as a result of his excessive consumption of Radithor. His death has been described as 'radiation poisoning.' Prior to his demise, his teeth fell out, his lower jaw was removed, and his bone tissue disintegrated. His funeral required that he be buried in a lead-lined coffin, to contain the radiation in his remains!

Call out these criminals!

In the interests of public health, it's time to call out these quacks and parasites who are living off the lifeblood of Melbourne's men, women, and children. We call on our citizens to support the introduction of new laws to regulate the trade in patent medicines and rid Victoria of this scourge.

[*The Argus* October 12, 1925]

Reggie looked up as his protégé, Dusty Rhodes, entered the office.

'Regulation can't come soon enough,' he declared, tapping the newspaper article that lay on his desk. 'What did you think of my report?'

'Hard-hitting,' replied Dusty as he took a seat on the other side of his mentor's desk. 'I particularly liked your last paragraph. "...it's time to call out these quacks and parasites who are living off the lifeblood of Melbourne's men, women, and children." Very *Truth*-like.'

Reggie chuckled. 'True. But it is a serious problem. What they're peddling is so dangerous. Who knows who will be struck down next? Hopefully, no one close to us.'

'I was in a chemist shop last week,' said Dusty, running his fingers through his mop of untidy hair. 'I asked the pharmacist about the proposed laws. He can't wait to see them implemented. He's frustrated that he has to keep a record of every prescription that he dispenses, but these charlatans don't. They can treat any disease or condition without being held accountable. Honestly, Reggie, I confess that I didn't realise how bad the present situation is. And how dangerous. I decided to put it to the test.'

'What did you do?'

'There's a herbalist's shop near my house. I went in yesterday and told him that I was feeling rundown. Do you know what he told me? That my bones were growing faster than my muscles, putting my muscles under strain. Imagine that? He offered to sell me a bottle of medicine for four shillings. I laughed in his face and left.'

Reggie nodded. 'The average patient doesn't realise what he's taking. They believe all the propaganda. They believe that these remedies are safe. And they're exposed to persuasive advertisements which spruik this stuff.'

'What do you hope to achieve?'

'I want to expose these frauds. Show the public that quacks can't be trusted. They pretend to have medical qualifications, even call themselves doctors, when they probably haven't finished Grade Eight. I want to make the public think!'

He pushed aside the laboratory's report. 'Now, enough about snake oil salesmen, what do you have for me?'

Dusty smiled and reached for his notebook. 'I had an interesting telephone call from one of Jasper Howard's victims. She was on holiday from Adelaide and saw his photograph in the newspaper. She knew him as Jasper Waters. He charmed her enough so that she sold her house and gave him the money, thinking that they'd buy a place together. Of course, his *wife* turned up on her doorstep. Unfortunately, the victim handed over another fifty quid to keep her quiet. The money from her house sale was gone, just like Howard.'

'No coppers, I guess?'

'As you'd expect. She didn't want the shame and mortification of being swindled and made to look like a fool.'

'Any name?'

'No luck there.'

'Understandable.'

'But she agreed that we could tell her story as a warning to other women.'

'Jasper Waters. That fits with the calling cards he was carrying.'

'Calling cards?'

Reggie explained about the documents that had been concealed in Jasper Howard's suitcase. 'There were letters, too,' he added, 'from his blackmail victims pleading for mercy. Ruby wants me to hand them over to the police. Or give them back to the victims.'

Dusty smiled. 'She would. What did you say?'

'What do you think? I told her that I need them if I'm going to track down some of Howard's victims, otherwise I have no evidence of their involvement. They would deny everything. But I will do something with the letters once I solve this case. Maybe I'll burn them.'

'You surprise me. Why would you do that?'

'Ruby's right. If the letters are made public, reputations would suffer, and lives would be open to scrutiny. Your sister made me think about the ramifications of that.'

'Better watch out. Ruby might teach you something about morality and ethics.'

Reggie's face softened. 'The love of a good woman.' He grinned. 'Can't have a crime reporter with a conscience, can we?' He looked at Dusty. 'No answer required.'

'What's next?'

'I fancy a train trip. There's one of Howard's associates that I'd like to have a chat to, as well as some of his victims. Find some answers to the mystery that was Jasper Howard.'

CHAPTER TWENTY-FOUR

Dusty nodded slowly. 'That sounds like a good next step.'

Reggie studied his assistant. 'Go out and buy yourself a new suit.'

'Why boss?'

'Because the patches on your trousers and that coat won't get you access to where we're going.'

'And that would be–?'

'Sydney, Dusty. Fancy a trip to Sydney?'

Chapter Twenty-Five

Curtis Flange sat back in his chair, a pile of newspaper clippings from *The Argus* in front of him. The frustration that he was feeling was showing on his face. His eyes narrowed, and the frown lines on his forehead gathered as he read the crime report from Saturday's edition of the newspaper.

'Damn,' he muttered under his breath. 'I told him what to do, and he ignores me.'

If Reggie had been aware of the reception he was about to receive when he entered Flange's office, he might have thought twice about putting forward his request to travel interstate. But unaware he was, and so he sailed in oblivious to the glacial reception he was about to receive.

'Have you got a moment for me, Curtis?'

'Reginald. Please address me as Mr Flange.'

'Have you got a moment for me, Mr Flange?' said Reggie, his lip curling contemptuously.

'Actually, I have. I need to discuss these reports with you.' He prodded the pile of clippings with his finger. 'I've been reading your reports on Squizzy Taylor and his appearance in court.'

'What about them? It's a straightforward case of his ex-wife asking for alimony and that dirty little rat of a gangster saying that he can't afford it. The judge rules in his favour, ignoring Squizzy's collection of cars and the gambling dens he runs in Fitzroy. Not to mention his association with jury-fixing, brothels, and illegal booze.'

'I understand that, but you need to get into the detail that our readers love.'

Reggie cocked his head. 'Which is–?'

'Now, Reginald, we know that Squizzy admires the American bootleggers. It's obvious from the clothing he wears and the way he acts. Only the other day, I saw him featured in *another* newspaper. The photograph said it all. Dressed as a toff. Wearing a quality suit in the finest fabric. Silk shirt. Silk tie. Silk socks. Patent leather shoes. Diamonds dripping off his fingers and his tie pin. Smoking a cigar. And seated in a classy American motorcar.'

Reggie nodded. 'It's true that he dresses to impress. I even heard that when Detective Piggott raided his home, Squizzy was in bed wearing pink silk pyjamas.' He chuckled, then noted the disapproving look on his boss's face. 'What's your point, Mr Flange?'

'My point, Reginald, is that you're missing the point! I told you that I want to give our readers a glimpse of the lifestyles of the rich and famous.'

'Rich and famous? Squizzy Taylor is a nasty little criminal who worms his way out of every charge brought against him. You want me to write about what he *wears?*' Reggie nearly choked at the thought.

'Indeed, I do. Haven't I made that clear to you? Now, I'm a busy man, so if you have something to say, make it quick.'

Reggie took a deep breath and tried to ignore his mounting frustration. 'I'm following some lines of inquiry regarding the Howard murder. You mentioned last month that you were at a charity function at The Windsor on the night of his murder. Do you keep records of those who attended it?'

'Of course, I do. Who was there, what they wore, what they said. It's what makes the social pages of *The Argus* sing.'

'Sing?' Reggie raised an eyebrow. 'Of course, sing. Metaphorically speaking.'

Flange smiled and reached into the filing cabinet positioned next to his desk. He removed a folder and flipped through the pages. 'January, 1925. February. June. Ah, here it is. Saturday, the 29th of August, 1925. The Lord Mayor's Fund charity ball. The Hotel Windsor.'

'Could I look at that list?'

'What does this have to do with a murder?'

'I'm not sure yet, but I'm following up leads.'

'If you wish.' Flange handed over the list and watched as Reggie scanned the names.

'Interesting,' the crime reporter said, although no other comment was forthcoming.

'Did you find what you wanted?'

'I did, thank you.'

'Now, if that's all that you need, you may go, Reginald.'

Reggie took a deep breath. 'One more thing, boss.'

'Mr Flange.'

'Yes, that, too. As I said, I'm continuing my investigation into the murder of Jasper Howard at The Hotel Windsor.'

'I thought we were through with that.'

'Certain information has come into my possession which makes an interstate trip a necessity. I want to go to Sydney after the Melbourne Cup and check out Howard's background. He lived there for a while. Bluey Talbot says he'll look after the crime desk while I'm away, so there's no problem there.'

'You want to do what?' Flange spluttered. He had gone so red that it appeared that his bow tie was strangling him.

'Take the train to Sydney,' replied Reggie coolly. 'Take young Dusty with me, too. We'll interview those who knew Jasper Howard. It will make for a great scoop.'

'What's the use of this? He was a nobody. You've already told me that he's not related to the Duke of Norfolk; in fact, he has no social connections except those he made when he was impersonating aristocracy. He was a confidence man. He was a phony.'

Reggie sighed, trying to keep calm. 'That's all true, but he's a mystery. And our readers love a mystery. He fooled Melbourne society. He stole their money. He blackmailed women, one of whom is now a suspect in his murder. Can't you see the immense interest this story will generate?'

'It's in the past, Reginald. Our readers want to know about the present. Who's going to what event? Who's hosting the Spring Racing Carnival parties? Who's wearing the latest Paris fashions? Who's going to be debutante of the year? And, if I might add, what Squizzy Taylor was wearing in court.'

Reggie scowled. 'If Kramer was here–'

'But he's not, and I am. And you've ignored what I've asked you to do. It was a simple request.'

Reggie struggled to regain control, casting his mind around for an argument that would change Flange's mind. 'I understand that, and I'll do better, I promise, Mr Flange. But perhaps I neglected to tell you that Howard was associated with Odette, the Marchioness de Montignac? And Odette is one of the first people I'll be interviewing.'

Flange sat upright. 'Why didn't you say so? She's in all the social pages. She's related to the French actress, Renée Adorée.' His eyes were nearly starting out of his head at the prospect.

Reggie sensed that now was not the time to tell his boss that Odette was a charlatan, whose real name was Lottie O'Leary. Or that she was an associate of Louie 'The Dodger' Hayes. And that she was facing charges of fraud and blackmail. And that he hadn't actually set up an interview with her at all.

'I might add that Howard mixed with the *crème de la crème* of Sydney society,' Reggie continued. 'It's such a pity that I'll have to refuse all those invitations that I've wrangled to some of the best houses around the Harbour. Vaucluse, Manly, Potts Point, Hunters Hill.'

Flange's eyes misted over. 'Now, now, I'm a reasonable man. This story sounds far more interesting than I first thought. You should explain yourself better, Reginald. Of course, you can go to Sydney, but I expect to hear all the gossip. You understand me?'

'Never in doubt.'

Flange's fat cheeks glowed with happiness. 'Sydney society. That will sell newspapers.' He cleared his throat and assumed an official tone of voice. 'You have my permission, Reginald. And you can take Dusty. One week, including travelling time. Would that suffice?'

Reggie calculated travel times. Two nights on the train, all up. Four days in Sydney. It wasn't long enough, but he might stretch it to eight or nine days overall. He'd get his story on Howard and keep Flange happy by providing him with a frivolous piece on Sydney society and photographs of the upper classes at play.

He smiled. 'That would be wonderful, Mr Flange. Thank you so much.'

As he exited the office, he raised his eyes to heaven. 'Get better soon, Kramer, or I might be guilty of murder myself!'

Chapter Twenty-Six

D r Hiram T Wishbone was in the small workshop behind Mr Higgs' engineering factory, staring in frustration at the Violet Ray machine that lay in pieces on the bench in front of him. His future in the patent medicine industry depended on his ability to diversify into medical machines and devices. Pills and lotions weren't enough to give him a reasonable standard of living, and he knew that side of the business was facing an uncertain future. Soon Regulation 79 would be law. Damned interference. What did the Government know about medicine? What did they know about the restorative and beneficial effects of cocaine, opium, and morphine?

The Bardsley Smiths and their friends, members of an exclusive Brighton coterie, had enthusiastically endorsed his extensive range of syrups, pills, lotions, and tonics, but the real money was in the hardware. Four Wishbone Electromagnetic Belts had been sold within the group, garnering him one hundred pounds, and only last week, Edith McGillicutty, a sour old puss if ever there was one, had embraced one of his cheaper contraptions: Dr Wishbone's Delicate Dimpler.

It was during a visit to the McGillicutty home when he was re-stocking her supplies of Dr Wishbone's Elixir of Youth that, in a moment of weakness, Edith had confided to the good doctor, 'You might find this hard to believe, Dr Wishbone, but I was not popular in my youth.'

'Impossible, dear lady. You have a most engaging personality.' He had almost choked on his words. But a sale was a sale, and he adhered to the maxim that honesty should never get in the way of a financial transaction.

'No, no,' Edith insisted. 'My lack of popularity had nothing to do with my character. It was my lack of dimples.' She leaned in, ready to impart a confidence. 'When I was a girl, a friend of mine captivated many young men by simply smiling and showing her dimples. I was far superior to her in terms of conversation and beauty. But as soon as she showed her dimples, the men would flock to her, like seagulls to a dead fish.'

Dr Wishbone stroked his beard, envisaging the scene. 'It's hard to imagine that any man would be able to resist you, Mrs McGillicutty. Yet, it is an amazing coincidence that I happen to have one of my Delicate Dimpler devices with me.'

He took it out of his bag and laid it on the table.

'How does it work?' asked Edith, marvelling at the contraption.

'It is quite simple to use, ma'am. The dimple producer is constructed of two pointed knobs fitted to a spring bow. The device is anchored under the chin, with the two knobs pushing into the cheeks.' Wishbone picked it up and demonstrated it as he spoke. His eyes watered as the metal points gouged into his face. 'You must wear it for two hours each day for it to be effective. It may feel uncomfortable,' Wishbone conceded, 'but this is the price you must pay for beauty. You will reap the benefits once the dimples become a permanent feature. Be assured, my dear lady, that my Delicate Dimpler works miracles.' He removed it quickly, relieved to have it off.

Edith was convinced. All those wasted years of her youth, lacking dimples, lay behind her. The future looked bright.

She shook her head in wonder. 'My husband,' she said in a whisper, 'seems oblivious to my presence. Call it the price of being married for twenty-five years. I know that this will spark his interest in me again.'

The doctor looked her up and down. Her dark button eyes beneath black hairy eyebrows blinked at him through the thick lens of her glasses, her crinkled hair hanging lifeless to her shoulders, her mouth in a perpetual scowl. Nothing there to spark interest, he thought.

Carefully, the doctor removed her glasses and fitted the device to Edith's face, screwing the points in until they dinted her cheeks. Her eyes watered, her lips were pursed, her eyebrows knitted, but any amount of pain was worth the addition of two beautiful dimples, the envy of all and sundry.

Dr Wishbone nodded slowly, admiring his handiwork. 'Excellent. That will be five pounds, please.' He raised a finger, as if struck by another thought. 'I just realised that I can do more to enhance your beauty, my dear lady. Would you like a chin dimple, too? It's an optional extra, so will cost another three pounds.'

Edith looked unsure, but soon acquiesced. Not two, but three dimples for the price of eight pounds. Beauty was just around the corner.

And then, he had left her, another satisfied customer.

Wishbone turned his attention back to the task at hand. Financial success depended on the safety and reliability of his devices, including those of his latest invention. It was the fourth time this week that he'd had to dismantle the Violet Ray machine and start again. How he wished that he had pursued engineering as a career rather than medicine. Or at least read a book on it. He couldn't seem to get the voltage right. The tube had glowed with a pretty purple light, making him believe all was well, but unexpectedly, sparks flew, and an acrid smell of burning preceded the nasty shock that it gave him when he tried to switch it off. It would sound the death knell for the machine if he couldn't iron out the problems.

Standing at the bench in his little workshop behind the factory, Wishbone shook his head and swore. How to make the Violet Ray machine work? He picked up a screwdriver and turned his attention back to the array of metal, rubber, and electrical fittings on the bench. Nothing seemed to fit properly. Perhaps he should ask Mr Higgs to assemble it for him, but that would cost money. Perhaps he needed to learn how to weld metal, but that would take time to learn. And time was precious when you were trying to make a living. There was no alternative but to muddle through himself.

Similarly, his relationship with the chemist, Mr Clegg, was problematic. Surely, he should be seeing more profits from the sale of his patent medicines, which were channelled through Clegg to grocery shops and pharmacies? And it struck him that the pharmacist's charges for compounding his products seemed inordinately high, compared to what he had outlaid in the

United States.

And how could he ignore Clegg's treatment of him when it came to Councillor Plumstead? Another source of dissatisfaction. Clegg had asked him to keep his eyes open and his ear to the ground should there be any gossip concerning the politicians who were opposed to the repeal of Regulation 79.

Usually, the private lives and activities of his patients were of little to no interest to Wishbone, unless they impacted on sales or the extension of his client list. But it was at Mavis da Costa's house, when he was supplying her with his new remedy for insomnia, that she mentioned in passing that her son was a crime reporter with *The Argus*.

'Reggie is investigating the murder of that man, Jasper Howard, the one who was killed at The Hotel Windsor. Ten times, he was stabbed. And he had a tarot card, the Ten of Swords, in his hand. Isn't that strange?'

Wishbone's eyes focused on the silver candelabra on the mantelpiece. It would fetch six pounds in a pawnbroker's, he estimated, as she rattled on.

'And what's even stranger was that the police suspect the daughter of Mrs Bardsley Smith's best friend, Mrs Plumstead. You know, the politician's wife?'

Wishbone pricked up his ears. 'Plumstead?' That name was on the list that Mr Clegg had given him.

'That's right. Reggie knows everyone and everything,' she added proudly.

Dr Wishbone's eyes twinkled. Now, he was paying attention. 'Mr Plumstead must be very concerned about his wife being accused of murder.'

'I believe so,' Mavis said. 'Reggie says that she was in Mr Howard's hotel room the day he was murdered.'

'Does Reggie think she did it?'

She shook her head. 'She's a respectable lady. No blot on her reputation except for this. Reggie says that she was being blackmailed. He doesn't think she was–'

Wishbone leaned forward. 'What, ma'am?'

'Committing adultery,' she whispered. 'Unlike her husband.'

'What do you mean? Her husband? Surely not–?' This sounded promising.

Something to take back to Clegg.

'Reggie says that Councillor Plumstead has a bit of a reputation. There are rumours about him. Reggie thinks he has a fancy woman somewhere.' She looked anxious and touched her mouth. 'I wouldn't want that to go any further, you understand.'

Doctor Wishbone patted her hand and gave her his most sincere look. 'Of course not, dear lady. Your secret is safe with me.'

Afterwards, when he had apprised Mr Clegg of that most tasty piece of gossip, he had expected some material change for the better in regard to his financial transactions with the chemist, but all he received was a nod and the insistence that he keep passing on any information that he collected. No reimbursement at all. Most frustrating!

Chapter Twenty-Seven

Clary Blain was in his usual spot, leaning up against the bar at the Duke of Wellington. His hand grasped a glass of whisky, which he had paid for, given that Reggie was running late. He checked his watch. Half-past four. Thirty minutes of paid drinking time wasted. He slipped off the stool and headed for the last remaining free table in the public bar, seeing that his conversations with *The Argus*'s crime reporter were confidential and he couldn't afford to be quoted by a member of the general public.

Three minutes later, Reggie strolled through the door, sighted Clary at the table, and stopped at the bar to order a beer and a whisky. He took a seat opposite the detective sergeant and lit up a cigarette.

'Sorry, but I was called in to a sub-editor's meeting. I couldn't avoid it.'

'No problem, mate,' Clary replied, draining his glass and eyeing the one being carried over to his table by the bartender. He looked at his watch again. 'Can't spare too much time. I thought we might be able to share some information on this Howard murder. You go first.'

Reggie nodded. 'Those suitcases that you were going to throw out. Remember I told you that I had them? There were a couple of photographs that I thought you might like to see. They were under the lining.'

Clary frowned. 'We shouldn't have missed that.'

Reggie handed over the picture of Dulcie with Jasper Howard. 'Seems like Dulcie Smith, who was staying in Room 101 of The Windsor, was Howard's partner. It's dated 1920 on the back, suggesting that they've known each other a while.'

Clary raised an eyebrow. 'Howard and Smith. An interesting connection. How do you know she's one and the same?'

'I showed her photograph to the concierge at The Windsor. He confirmed that it was Miss Smith.'

Clary took a sip of whisky and smacked his lips in satisfaction. 'I checked the departures after the murder. Miss Smith left the morning that the body was discovered. No forwarding address, unfortunately. I might have to dig a bit deeper.' He took another look at the photograph. 'She's a good-looking woman. Expensive outfit.'

'Between them, they must have been making a lot of money from their blackmail targets.'

'Who's in the other one?' asked Clary, pointing at the second photograph.

'I reckon that you'll know her.' Reggie handed over the photograph of Lottie O'Leary.

'Well, well,' said Clary, a smile on his lips. 'Odette de la Tours, the Marchioness de Montignac. Or should I say, Lottie O'Leary. Associate of blackmailer and fraudster, Louie 'The Dodger' Hayes. She's in prison awaiting sentencing, I believe.' He turned the photograph over and read what was written on the back, '"Love, Lottie. January 1923."'

Reggie leaned forward. 'Our friend Jasper Howard knew her well, I'd suggest.'

'I wasn't aware that she ever visited Melbourne.'

'I don't think she did. I believe Jasper knew her in Sydney.'

'Lottie O'Leary and Jasper Howard.' Clary downed his glass and beckoned to the bartender for a refill. 'I doubt if my bosses will let me go up there to interview her.'

'But mine will. I'm going with Dusty Rhodes the day after the Melbourne Cup.'

Clary chuckled. 'A horse race is more important than a crime story? Who would have thought?' He nodded at the photographs. 'I'll need these.'

Reggie wasn't about to let them go. 'Let me have the photographs for the Sydney trip, then I'll hand them over when I get back. I plan to interview Lottie. I might need these to persuade her to speak to me. She might deny knowing him, otherwise.'

'Anything else in those suitcases?'

'Nothing.' Reggie blew a smoke ring, then butted out the cigarette. 'Now, what have you got for me?'

'We interviewed Sir Ambrose Beauchamp Kiddle two weeks ago. He invested in one of Howard's schemes and lost a lot. I asked him when he knew that he was being swindled. Before or after Howard's death?'

'And what did he say?'

'*After*, according to him.'

'He's lying, Clary. I had an anonymous telephone call a week and a half ago. It was from a woman who overheard Howard and Kiddle arguing at a soirée. Apparently, he threatened Howard. Told him that he would kill him if he didn't get his money back.'

'Interesting.' Clary nodded and made a note. 'Thanks, Reggie. That tallies with what some of his cronies at the exclusive Melbourne Club said. They reckon that he was getting suspicious, what with the lack of progress in closing the deal and an absence of documentation from Howard. Kiddle complained to one colleague that his wife was angry, thinking he'd thrown away their money again. You know that he lost thousands in that Sandridge Bridge fiasco?'

Reggie nodded. 'Does Kiddle have an alibi for the 29th of August?'

'Says he was at a charitable event.'

'He didn't mention that it was at The Hotel Windsor? A fund-raiser for the Lord Mayor's Fund.'

'Well, well. I might have another word or two with Sir Ambrose.'

'Do you know how much he lost investing in Howard's scheme?'

'About six thousand pounds.'

Reggie whistled. 'Worth killing for.' He lit up another cigarette. 'Do you regard him as a suspect?'

'We couldn't place him at the scene of the crime until now.'

'What about Mrs Plumstead? Did her husband know that she was being blackmailed?'

'Not until *after* the murder. She claims that she was hoping that it would all go away if she refused to pay, and, in a sense, it did. With the blackmailer dead, she didn't lose a penny.'

'But now she's in the newspapers, and her husband is very unhappy.'

'He's been bending the ear of the Chief Commissioner to solve the case quickly and get his wife out of the headlines.' Clary scratched his nose. 'An unpleasant character, Councillor Plumstead.'

'I agree. Only likes the press when it suits him. His wife asked me to investigate on her behalf, but this case is complicated. It's not easy to see the wood for the trees. Howard upset a lot of people: investors, errant wives and husbands, and trusting salesmen who lent him their goods and never saw them again.'

'What do you hope to achieve in Sydney?' asked Clary, downing the rest of his Scotch.

'Get some background on Howard. Find out who he really was and where he came from. Interview Lottie O'Leary and track down some of Howard's victims in Sydney. One of my newspaper colleagues reckons that he might have some leads for me. I suspect that what we've seen Howard do in Melbourne would have been replicated in New South Wales.'

Clary nodded. 'Confidence men take years to perfect their techniques. I reckon that you'll find plenty of evidence to prove that Howard was up to his tricks in Sydney, but under another name. I'd appreciate it if you'd share what you find with me, Reggie. Chief Commissioner Blamey is breathing down my neck. And, when you're back, you might tell me what else you found in Howard's suitcases.'

Reggie shook his head and grinned. 'Really, Clary? You don't trust me?'

Clary wiped his mouth with the back of his hand. 'Do you really expect me to answer that question?'

With that, he pushed his glass into the middle of the table and stood up.

'Enjoy your trip to the Harbour City, Reggie. And don't fall for Lottie O'Leary. They say she's a real *femme fatale*.'

Chapter Twenty-Eight

Horace Striker was a major player in Melbourne's underworld who, unlike Squizzy Taylor, preferred to keep a low profile. Not for him, the outrageous behaviour and flashy dress of his major competitor in illegal gambling, prostitution, and bootlegging.

Horace resided in a nondescript terrace house in Shamrock Street, Richmond, from where he controlled his empire. The tentacles of his influence extended into the upper levels of Melbourne's political and legal classes, aided by the tools of his trade: bribery, intimidation, and blackmail. Amongst his peers, Horace Striker was regarded with grudging respect borne of fear.

Ruby Rhodes' friendship with the gangster appeared incongruous to outsiders. A secretary and a gangster? Most unusual. But it was unique circumstances that had brought them together, enabled by the inimitable Reggie da Costa, whose contacts and acquaintances extended into the seedy environs of Melbourne's criminal underworld. Katherine, Ruby's sister, and her fiancé, Stanley Duggan, who was also Horace Striker's nephew, had been murdered. To track down the killer, Ruby had enlisted Striker's help, so that she could carry off a credible impersonation of her identical twin when visiting the gambling dens and clubs frequented by Katherine. Without Horace's support, her efforts would not have succeeded. In the process, Striker had developed a respect for her which he did not often have for the rest of the human race. And she, despite her knowledge of his nefarious and shady activities, regarded him with something akin to affection.

Horace Striker owned a club, The Stockade, in the back blocks of

Richmond. Entry was by invitation only. Originally a warehouse built in the 1870s, it had undergone an expensive renovation in recent years, converted into a venue for Horace's close friends, acolytes, and influential acquaintances. A large central space, with handmade red brick walls, rose over two storeys in height, lit primarily by large skylights in the ceiling. Behind a bar, on Friday and Saturday nights, could be found four or five bartenders, blending cocktails, pouring beers, and popping champagne corks, while a bevy of eager patrons took advantage of Horace Striker's generosity. In three smaller rooms off the main space, baccarat, 'two-up,' blackjack, or poker were being played, whilst in another room, bookies took bets on horse races.

When the mood took him, Striker threw some of the best parties in all of Melbourne, themed costume events which attracted the wealthiest, powerful, and most beautiful of the social set. Money could not necessarily buy an invitation to one of these nights, but those who aided and abetted Horace's steady climb in influence were always welcome.

* * *

It was the last Saturday in October and excited guests were lining up outside The Stockade waiting to be admitted to Horace Striker's Melbourne Cup party, held to celebrate the running of Australia's richest horse race. The event was one of the unofficial highlights of Melbourne's social calendar and part of the Melbourne Cup festivities to be held over four days.

Amongst those queuing outside The Stockade were Ruby and her beau, Reggie. In her hand Ruby clutched an invitation to the party, signed by the host himself. As they waited, the couple commented on the costumes of the guests, for the dress code was the stars of moving pictures.

'You look wonderful, Reggie,' said Ruby, admiring his costume. 'Douglas Fairbanks looks ordinary compared to you. All you need is a sword.'

Reggie grinned, showing off his perfect white teeth. 'Thank you, my dear, but it's in the scabbard.' He withdrew it and slashed the air in the shape of a 'Z.'

'Watch out, mister!' cried Charlie Chaplin, the next along. 'You could do some damage with that.'

Reggie laughed, imitating the devil-may-care attitude of the eponymous lead in The Mark of Zorro. He knew that he looked the part. His dark satin shirt, red sash and headscarf, cape, and black mask showed off his aristocratic and classic features, as well as his manly physique.

Next to him was Ruby, dressed as the princess from The Thief of Bagdad, in flowing robes and an abundance of jewellery, her crimped red hair partially hidden by a translucent long veil.

'Very Arabian Nights. Very romantic,' Reggie had commented when he collected her in the Hupmobile. He had kissed her hand and looked deep into her eyes through his mask. It had only made Ruby giggle.

Their invitations checked, they entered the lobby of The Stockade and deposited their coats in the cloakroom.

The large double doors to the club swung wide, and a wall of noise struck them as they entered.

'Isn't it wonderful?' asked Ruby, her eyes shining as she took in the scene.

Outside on the street it had been relatively quiet, but inside a mass of people laughed and chatted and danced to the band, which was playing popular songs from the 1920s. Cigarette smoke swirled in the air, as jockey-clad waiters, dressed in silks, white riding pants, and long brown leather boots, in a nod to the upcoming Melbourne Cup horse race, made their way amongst the guests, offering them glasses of champagne and hors d'oeuvres from silver trays.

The Stockade was decorated accordingly for the theme, with large colourful movie posters on the walls. Rudolph Valentino smouldered down at them in scenes from The Sheik. One of the walls had been decorated with a mural of The Thief of Bagdad, portraying the magical elements of the film: its smoke-belching dragons, underwater spiders, magic carpets, and flying horses.

'Look, Reggie, there's you!' cried Ruby, pointing at the poster of Douglas Fairbanks, disguised as Zorro, the masked avenger.

Reggie smiled appreciatively and took her hand. 'He does look like me, doesn't he?'

Pictures of Clara Bow, Charlie Chaplin's little tramp, and Mary Pickford were interspersed with scenes from Cecil B. DeMille's The Ten Commandments and Ben-Hur.

'We must see Ben-Hur,' remarked Reggie. 'It's supposed to be amazing. DeMille spent nearly $4 million on making it, you know.'

The room was full of Robin Hoods, walking-stick-twirling little Tramps, red-headed Clara Bows, Alaskan prospectors from The Gold Rush, and dashing Sheiks. There was even the occasional dinosaur from The Lost World and one or two Hunchbacks of Notre Dame.

'Watch out, Ruby!' cried Reggie, as the Phantom of the Opera, his cape billowing behind him, barrelled past, pursuing a beautiful young woman who could only have been his love interest, Christine.

'Isn't that Lady Beauchamp Kiddle, dressed as Gloria Swanson from Zaza?' asked Ruby.

Reggie smiled. 'It definitely is. And her husband is nowhere to be seen. This might be an opportune time to have a chat with her.'

The lady herself was standing in the middle of the room, resplendent in a beaded dress, long string of pearls, Z-shaped earrings, and the outlandish feathered hat worn by Swanson in her role as Zaza. Next to her was an attractive woman, adorned in furs and a flapper-style dress hemmed in gold fringe, holding a ridiculously long silver cigarette holder between her manicured fingernails.

'Lady Beauchamp Kiddle,' oozed Reggie, taking her hand. 'It's as if Gloria herself has come to Melbourne. You look radiant.'

She looked uncertainly at Reggie, not recognising Melbourne's premier crime reporter beneath his Zorro costume.

'Thank you so much, Mr–'

'Reggie da Costa of The Argus. And this is my companion, Miss Rhodes. I just had to introduce myself. Your reputation as a pillar of Melbourne society is unsurpassed.'

'Why, thank you. And I am familiar with you, too. Who can't remember your articles on the Death Mask Murderer and the Basement Murder? Quite thrilling. May I introduce my friend, Mrs Bentinck Jones.'

Reggie nodded his head. 'Pleased to meet you. As a matter of fact, I'm investigating the murder of Mr Jasper Howard. I believe that he was a mutual friend of both of you.'

Lady Beauchamp Kiddle frowned. 'No longer a friend, I can assure you. I regret that I was completely taken in by him. Simply shocking.'

'I agree,' said Mrs Bentinck Jones, her distaste evident.

Reggie addressed Lady Beauchamp Kiddle. 'Would it be an intrusion if I asked you for your impressions of the man? It's rare to find someone who has known him as intimately as you.'

'Intimately? Oh no. Purely in social circles.'

'Of course. I didn't mean to imply–'

Lady Beauchamp Kiddle recovered quickly, appeased by Reggie's quick rejoinder. 'You understand that I am a happily married woman. But Mr Howard was a charmer. Well-spoken, handsome, polite, beautifully groomed, a good conversationalist. But now, when I look back, I can see that he was a manipulator. He never stated an opinion on anything until he knew what I thought. At the time, I thought he was an agreeable person; now, I know it was a sham.' She turned to her companion. 'Wouldn't you agree, Seraphina?'

Mrs Bentinck Jones nodded her head. 'A nasty man.'

'Did Sir Ambrose enjoy his company?'

'Indeed, he did,' replied Lady Beauchamp Kiddle. 'He invited him along to the Melbourne Club and made him most welcome. It's shocking that Mr Howard should have taken advantage of my husband's good nature. Sir Ambrose tends to be a little too trusting at times.'

'I believe your husband is most generous when it comes to those in need. I heard that you both attended the Lord Mayor's Fund charity ball back in August.'

'It was a wonderful event, wouldn't you agree, Seraphina?'

Mrs Bentinck Jones smiled. 'The Grand Ballroom looked a picture. The Windsor does things so well.'

'And did Mr Howard attend?' Reggie asked.

'He was supposed to be at our table, but he didn't show up,' replied Lady Beauchamp Kiddle.

'What a disappointment for you.'

'It was, at the time. My husband even offered to go upstairs and check Mr Howard's whereabouts.'

'And what happened?'

'He came back shortly after. Mr Howard didn't answer his knock on the door.' She lowered her voice. 'The next morning, they found Mr Howard dead in his room. But you must know that?'

'Of course. A dreadful business.'

Mrs Bentinck Jones had gone pale. 'Do we need to discuss this?' she asked.

Reggie changed tack, interested to know what she knew about Madame Esmeralda.

'I believe that you invited a fortune-teller to your soirée in July?'

'That's right. Madame Esmeralda,' replied Mrs Bentinck Jones. 'She was recommended by a friend of mine. It's nice to offer my guests something that's a little bit different.' She looked puzzled. 'Why would you want to know about her?'

'She appears to have been connected with this case. Madame Esmeralda predicted that Mrs Van Cooth would meet a handsome stranger, and there he was: Jasper Howard.'

Mrs Bentinck Jones looked Reggie up and down. 'Perhaps it was pure coincidence, not planned. I dislike the suggestion that I was responsible for Mrs Van Cooth meeting a confidence man.'

'It's an interesting proposition though, don't you think? That Madame Esmeralda and Mr Howard knew each other?' asked Reggie.

'You're suggesting that they were in cahoots?'

'I suppose I am.'

'I wouldn't know, as I said before.'

'Come now,' said Lady Beauchamp Kiddle. 'Enough of this. Seraphina is relatively new to Melbourne, and I'd like to introduce her to some of the other guests.'

'Where do you come from, Mrs Bentinck Jones?' inquired Reggie.

'Sydney, she comes from Sydney.' Lady Beauchamp Kiddle took Seraphina's arm. 'There's Sir Ambrose. We really must go. He'll want my opinion on who's going to win the Cup.'

Reggie smiled. 'It's been lovely speaking to you both. Hopefully, we can have another chat again soon.'

Lady Beauchamp Kiddle shrugged her shoulders and led Seraphina away.

When they had gone, Ruby leaned in. 'Now, that was interesting. Mrs Bentinck Jones is a bit of a mystery woman. Did you notice that she went pale when you talked about the murder? And she attended the Lord Mayor's charity ball, the same night that Howard was murdered.'

'As did the Beauchamp Kiddles,' added Reggie. 'And Sir Ambrose went up to Howard's room. We know that he was angry with Howard over their business deal. But angry enough to kill him? The one thing that points to someone else being involved is the tarot card. It doesn't fit with my vision of Sir Ambrose.'

'Unless two people were involved,' suggested Ruby. 'Perhaps the killer stabbed him to death, and someone else put the Ten of Swords in his hand. Maybe they even came separately.'

Reggie nodded. 'Definitely worth considering. Two people. Hmmm.'

Chapter Twenty-Nine

A hush fell over the crowd at The Stockade as the doors swung wide and two of Striker's most trusted bodyguards entered the room. They were Burke and Hare, both Scots, nicknamed for the grave robbers who had killed innocent victims and sold their bodies to the Edinburgh Medical College for dissection. It was a known fact that Horace Striker and his two henchmen were inseparable, such was the threat from his enemies in Melbourne's underworld. And, sure enough, the man himself strode in behind them.

Heads turned, the room buzzed with excitement, and spontaneous applause broke out as he stepped into the room. Immediately, he was surrounded by a bevy of people seeking his attention, determined to ingratiate themselves with the influential, but shady Horace Striker.

He was anything but the image of the archetypal gangster. Unlike Squizzy Taylor, who was attention-seeking, vulgar, and flashy, Striker looked more like a banker or the manager of a respectable company. Clean-shaven, tall, and lean, Horace was a striking figure, dressed in a well-cut tuxedo, his shoes highly polished. He never missed a trick, as his gaze swept across the multitude of admirers, sycophants, and gamblers who had gathered in response to his invitation.

Within a few short minutes, Striker was making his way towards Ruby, with the red-haired bodyguard, Hare, behind him.

'Miss Ruby, you do look delightful. Who are you today? Bagdad's princess, if I'm any judge of beauty and costume.'

Ruby laughed. 'It's the costume, Horace, nothing more.'

'You do yourself an injustice,' he replied. 'Don't you think so, Reggie?' He glanced briefly at the crime reporter.

'Indeed, she looks beautiful. But she's more than that.'

'Ah, you finally see that, do you? I would never underestimate this young lady.'

Ruby smiled. 'And what of you, Horace? No fancy dress for you?'

'You know me well.'

Ruby knew from her past encounters with Striker that he preferred to set himself apart from the mob, by distancing himself from the follies and antics of those who surrounded him. He would never be found in a costume, preferring the dignity and elegance of a tuxedo. Control and self-discipline were Horace's watchwords. In company, he didn't smoke, drink, womanise, or swear. But although his expression looked relaxed, his eyes were ever vigilant, ever watchful.

A waiter, clad in the colours of the favourite for the Melbourne Cup, hovered at his elbow, offering champagne. Horace took a glass and handed it to Ruby, while Reggie helped himself.

'Who do you think will win the Cup, Horace?' asked Reggie, as he put down his glass and lit a cigarette.

'Windbag. But it will be close. Manfred will give him a run for his money.'

'In that case, I'll go and place a bet. Your word is good enough for me.'

Horace placed a hand on his arm as he was about to leave. 'While you're there, ten pounds on Windbag for the win. Five pounds each on Manfred and Pilliewinkie for a place.' He snapped his fingers, and Hare responded, handing over twenty pounds to the crime reporter. 'Put the bet in Miss Ruby's name. A little something to make this little lady happy.'

'Horace, you don't need to do that,' protested Ruby, blushing.

The gangster smiled down on her. 'You're the only person in this room who doesn't want something from me. Now, say "thank you" and accept it gracefully.'

'Thank you, Horace.'

'I think that you're having a good influence on Melbourne's senior crime reporter,' he commented, watching as Reggie approached the bookmaker, his Zorro cape fluttering behind him. 'He seems to be settling down a little.'

'He's a good man, Horace.'

'What story is he working on? Not me, I hope.' Striker's eyes narrowed.

'Not you. Reggie's working on the Jasper Howard case.'

'The confidence man? No loss to society.'

'You think that?'

'These confidence men are scum. Pretending to be someone they're not; leading their victims up the garden path. Both the perpetrator and his victim should know where they stand. Crime should be straightforward, not this devious business where you set people up to cheat them.'

Ruby raised an eyebrow. 'Ethics in crime? A straightforward robbery? A straightforward murder?'

Horace smirked. 'Only you can get away with that, Ruby. But the fact is that confidence men and women lack honesty.'

'There's no point arguing with you. But I do believe that you are basically honest in your dealings with me, even if your activities, for want of a better word, leave a lot to be desired.'

The gangster laughed, a rare event indeed, causing Hare, who was standing on the other side of him, to look startled.

'Here comes your beau.' Horace waited till Reggie returned. 'I must be off, now. It's always a pleasure seeing you. There's flesh to press and pressure to be exerted. Back to work.'

Horace kissed Ruby's hand and strode off.

'Did Striker tell you anything useful?' asked Reggie, watching a circle of admirers cluster around the gangster.

Ruby looked at him enigmatically. 'I will say this: Horace doesn't like confidence men. He has some interesting views on crime in general.'

'Is that right? That doesn't surprise me.' Reggie lit a cigarette and blew a smoke ring in the air. 'By the way, you'll never guess who I saw when I passed the baccarat table. The Honourable Councillor Plumstead. He was dressed as Tom Mix. White suit and ten-gallon hat. All that was missing was a horse.'

Ruby laughed. 'That's funny.'

Reggie took a sip of champagne and leaned in towards her. 'And he was with a woman who was not his wife.'

'Now, that isn't funny. What's he doing here? Surely, he must be worried about Mrs Plumstead. Why would he leave her when she's a suspect in a murder case?'

'Take it from me, Ruby, there's no love lost between those two. And he is renowned for not letting marriage stand in the way of…liaisons, if you know what I mean?'

'Did he recognise you?'

'Luckily, I'm Zorro tonight, not Reggie da Costa. It would have been a chilly reception if I'd been me.'

'Isn't that him? Walking towards the exit?' she asked, pointing at a rotund little fellow, wearing an enormous white hat, his arm encircling the waist of Robin Hood's Lady Marian.

As Ruby spoke, the woman in question turned around, facing in their direction. Her long, dark, wavy hair hung down over her shoulders, a coronet on her head. She was wearing a medieval gown in green velvet with a cord tied around her waist.

Ruby stared in shock. 'Reggie. That's the woman in Howard's photograph. Dulcie.'

Reggie shook his head in wonder. 'You're right. Miss Smith from Room 101 at The Windsor. Now, isn't that interesting?'

Reggie hesitated. He looked at Ruby, then across at the departing politician and his friend.

Ruby tapped him on the arm. 'What are we waiting for? Let's go before they get away.'

'You really are special,' he said, taking her hand. 'The Hupmobile is waiting.'

* * *

Reggie gripped the wooden steering wheel of his prized Hupmobile and slammed his foot down hard on the accelerator pedal. Up ahead, the councillor's crimson Pontiac had already made the turn into Church Street.

'Hold on, Ruby. We have to catch him,' he cried. 'He's heading towards Melbourne.'

Within seconds, the motorcar had covered the length of the street, but came to a shuddering halt at the T-intersection with Church Street. The Hupmobile growled, waiting to be unleashed, Reggie swearing under his breath as an unbroken phalanx of traffic surged past them towards the city. Seeing a gap in the pack of trucks, automobiles, and horse-drawn carts, Reggie executed a sharp right turn, narrowly missing a Dodge. He jammed his foot down on the accelerator, and the Hupmobile swept past a Model T Ford that was hugging the curb, only to confront a Summit coming straight at him in the opposite lane.

Ruby clung on to the edge of her seat as she braced for the crash. In the last second or two, before a collision was imminent, a space opened up, and Reggie expertly threaded the motorcar through the gap, bringing them back into the left lane.

'I could see the whites of his eyes,' Ruby protested. 'For goodness' sake, Reggie, you'll get us killed.'

'Hold on, my love. We can't afford to lose them.' He threw the car into third gear and pressed down on the accelerator.

Ruby shook her head in disbelief and sank down in the seat, trying not to watch. But the driver of the Hupmobile was not the only thing that was out of her control that night. The wind was gusting, causing her costume to take on a life of its own as the motorcar tore up Church Street. The flimsy diaphanous veil that she wore on her head was threatening to blow away while her dress wrapped itself around her legs. She hung onto the veil with one hand while anchoring her dress with the other, but the wind caught the headdress, ripping it from her grasp. It flew out the side window, smack into the windscreen of the car following them, catching on a windscreen wiper and obscuring the driver's view of the road. He made frantic efforts to pull it off but to no avail, as the automobile swerved and hit the curb, then bounced back into the left lane.

Just when it seemed that the driver would lose control, the wind whipped up and ripped the veil off the wiper, sending it wafting away into the gutter.

Ruby breathed a sigh of relief and turned her attention back to the road ahead. At least no one had been hurt, she thought, although she would have to reimburse the costume hire shop for a lost veil.

'Isn't that him up ahead?' cried Reggie above the roar of the engine.

'I don't know, it's so dark.'

The stop lights of a car came on in front of them, as the driver did the turn towards the city.

'It's the Pontiac!' Reggie was exultant. He slowed as they came to the Bridge Road corner, then planted his foot on the throttle, taking the turn too fast, the rubber tyres squealing in protest. The rear of the car flipped out as Reggie battled to regain control of the steering. He double de-clutched, shifting into third gear, the Hupmobile powering forward as he stepped on the accelerator, gaining on the vehicle driven by Councillor Plumstead.

'Pull back, Reggie!' cried Ruby. 'Otherwise, he'll get suspicious.'

'Quite right, my love. The first rule of tailing a suspect.' He slowed the car so that they were a respectable distance behind the Pontiac.

They passed parkland, then the Melbourne Cricket Ground to their left and the Fitzroy Gardens to their right, continuing along Wellington Parade up to the edge of the city. They crossed Spring Street, home to The Hotel Windsor and the scene of Jasper Howard's murder, and continued two miles down Flinders Street. The Pontiac turned into William Street, haven to the mahogany desks, brass plaques, and expensive offices of the legal fraternity, and pulled into the curb of yet another of Melbourne's grandest hotels, The Menzies.

'She likes to live well. First, The Windsor, and now, The Menzies,' commented Reggie as they drove slowly past and parked on the other side of the intersection.

'Perhaps the councillor likes to live well, too,' Ruby said. They watched on as the couple walked in through the hotel's main entrance. 'What do we do now?'

'I'll have a word with the bellboy.'

'Dressed as Zorro?'

Reggie laughed, his white teeth sparkling in the darkness. 'Just a moment.' He removed the headscarf, mask, and cape and reached into the back seat for his coat. He gave Ruby a quick kiss on the cheek and exited the car. Ruby poked her head out of the side window and watched as Reggie approached the hotel's bellboy. A short conversation took place, and very soon, he was striding back, his long leather boots and sword within the scabbard incongruous against his smartly tailored coat.

'All done,' he said. 'Miss Smith is in Room 305. She arrived at the end of August, which fits in nicely with the date of Howard's murder.'

'How did you find that out?'

'It's amazing what five shillings can buy you these days.' He laughed as she shook her head at him. 'It's ten o'clock. If we hurry, we'll be back at The Stockade in time to enjoy the rest of the party.'

'Let's go,' said Ruby.

With that, Reggie started the engine, and the Hupmobile roared its approval.

Chapter Thirty

Detective Sergeant Clary Blain stared down at the body and felt a cold shiver go through him. Only two months before, he had attended an almost identical crime scene. A body, lying face down, with multiple stab wounds in the back and a tarot card clutched in the right hand. The Ten of Swords. Blood splatter was confined to the wall behind the body and the floor, but in this case, the deceased was female, not male. Yet another dead body in another exclusive Melbourne hotel.

The doctor was due at any moment, but the cause of death was obvious. In his newspaper report, Reggie da Costa had described the previous killing as a crime of passion. In this case, too, the perpetrator had wanted his victim dead.

The photograph that Reggie had shown him made it clear that Jasper Howard and this woman in Room 305, Dulcie Smith, knew each other, but what was their connection to the killer? The *modus operandi* was the same, as was the tarot card found at both crime scenes.

Blain moved slowly around the room, looking for clues. The lock had not been forced, so the victim had opened the door to her killer. The weapon was missing, but Blain suspected that the autopsy would show that a knife had been used. He would bet his next glass of whisky that ten stab wounds would be found on the body. As with the murder of Jasper Howard, there was no trail of bloodied footprints leading to the door, so the killer had again come prepared and changed their shoes. Most probably their clothing, too, given that a blood-soaked killer would draw the attention of the staff in the lobby.

In the wardrobe and chest of drawers Blain found an array of good quality clothing, including some European labels, recently laundered and pressed. He went through the pockets of her coats, looking for some form of identification or indications of places she had visited in Melbourne. But there were none. Her handbag contained the usual female paraphernalia: lipstick, a mirror, a handkerchief, and a small hairbrush. But, at the bottom of the bag, Blain's fingers closed over a leather notebook.

He smiled grimly. 'That's better.'

He sat down in one of The Menzies' comfortable armchairs and thumbed through it, whistling in surprise at the names and addresses that were listed within its pages; a snapshot of elite Melbourne society. Next to some of the names were symbols, perhaps a code, unfamiliar to the detective sergeant, but undoubtedly meaningful to the dead woman. He put the notebook in his pocket.

Her suitcases were unpacked, indicating that she was intending to stay at the hotel for an extended period of time. There were no compartments in them containing documents or a passport. Inside the top drawer of the tallboy was a collection of Vice Regal clippings from Melbourne newspapers as well as torn-out sections of the social pages. This was a woman, Clary concluded, who was particularly interested in the goings-on of the city's rich and powerful. Apart from that, there were no photographs, no letters, nothing that could further identify who she was or what she was doing in Melbourne. However, her purse was stuffed with Australian bank notes so it was apparent that money was no object when it came to this lady. But where had she acquired the cash to stay in one of the most exclusive hotels in Victoria?

There was a knock on the door. Blain looked up.

'Come in.'

The doctor entered, carrying a black medical bag. He raised his hat to the detective and placed it on the table, then eyed the body on the floor. 'She's dead?'

'Cold as the grave. I'll leave you to do the examination while I have a chat with the staff.'

The doctor nodded and went to work. Clary Blain headed out the door.

Down in the lobby, Mr James, the hotel manager, well-dressed and imperious, showed the detective to his office.

'This is terrible, detective sergeant. The Menzies has an impeccable reputation. I simply cannot understand how a murder could happen within our walls.'

'Indeed? In my experience, murder knows no boundaries. Now, a few questions if you please. Under what name did the lady check in?'

'Miss Dulcie Smith.'

'I thought as much. And when did she arrive?'

'At the end of August.'

Blain scratched his nose and licked the end of his pencil. '*Very* interesting.' He scribbled in his notebook. 'Any address for the lady? Any personal details?'

'An address in Sydney. Nothing apart from that.' He jotted it down and handed over the slip of paper, which Clary glanced at, then put in his pocket.

'Anything that you can add, which might help in our investigation?'

The hotel manager shook his head. 'If you could hurry things up here, I'd be grateful.'

Clary gave him a disparaging look. 'There's been a murder, Mr James, so it will take time. I would like to speak to the maid who found her, please.'

A young girl, aged about fifteen, was shown into the room. She was wiping her eyes and blowing her nose into a large handkerchief. She had a ruddy complexion, made worse by the state she was in.

'Can you answer some questions for me, Miss–?'

'Hyacinth, sir. I will, sir. It was awful, sir. I've never seen anything like that in my life.' Tears rolled down her cheeks.

'When did you discover Miss Smith?'

'It was after eleven o'clock this morning. I'd knocked on her door about an hour before, but there wasn't any answer. I thought she might be sleeping. I went and did some other rooms, then I went back there. This time, I let myself in.'

'Did you use your master key?'

'No need, sir. The door was open. I thought that was strange. Miss Smith was particular about such things.'

'And what did you do then?'

'It was dark inside. The blind was down. I called out to her, "Miss Smith. Maid service." I turned on the light. She wasn't in bed. I pushed the trolley into the room, and I knocked up against her. I screamed, and the other maid came running. Mr James, the hotel manager, came up. It was a right bunfight, sir.'

Clary smiled. 'I'm sure it was. Were you on duty last night?'

'Yes, I was. I went in and turned down her bed. She had gone out, so I didn't see her.'

'And when was that?'

'About five o'clock.'

'Did you ever have a conversation with Miss Smith?'

'Who me, sir? No, sir.'

'Did you notice anything or anyone last night? Something out of the ordinary?'

She shook her head. Blain patted her on the arm. 'Good girl. You can go.' He turned to the hotel manager, who was hovering in the doorway. 'You should let her have the rest of the day off. She's had a terrible fright, poor girl.'

'Please send in the concierge. And then, you can go.'

Mr James looked put out, but Blain's tone of voice offered no room to argue.

The concierge, decked out in his smart uniform, strode in.

'The name's Dexter, sir,' he said, doffing his hat to the detective. 'Anything that you want to know, I'm your man.'

It was clear that the concierge was enjoying the excitement of having a murder occur on his patch. As the questioning proceeded, it was also apparent that he thrived on any juicy tidbits of gossip and innuendo that The Menzies provided. Clary doubted that the hotel manager would approve.

'Has Miss Smith received any regular visitors during her time at the hotel?' asked Clary.

'Miss Smith has quite a few gentlemen calling on her,' he said, 'but there's one in particular who accompanies her.'

'Do you know his name?'

The concierge glowed with excitement and anticipation. 'I do, sir. Councillor Plumstead, the politician. I recognised him from the newspapers.' His chest swelled with pride.

'How often did you see him?'

'Twice a week. Often three. They were friendly, if you know what I mean.' He gave Blain a salacious wink.

The detective nodded. 'Did you see Councillor Plumstead last night?'

'He and Miss Smith came back from a party about ten o'clock. They were all dressed up. He was Tom Mix. She looked straight out of the Middle Ages. And very nice, too.'

'You saw him leave?'

'I tipped my hat at him and followed him out. He seemed angry. I thought they must have had an argument. I offered to help him into his motorcar, but he was rather rude. Told me that he didn't need anyone's help, thank you.'

'Did he have any blood on him?'

The concierge's eyes opened wide. 'You don't think–?'

'Answer the question, please.'

'No blood, sir. None.'

The rest of the interviews didn't elicit any further information, but Blain was satisfied with what he had learned. Now, he knew where Miss Dulcie Smith had gone after she left The Windsor. And he could safely assume that the murderer of Miss Smith and Mr Howard was the same person, based on the nature of the killing and the presence of the tarot card.

The case against the Plumsteads was building. Each had been in the vicinity of the crime scenes around the time they happened: Mrs Plumstead at The Windsor and her husband at The Menzies. This put them firmly in the frame as suspects in the murders of Mr Jasper Howard and Miss Dulcie Smith, respectively. But he needed more than circumstantial evidence to pin the crimes on them, taking into consideration their status in society and their links with people in positions of power.

Back at police headquarters, Clary picked up the telephone. 'Give Reggie da Costa a message. Tell him I'll be at The Duke at four o'clock.'

Chapter Thirty-One

Flemington racecourse, with its roses in bloom, was looking a treat for the running of The Melbourne Cup. It was the premier day of the Spring Racing Carnival, so important to Victorians that it had been declared a public holiday. Government offices, banks, and most businesses and shops were closed, and even children had been granted a break from the rigours of their schooling. Trains and special trams ferried race-goers to the big event. For those whose tastes were not for horse racing, the beach or picnics beckoned, given that the promise of summer was in the air. Bay steamers were crowded with holidaymakers, merrily setting out on a day's visit to Queenscliff or Sorrento. Some ventured to the hills or close mountain resorts, such as Healesville, Fern Tree Gully, and Warburton. Others gathered at sports meetings, or attended matinee performances at cinemas or live productions. But the burning question on the lips of every Melburnian was: Who would win the Melbourne Cup?

For the first time in history, the running of the Cup was being broadcast by wireless telegraphy, with thousands listening in to the race call. They were promised a graphic description of the big race and would hear the raucous voices of the bookmakers calling the odds, the thundering of the hooves, and the cheering of the crowds as the horses turned into the straight.

The crowd was pouring into Flemington racecourse from the time it opened, all keen to secure a good view of the track. By twelve o'clock, three and a half hours before the starting time for the big race, it was estimated that the size of the crowd would eclipse that of the previous year's attendance, with over 100,000 people squeezing themselves through the entrance gates.

Over in the Members' Enclosure, or 'birdcage' as it was known colloquially, behaviour was more sedate, the *crème de la crème* of Melbourne society rubbing shoulders with titans of industry, senior politicians, visiting aristocracy and, of course, *The Argus*'s senior crime reporter, Reggie da Costa, and his lady friend, Miss Ruby Rhodes.

Reggie had been quite overcome with joy when Horace Striker offered them guest passes to the select members' stand and enclosure, where he and Ruby could mingle with the upper classes and rub shoulders with those who graced the social pages. Not even Curtis Flange, society gossip, and temporary crime desk boss, had been invited, and he had expressed his disapproval in no uncertain terms.

'How did *you* get a guest pass?'

Reggie had enjoyed Flange's flash of jealousy and had not satisfied his curiosity at all, giving him a knowing smile, but no explanation.

It had been a torturous process selecting the right suit to wear to such an august occasion, but Reggie had decided on pin-striped dark grey trousers, with a black cutaway morning coat and matching waistcoat edged in dark grey satin. His silver bow tie, crisp white dress shirt, and smart top hat were the finishing touches. With his Ronald Colman moustache trimmed and his thick black hair slicked with Brilliantine, Reggie was pleased with his presentation. Similarly, the Hupmobile had undergone an intensive spit and polish, its forest green finish, white wall tyres, and chrome headlights gleaming under the sunny skies of Cup Day.

Next to Reggie in the Members' Enclosure stood Ruby, looking particularly attractive in an elegant frock of emerald green georgette, worn beneath a long race coat of black ottoman silk, with a full collar. Her large black hat was decorated with an ostrich plume. Reggie was pleased to see that his companion was embracing the occasion and enjoying herself. By impersonating 'Miss Kitty', her sister Katherine's alter ego, and visiting the gambling dens and social clubs frequented by Melbourne's criminal classes, Ruby had acquired a taste of what life could be like if she would throw off her natural reticence. And it was apparent that she had found a middle way between the self-consciousness and reserve of the 'old' Ruby and the excesses of 'Miss Kitty.'

'Reggie, look who's arriving?' Ruby interrupted his reverie, bringing him back to the delightful realities of being in the Members' Enclosure.

The State coach drove past, bearing the Governor-General and Lady Stonehaven, attended by a retinue of staff and guests. As they made their way to their reserved seats in the grandstand, admiring glances followed Lady Stonehaven, who looked striking in a scintillating silver cloak, beneath which was a gown in Havana brown.

'Isn't that Mrs Van Cooth?' Ruby asked, pointing at a woman wearing a vivid dress in lime green, set off by a straw hat covered in red silk flowers. Her parasol was decorated with tufts of ostrich feathers, dyed yellow.

'She looks like she's escaped from an aviary,' observed Reggie.

'Who's that she's talking to?'

'Well, well, it's the Plumsteads. They must be friends again. Let's go and have a chat, shall we?'

They strolled over towards the group. The politician's reaction, when he saw Reggie coming his way, was not welcoming, but that didn't discourage Melbourne's premier crime reporter.

He tipped his top hat to the ladies. 'Councillor and Mrs Plumstead. Mrs Van Cooth. What a delightful surprise.'

Beatrice simpered and smiled and stretched out a red-gloved hand to shake his.

'Mr da Costa. And–' She looked Ruby up and down.

'This is my friend, Miss Rhodes.' Reggie proceeded to introduce her to the Plumsteads.

As they chatted about the likely winner of the Melbourne Cup, the fashions, the weather, and the roses, Peggy Plumstead and Beatrice Van Cooth engaged with their new acquaintance, Miss Rhodes. Beatrice in particular interrogated Ruby as to her social connections and her family.

'You work? You're a secretary?' Mrs Van Cooth was horrified.

Peggy Plumstead was, however, having none of that. 'You must be a very capable woman, Miss Rhodes. Holding down a job and having that independence. I envy you.' She looked sideways at her husband.

'Thank you,' replied Ruby. 'I had no choice except to work. My parents died when I was young, so my younger brother and I would have starved otherwise.'

'Admirable. And you seem to have a very capable friend in Mr da Costa.'

Ruby smiled. 'Indeed, I do. He's been a great support through my trials and tribulations.' She glanced at Reggie, who smiled back at her.

Mrs Van Cooth was getting bored with the focus being on someone apart from herself. 'There's Lady Beauchamp Kiddle with her husband!' she exclaimed. 'I simply must go and offer them my best wishes.'

With that, she sashayed across the lawn, leaving the Plumsteads alone with Reggie and Ruby.

'Can I ask how your investigation is going, Mr da Costa?' asked Mrs Plumstead. 'Have you found out anything that might help my case?'

'Apart from the letter and your visit to The Windsor prior to Mr Howard's death, there's nothing of a physical nature tying you to his death. I believe that the police are treading gently in that area. However, I want to assure you that I am following up any leads that will uncover the real murderer and prove your innocence.'

'It's totally ridiculous suggesting that my wife had anything to do with murder,' Plumstead retorted. 'She's made a statement to the police, and that's where it should end. I might add that there are others in this city who had greater grievances against the man and motivation to kill him.'

'Including yourself, councillor?' asked Reggie, smirking. 'I believe that you lost a large sum of money investing in one of Howard's schemes.'

'Pure rubbish. As if–,' Plumstead spluttered.

'Along with Sir Ambrose Beauchamp Kiddle. The rumours are that you are quite strapped for cash.'

Mrs Plumstead interrupted him. 'That's enough, Mr da Costa. I think that you're being very rude. The agreement was that you would assist me, not implicate my husband. If that's all you have against him, I'd ask you to desist.'

'Unfortunately, there is something else,' said Reggie, watching the politician closely. 'A certain lady was found murdered at the Menzies Hotel on

Sunday morning.'

'Who was she?' asked Mrs Plumstead.

'She'd checked in as Miss Dulcie Smith.'

'What's that got to do with me?' Plumstead leaned forward and poked Reggie in the chest.

Around them, the babble of voices had died away, their attention drawn to the argument brewing in their midst.

'Donald. Calm down. People are watching.'

Reggie continued, ignoring Plumstead's provocation. 'A man answering your description was seen entering the hotel with that lady on Saturday night.'

The councillor regained control. 'There are plenty of men who look like me.'

Reggie paused for effect. 'Tom Mix?'

Plumstead went pale. 'I don't know what you're talking about.'

'I think you do, councillor. This is going to come out in the papers in the next day or so. I suggest you have a little chat with your wife before it does.'

Peggy Plumstead stared at her husband, her lips pursed. 'Is she–?'

'Not here, Peggy. Wait till we get home.'

'She's dead, Mrs Plumstead,' continued Reggie. 'And the police know now that she was an associate of Jasper Fitzalan Howard. Dulcie Smith was Jasper Howard's partner in crime and his so-called wife in their blackmail racket. Sometimes, their roles were reversed. Is that what happened to you, councillor? Did she threaten to expose you publicly because of your tawdry affair?'

The atmosphere was growing heated. Councillor Plumstead's face had drained of colour, and his hands were trembling.

Ruby took Reggie's arm. 'Enough. This is the police's job. Let them deal with it.'

Reggie raised his hat. 'I apologise, Mrs Plumstead. I regret that I embarrassed you. You are the innocent party in this. I believe that there is no case against you, but there may be against your husband.' He turned to the politician. 'Get a lawyer, *Mister* Plumstead. That would be my advice.'

As they were about to walk away, Mrs Plumstead touched Reggie's arm. 'Mr da Costa, despite everything that you've just said, there's something you should know.'

Surprised, Reggie faced her. 'What is it?' He glanced across at Councillor Plumstead, who had turned his back on him.

'Donald received a threatening letter yesterday. He wouldn't tell me the details, but the gist of it was that he would find himself in a lot of trouble if he didn't vote in favour of keeping the status quo for patent medicines.'

'They wanted him to vote for repealing the law?'

'That's right.'

'And what was this trouble that they talked about?'

'He wouldn't tell me, but it's obvious, isn't it?'

'The murder of Dulcie Smith?'

'How can you doubt that?'

'Does he know who sent the letter?'

'It was anonymous, but he thinks there's some group of people with vested interests stirring up trouble. There's talk in the parliament.'

She looked back at her husband. 'I have to go. Donald's not happy with me talking to you. Help us, Mr da Costa.'

She walked away. Reggie turned to Ruby and raised an eyebrow. He took her arm, and they climbed the stairs of the grandstand to take their seats for the running of the next race.

'That was interesting,' said Reggie. When she remained silent, he took her hand. 'I'm sorry, my love. Have I ruined your day?'

She shrugged her shoulders. 'I would have liked a crime-free day, Reggie, but it's inescapable even if we're at the Melbourne Cup. Was that really necessary?' she asked, indicating the Plumsteads, who were standing at the rails watching the horses go up towards the barrier.

'I can't bear that man. He gets up there and spouts this rubbish about the value of families and ethical behaviour, and then, he cheats on his wife. He's disgusting.'

Ruby frowned. 'I understand that, but berating him in front of his wife was wrong.'

'Perhaps I let my feelings get the better of me. But the police will be waiting this evening when he gets home. It's probably better that she's forewarned about what's coming. He's not likely to tell her otherwise.'

'I'd judge from her reaction that she already knows about his affairs. Do you think he killed Miss Smith?'

'I'd say he knew who Dulcie really was. That she was an accomplice of Jasper Howard. He didn't look surprised or shocked, rather that he was afraid of being exposed publicly. And, if that's true, then he'd be angry. But angry enough to kill her? I don't know.'

Ruby looked thoughtful. 'Is it possible that he had something to do with Howard's murder? He did lose most of his money.'

'There's one thing for sure. The two deaths are linked. Not only because the victims knew each other, but because they were stabbed to death and both were clutching tarot cards: the Ten of Swords.'

'I know that I lack your experience in investigating crime,' said Ruby, 'but I think you're being hasty in ruling out Mrs Plumstead as a killer. Both of them had motives for killing Mr Howard and Miss Smith.'

'Go on,' said Reggie, giving her his full attention.

'On the one hand, we have the husband. He was financially ruined by Howard, so he killed him. He discovers afterwards that Miss Smith was Howard's accomplice. By that stage, he knows that Howard had been blackmailing his wife as well as swindling him. He kills Miss Smith in a fit of rage because she makes a fool of him.

'On the other hand, we have the wife. She's being blackmailed by Howard. She kills him. Then, she finds out that her husband is having an affair with Miss Smith. She's angry, jealous. How could he do that to her, she asks herself? She follows him and takes out her anger on the woman. Perhaps she even thinks that the police will charge her husband with Miss Smith's murder, so that she will get her revenge on him without lifting a finger.'

Reggie smiled. 'You have an unhealthy interest in crime, my love.'

'You disagree with me?'

'On the contrary, what you say is possible. You offer good points against Mrs Plumstead, although I'm not sure that she's a killer. She's a very attractive woman.'

'You're letting a pretty face override motive?'

'You've found my weakness. However, both crimes were premeditated. The killer had the tarot card, the knife, and the change of clothes when he or she did the dirty deed. You have to wonder if the Plumsteads were capable of that, but it's certainly worth considering. But let's put aside our murder investigation for the next few hours and give our attention to what's important in life.'

'And what's that?'

'The Melbourne Cup, of course.'

Chapter Thirty-Two

Ruby was sitting in her office at Smith and Sons, typing up the monthly report. As she pulled the finished document from the typewriter roller and placed it in the metal tray awaiting her boss's signature, she let her mind drift back to the previous day.

Her attendance at the Melbourne Cup had offered both excitement and intrigue. Apart from the questions surrounding the guilt, or otherwise, of Councillor Plumstead and his wife, there was the enjoyment and luxury of experiencing the Members' Enclosure, surrounded by the cream of Melbourne society, whilst watching the running of the Cup itself.

By half-past three, the unpleasantness of the exchange between Reggie and Councillor Plumstead had worn off. The horses were led into the starting barrier, ready for the long race to the finishing post, two miles in all. With a purse of over ten thousand pounds for the winner, Australia's premier horse race was being keenly contested. The favourite, Manfred, had been heavily backed, having won the Derby the week before. But a two-mile race was a different affair, and Windbag was also a favourite with the punters.

Reggie had just returned from the betting ring when the cry rose up from the crowd, 'They're off!'

Down the straight, the horses thundered, with the pace hot in the early stages. The crowd roared as the horses swept past the grandstand, all eyes on the leaders that were about twenty lengths ahead of the tail of the field. Manfred was in the lead, pulling hard, with Friarsdale, Pilliewinkie, and Windbag in hot pursuit. The lead changed again as Friarsdale dropped back, with Manfred out front and Windbag striding comfortably ahead of

Pilliewinkie.

Ruby rose to her feet, watching excitedly as the two champions fought it out. 'Come on, Windbag!' she cried.

Windbag, the four-year-old bay stallion, carrying over nine pounds in lead weight, started to gain on Manfred, every stride bringing him closer. The horses rounded the bend and turned into the straight. The jockeys, in their brightly coloured silks, spurred on their mounts, the thudding of the hooves reverberating on the track, whilst the cheering of the crowd was deafening.

All sense of decorum had deserted those in the Members' Enclosure. Waving their betting tickets, yelling, jumping up and down, the excited crowd was focused solely on the progress of the horses as they raced down the straight, each person vying for the thrill of betting on the winner of the celebrated Melbourne Cup.

Down on the lawns, spectators were packed twenty deep against the fence, a sea of faces watching expectantly as the thoroughbreds pounded the turf, their jockeys urging them on, with only two hundred yards between them and the thrill of holding the Cup aloft.

Windbag drew level. Then, as the finishing post rose up in front of them, the horse flashed past Manfred with a half a length to spare, Pilliewinkie only a length behind in third place.

Champagne corks popped, the winner was toasted, and gentlemen threw their hats in the air.

'You've won fifty pounds on Windbag alone!' cried Reggie above the din.

Ruby danced up and down, ecstatic in her win. She hugged Reggie, who took advantage of her enthusiasm and hugged her back.

He stopped suddenly and dropped to one knee. 'Will you marry me, Ruby?'

She stared down at him and smiled. 'You'd do anything to get your hands on my winnings.'

He chuckled. 'But will you marry me anyway?'

'Of course, I will. Yes, Reggie, yes.'

* * *

One of the typists was standing next to her. 'Why are you smiling?'

Ruby blinked, brought back to the present. 'I was thinking about yesterday. I had such a wonderful time at the Cup.'

'Lucky girl. But you better get the monthly report on the boss's desk. I've heard that Mr Smith is on the warpath.' She paused. 'How's that Reggie of yours? He's off to Sydney, you said?'

Ruby nodded. She was about to slide a paperclip onto the pages of the report when a troubling thought crossed her mind.

'Oh dear,' she whispered and put her hand to her mouth.

In all the excitement at the Cup, and Reggie's surprise proposal, Ruby had forgotten to ask him about his mother. The last time they'd seen Mavis, over afternoon tea a week before, Ruby had thought that Mrs da Costa looked lethargic and had struggled to follow the conversation. Reggie had been so caught up in discussing his latest case that he didn't appear to notice. And now, he was leaving for Sydney the next day, searching for evidence related to the Howard-Smith murders, and there wouldn't be an opportunity to talk to him about it until he returned.

Chapter Thirty-Three

S pencer Street railway station was buzzing with people as the Sydney Express belched steam into the sky, waiting for the station master to blow his whistle and wave his flag for its departure. Along the platform, porters pushed trolleys laden with suitcases down to the baggage van, while passengers climbed aboard the train that would deposit them in the Harbour City the next morning. With only fifteen minutes to go until the station clock ticked over to five o'clock, expectation was in the smoky air.

Reggie and Dusty stood on the platform, saying their farewells to Ruby, who had accompanied them to the station, having been allowed to get off work early.

'Thanks for looking after the Australian Six while I'm away,' said Dusty. 'You'll be careful driving it home, won't you?'

Ruby laughed. 'You're starting to sound like Reggie, obsessing about a motorcar.' She turned to her beau, the glimmer of a smile on her lips. 'I notice you didn't offer me the Hupmobile.'

Reggie chuckled nervously. 'It's not that I don't trust you–'

She leaned in and kissed him on the cheek. 'It's alright. I've accepted that you love your motorcar more than me.'

'Don't be ridiculous. As if I'd love the Hupmobile more than you.'

'Enough, Reggie. I'm sure your mother wouldn't like you telling lies.'

'About Mother. Could you keep an eye on her for me? I know that it's a lot to ask in the circumstances.'

'I will do that. I'll telephone her in a couple of days. By the way, where are you staying?'

'The Hero of Waterloo Hotel at Millers Point. It's close to Circular Quay and Sydney Harbour.'

'Take care, both of you. And have a good trip.'

They exchanged kisses then Reggie and Dusty boarded the train and were shown to their first-class sleepers by the conductor.

'I thought that we'd be going second class,' commented Dusty, standing in the corridor outside Reggie's compartment.

Reggie chuckled. 'Flange agreed to an upgrade when I told him that arriving in Sydney after sitting up all night was not conducive to good reporting.

'I'll see you at dinner,' he added.

The whistle blew, and the Sydney Express chugged out of the station, gathering speed as they left behind the city of Melbourne. Pleased with the amenities of his first-class compartment, Reggie unpacked his toiletries, stowed his belongings in the small locker, and hung up the suit that he would wear on arrival in Sydney. He pulled out a copy of the Victoria Police Gazette and spent the next hour updating himself on the recent criminal activities of those offenders who had failed to evade the police. In some respects, he found it more interesting than the Foy & Gibson catalogue, although keeping up with the latest fashions in menswear was important to him, too.

At seven o'clock, Reggie and Dusty made their way to the dining car and were shown to their seats. Whilst partaking of a flavoursome meal of ribs of beef, followed by bread-and-butter pudding with lashings of cream, the two men discussed their plans for Sydney, mostly pertaining as to whom amongst Howard's victims they needed to interview.

'I'm keen to meet with Lottie O'Leary,' Reggie said.

'Remind me about her,' replied Dusty, spearing a juicy bean with his fork.

'Ruby and I found a photograph of her in Howard's secret stash. They had an affair, judging by what was written on the back of her photograph. She operates out of Sydney, so Howard must have lived there at some stage. Lottie's a fraudster and a blackmailer. Goes by the name of Odette de la

Tours, Marchioness de Montignac. Supposedly related to the French actress, Renée Adorée.'

Reggie paused to sample the glass of French Bordeaux that the waiter had poured for them.

'Lottie became a fixture in Sydney society,' he said, setting his glass on the table. 'She seduced and blackmailed a number of prominent businessmen until one called her bluff, and she was arrested. Her partner was Louie "The Dodger" Hayes.'

'She did the seducing, while Louie was the standover man. Is that the way it worked?' asked Dusty.

'That's right. As I said, they picked the wrong target. Louie got a beating, and now, they're facing jail. Lottie's in the Women's Reformatory.'

'Can we meet her?'

'I have contacts in Sydney who can arrange that for us.'

'These victims. When are you going to tell them about the incriminating letters you found in Howard's suitcase?' asked Dusty, pushing his plate away and wiping his mouth with a napkin.

'Only if they deny knowledge of Howard. It's a means of getting information from them. But I'll have to convince them that I only want their cooperation, not their money. I'll hand over the letters once they've told their story. That way, the evidence will be destroyed, and they can live their lives without fear of discovery.'

'Ruby's suggestion,' observed Dusty.

'I have to hand it to your sister: she can make a convincing argument.'

'You like her a lot, don't you.' It was a statement, not a question.

'Indeed, I do. I have to say that I've never met anyone like her. In fact–'

Dusty interrupted him. 'She basically raised me after Mum died. I owe her a lot.'

Reggie took a moment and decided that it was perhaps for the best that he hadn't told Dusty about their engagement. He'd leave that up to Ruby.

Dinner drew to a close, and the two men walked down the corridor, then went to their respective compartments, as the locomotive barrelled along the tracks doing sixty miles per hour. The conductor had made up their beds while they were at dinner, and so they settled down for a sleep before they reached the State border, where it was necessary to change trains because of the different gauges used in each state. Despite the inconvenience and delay, the train pulled into Central Station, Sydney, on time at exactly eleven o'clock the next morning.

After collecting their luggage, the two crime reporters took a taxi to a hotel recommended by one of Reggie's Sydney colleagues. Situated at Millers Point, also known as The Rocks, The Hero of Waterloo Hotel, named after the Duke of Wellington, was a three-storey building, in the Old Colonial Regency style, made of sandstone chiselled by convicts. The publican was a jovial chap, in striped shirt and brown trousers, his large beer belly visible beneath a generous white apron. Encouraged by Reggie, he took the two reporters on a tour of the pub, before showing them to their rooms.

'The Hero was built in 1842 using convict labour,' he told them. 'It's amazing that it's still here. This is one of the few hotels in the area not demolished when the bubonic plague broke out in 1901.'

'My friend at *The Sydney Morning Herald* told me there's a tunnel running from the cellar to Sydney Harbour.'

'That's right,' said the publican. 'They used it to smuggle rum.' He pointed to a set of steps leading downstairs. 'Let's start with the cellar.'

It was a gloomy and forbidding room lit sparingly by electric light, with shackles still attached to the walls bearing silent witness to its notorious past. A large open fireplace dominated the room, which was paved with sandstone.

'The tunnel entrance is over there,' he said pointing to an opening fitted with a metal grille door. 'They reckon that if a young man got drunk in the public bar, he'd be dropped through a trapdoor into this cellar. He'd be dragged along that tunnel to the harbour, and next morning, when he came to, he'd discover that he was now a sailor on a ship out on the high seas, looking forward to a future of enforced labour.'

Dusty was shocked. 'Press-ganged?'

'That's right. It happened a lot in the past.'

The landlord was warming to his role as story-teller. 'Not only that, but we've got a genuine ghost at The Hero.'

Reggie was intrigued. 'Do tell.'

'It was 1849, and one of my predecessors was Thomas Kirkman. He and his wife, Anne, weren't getting on too well. Anyway, Thomas pushed her down the stairs, and she hit her head and died. No one has ever seen Anne's ghost, but they say that her presence can be felt. In one of the upstairs rooms, you might find that the chairs have been moved from their usual position, so that they face the fireplace. And sometimes, in the middle of the night, you might hear the piano being played in the bar. When you go in, there's no one there, but the lid of the piano is open.' He winked. 'What do you reckon?'

Dusty grinned. 'I reckon they've had a few too many beers.'

'What about you, Reggie? Believe in ghosts?'

'I'd need to see one with my own two eyes.'

The landlord nodded sagely. 'You might change your tune. How long are you here for?'

'A week.'

'That will be long enough. I'll take you up to your rooms.'

They followed him upstairs, smirking at each other. A ghost? Not likely.

Chapter Thirty-Four

While Reggie and Dusty were spending their first afternoon in Sydney, Detective Sergeant Clary Blain was at his desk studying the file on the Howard and Smith murders. He had decided to combine the two cases given the parallels between them: the weapon, the number of wounds, the presence of the same tarot card, and the fact that Miss Smith had also lodged at The Hotel Windsor and had departed the morning that Howard's body was found. There was also the photograph of Smith and Howard together, indicating that they had known each other.

The list of suspects was growing, as the extent of Howard's illegal activities became clearer. Firstly, there were those who had been affected by his suspect property investment schemes. They included, in the main, Councillor Plumstead and Sir Ambrose Beauchamp Kiddle, among others from the Melbourne Club. Secondly, there were the women who had been seduced by Howard and had fallen for his charms, becoming the target of blackmail.

The prime suspect in the second category was Mrs Plumstead. But there was also Mrs Van Cooth, who had become enamoured with Jasper Howard and had not taken it well when Mrs Plumstead had become the object of Howard's affections.

Another suspect was Madame Esmeralda, a name given to him by Reggie. His investigation showed that the fortune-teller had worked in tandem with Howard, directing susceptible women to make his acquaintance. It was possible that things had soured between the two of them, causing her to kill him. That hypothesis presented him with the perfect explanation for the presence of the tarot card. It was a setback that the woman had disappeared, no longer occupying rooms in the Eastern Arcade.

Blain looked up at the clock. His first interview for the day was due to start in two minutes. Councillor Plumstead had been shown to the interview room fifteen minutes earlier and was waiting for him. Let him wait, Blain thought. The man was known to be difficult, so let him take a sample of his own medicine. The detective picked up a pen and notepad, and the folder containing the Howard case notes. Time to go to work.

Plumstead looked up when Blain entered the room, appraising him with cold blue eyes.

'It's about time,' he said, tapping the table with his finger.

The detective remained silent, as he made himself comfortable and organised his notes.

'Thank you for coming in today, Mr Plumstead.'

'It's not as if I had much choice. And it's Councillor Plumstead to you.' He glanced around the room, noting the bars on the windows and the pale green walls. 'It's cold in here.'

Blain cleared his throat. 'I've asked you to attend to answer some questions pertaining to the Jasper Howard case. In particular, I'm interested in your association with the man.'

'There was no association,' replied Plumstead, looking defiantly across the table at the policeman. 'It was a business deal, which was completed to our mutual satisfaction.'

'Is that so?' Blain scratched his nose and shuffled his notes. 'According to our enquiries, sir, you lost a considerable sum of money investing in Howard's scheme. Is that correct?'

'Who gave you that information? I have a right to know.' Plumstead shifted in his chair.

'There are others who were parties to this venture and suffered losses,' said the detective, tapping his notes with the pen. 'They have made statements to us regarding the amounts that they invested. There was no acquisition of a Western District sheep farm. We now know that it was an elaborate swindle perpetrated by Jasper Howard. Therefore, I find it hard to believe that this business deal was completed to your satisfaction.' Blain studied the man opposite him. 'One might suggest that being defrauded gives a person a powerful motive to kill, wouldn't you agree?'

'How dare you!' Plumstead cried, going red in the face. 'I will report you to your superiors.'

'Calm down, sir,' replied Blain coolly. 'No need to get hot under the collar. I was speaking hypothetically, of course.' He paused, referring to his notes. 'Were you aware that Jasper Howard was blackmailing your wife?'

'Not until after he was found dead.'

'Your wife didn't confide in you?'

'Peggy has never confided in me. And I don't confide in her. That's how we are.'

'Your marriage is, if I may be so bold, one of convenience?'

'That's none of your business. Have you finished? I'm a busy man.'

Blain shuffled his notes, buying time, then fixed his eyes on Plumstead's face, watching for the reaction to his next question. 'Now, regarding your relationship with Miss Dulcie Smith. We have a witness who places you at the Menzies Hotel on the night of her murder. Can you explain that?'

His final question brought the interview to a shuddering halt. Councillor Plumstead rose to his feet, his whole body shaking with anger. 'If you wish to question me again, I will be bringing my legal representative with me. Is that clear?'

He shook his fist at the policeman. 'Watch your step, Detective Sergeant Blain. I will fight you every step of the way if you try to implicate me or my wife in these murders. I have friends in high places.'

Blain didn't blink. He was not going to be intimidated by the bullying tactics of this man. He felt justified in asking questions, given that two people were dead, and the man with a motive to kill both was standing in front of him, even if he were a member of the Victorian Legislative Council.

Blain sat back, calm in the face of Plumstead's threats.

'Thank you for attending today.' Blain got to his feet and nodded at the portly figure who stood glaring at him. 'I will be in touch with you again, sir, should it be necessary.'

He opened the door and stood aside as Plumstead stormed past.

Blain stared after him, analysing the character of the man he had just interviewed. A man in a loveless marriage. A man who lacked self-control, was used to getting his own way and had a firecracker temper. A cold man, too, who showed neither concern nor compassion for anyone, except himself. To Blain, Plumstead's responses and behaviour added weight to the case against him. Judging by his response, it was apparent that the councillor was under pressure. His financial situation must be in a perilous state for him to lie about his dealings with Howard, and he was obviously deeply concerned that his dalliance with the now-deceased Dulcie Smith would put his political career in jeopardy.

'Constable,' he said to the policeman on duty outside the room. 'Send in Sir Ambrose Beauchamp Kiddle, please.'

* * *

Kiddle was certainly a different proposition to Councillor Plumstead. He greeted Blain politely, seemingly overawed by his intimidating surroundings: the pale green walls, the barred windows and the spartan table and chairs, as well as the presence of a uniformed policeman guarding the door. Blain stood and shook his hand, then beckoned for him to take the seat opposite.

It was the detective's first chance to get a good look at his next suspect. Kiddle was in his early forties, of solid build, and going prematurely bald. He was dressed in a double-breasted pinstripe suit in dark grey, with a black waistcoat and black tie, almost funereal in appearance, but it was his hands that caught Blain's eye: very hairy with short, stubby fingers. The hands of a strangler.

'It's good of you to come in, Sir Ambrose.'

The man nodded. 'I'm not sure why I'm here.'

'It's in regard to Mr Jasper Howard. I believe that you knew him?'

'Barely.'

Blain sighed. More obstruction. He opened the file again and shuffled some papers. 'Is that right? I have it on good authority that you and he were business partners.'

'In a manner of speaking. However, the deal never went through.'

'Sheep? Wool production? In the Western District?'

Kiddle's face was a mask. 'It never happened.'

'You did invest in it, though?'

'A paltry amount.'

Blain ran his finger down the page, then tapped on it, as if he had found something of consequence. He looked up. 'Six thousand pounds is hardly a paltry amount. Or it's not in my world.'

Kiddle shifted in his chair. 'Wasn't that Councillor Plumstead whom I saw walking out of the front door?'

Blain fixed him with a look. 'You must have been very angry when you realised that you'd been duped.'

He shrugged his shoulders, looking elsewhere. 'I wasn't happy, no.'

'We've been informed that you threatened Howard.'

Kiddle ran his tongue over his lips. 'Who told you that?'

'You were overheard having an argument with him. You told him that you would kill him if you didn't get your money back.'

'That's ridiculous. I would never threaten anyone. I have never hurt anyone. My record speaks for itself.'

Blain turned over a few pages until he found the one that he wanted. Kiddle tried to read it upside down and blanched when he realised what it was.

'Your military record says otherwise. It says that you punched one of your men senseless.'

Kiddle snickered. 'You've obviously never served in a war. It's called discipline.'

'This was during training. It was not on the battlefield. The soldier was hospitalised.'

Kiddle leaned forward, a glimpse of steely reserve in his voice. 'I gave him an order, and he refused.'

'You were reprimanded.' Blain sat back in his chair. 'It seems that you have a temper, Sir Ambrose. I'd suggest that you were angry with Jasper Howard. He dangled a tempting proposition in front of you, and you fell for it, hook, line, and sinker. And when it became obvious that you'd been swindled, you decided to pay him back. It was at the Lord Mayor's charity ball at The Windsor. You left your table on the pretence of finding out where Howard was. You went up to his room, you knocked on his door, and you stabbed him to death.'

Kiddle went silent, withdrawing into himself. After a moment, he spoke haltingly. 'I admit that I went to see him. The door was locked. He never answered it. Ask my wife, she'll tell you.'

'Did you know Miss Dulcie Smith?'

'Who?' Kiddle looked bewildered.

Clary Blain studied the man on the other side of the table. Here was a man that he couldn't read, nervous and defensive at the idea that he was under suspicion for murder, and yet possessing somewhere deep inside him a tendency to violence, as evidenced by his treatment of the soldier under his command. He was a gullible fool when it came to investing in dodgy schemes, but did his impulsiveness translate into committing murder?

Blain knew that his allegation was full of holes and couldn't be proven. Where was the knife that Kiddle used? How could he have left a bloody crime scene and returned to the charity ball so quickly without a speck of blood on him? And what about the tarot card? Where did that fit in? And what was the link between Dulcie Smith and Kiddle?

Blain stood. 'Thank you for coming today. You may go now.'

The man looked confused and uncertain as he rose and nodded at Blain. He didn't strike the detective as a cold-blooded killer, a man who could commit premeditated murder.

Blain checked his watch. Five o'clock. A wasted afternoon with regard to the case. Both interviews had offered little to support the proposition that either man was a murderer. Although the motivation was there, the evidence wasn't. However, there was still something he could salvage from the day. There was enough time to get down to the pub and have a glass or two or three of whisky. And, with a bit of luck, Reggie would be back from

Sydney to pick up the bill next time.

Chapter Thirty-Five

It was late Friday afternoon, and Ruby had finished work for the day. She was walking up Bourke Street towards the Eastern Arcade, Madame Esmeralda's business card in her hand.

At home that morning, she had carried the suitcase, with the false bottom, into the sitting room and opened it. Inside were the business cards and letters belonging to Howard. Any which Reggie had deemed useful for his interstate investigation, those which linked the dead man with Sydney identities, he had taken with him.

Ruby didn't like to meddle, but Madame Esmeralda's business card had stuck in her mind. Reggie had mentioned that confidence men and women had associates, who helped them in the execution of their blackmail attempts and dodgy ventures, such as the man who had winked at Mrs Plumstead at the Hotel Continental in Sorrento.

Perhaps she could gather some information about the fortune-teller before Reggie's return, perhaps as early as tonight after work, confirming whether or not it was the same woman to whom Mrs Van Cooth was referring. Surely it wouldn't hurt, and besides, she argued, it was she who had discovered the false bottom of the suitcase, with its evidence of Howard's wrong-doing, not Reggie. She had a right to do some investigating of her own, and it would undoubtedly relieve the boredom of her social life while her beau was away. The fact was that she was feeling at a loose end, with her brother and Reggie in Sydney.

Unbeknown to Ruby, she was treading the same path as Reggie's mother, Mavis, some two months earlier, as she entered the Eastern Arcade, off

Bourke Street in the city. Nothing much had changed in that time, except for the occasional foot patrols of constables on the beat, cracking down on the prevalence of undesirable characters who had made the arcade their home.

Lit by glass panes in the roof, the arcade appeared deserted except for a man who was sweeping the promenade outside his chemist shop. He leaned on his broom and spoke to her as she passed.

'Can I help you, miss? Are you lost?'

'I'm looking for Madame Esmeralda. Can you direct me, please?'

'She's packed up and gone. The landlord wasn't too happy. She didn't give notice, and he's been left out of pocket.'

Ruby shook her head. 'I've come all this way for nothing.'

'If you're here to have your fortune told, then you're out of luck.'

Ruby thought fast. 'My mother came here two weeks ago. She thinks that she left her coat behind. I offered to come, given that I work close by. And now, there's nothing I can do.'

His mind made up, the chemist searched in his pocket for the key. 'I can let you in, but you'll have to be quick.'

'That would be wonderful. Thank you so much.'

He unlocked the door and pushed it open. 'Let me know when you've finished, and I'll lock it up again.'

Ruby flicked the switch, but the electricity had been disconnected. Leaving the front door open, which allowed some light into the premises, she could see that she was in a small waiting room, with chairs set out around the walls. There was a door to an adjoining room, with a sign attached to it. 'Madame Esmeralda. Character reader. Please wait until you are called.'

She opened the door and passed into a bigger room, where a circular table covered by a black velvet tablecloth occupied the middle of the room. Two chairs were placed opposite each other. Heavy curtains blanketed the windows. She pulled them back, but the glass had been covered in newspaper. On the table was a candle in a bottle and a box of Bryant & May safety matches. Ruby lit the candle and looked around her as the flame breached the shadows. It appeared that the occupant had left in a hurry.

The tools of the fortune-telling trade had been left behind: two packs of tarot cards, a Ouija board, sticks of incense, and a couple of cheap oriental statues of a dragon and a Hindu god.

Ruby had always been sceptical about the claims of those who read palms or saw answers in the stars. It was trickery, in her view, reliant on calculated questioning, perceptive observation, and sleight of hand, such as magicians used. Taking the chair where Madame Esmeralda sat, Ruby decided to test the possibility that the woman concealed items beneath the table, but when she lifted the tablecloth, she was disappointed to see that nothing was hidden there, except for a small basket containing a range of potions and pills. Inside were bottles of Dr Wishbone's Restorative Syrup and boxes of Dr Wishbone's Pills for Feeble People. At the bottom of the basket were the doctor's business cards.

It was time to leave, although she had learned almost nothing. The chemist, who had let her in, would be getting suspicious. She glanced at the packs of tarot cards, and a thought crossed her mind. Was it possible that the Ten of Swords, left at the murder scenes, was missing from these packs? Would that prove a connection to the killing of Jasper Howard and Dulcie Smith?

A voice came from the waiting room. 'Miss, did you find the coat?'

She swept the cards into her handbag and hurried outside. 'Thank you so much,' she said, smiling at the shopkeeper. 'My mother must have made a mistake. She probably left it elsewhere.'

* * *

Back at home, Ruby sat at the kitchen table after finishing her dinner. She eyed the pack of tarot cards. In truth, she was not familiar with how many cards were in the set, but she did know that there was only one of each card. She undid the first pack and lay each card down, looking for the illustration of the Ten of Swords: a man lying face down, lifeless, with ten swords protruding from his back. It was in the first pack, but the second one was a different matter. The Ten of Swords was missing.

Her thoughts turned to Reggie. No doubt, he'd find the absence of the tarot card interesting, as well as the departure of Madame Esmeralda from the Eastern Arcade. It bothered her that he hadn't telephoned since he had arrived in Sydney. But then, she hadn't rung his mother, which she had promised that she would do.

She tidied up the kitchen and walked reluctantly to the telephone, where she gave the operator the number. The telephone was answered almost immediately.

'Is that you, Reggie?' Mavis sounded fatigued.

'It's me, Mrs da Costa. Ruby.'

There was silence at the other end.

'Who?'

She sighed in frustration. 'Ruby Rhodes. Reggie asked me to ring you.'

'I don't understand. I spoke to Reggie today.'

'He's telephoned you?'

'Why wouldn't he? I'm his mother.' She was slurring her words. 'Hasn't he rung you?'

'Not yet. I expect that he will soon.'

'Where is he again?'

'Sydney. Reggie's in Sydney.'

'That's nice. I'm busy. Must go.' She hung up, leaving Ruby indignant.

'Wretched woman,' she muttered as she replaced the earpiece. 'Reggie's rung her and not me?' She stared at the telephone, not sure who annoyed her more: the mother or the son. She walked away, but then, the telephone started to ring. Not Mavis again?

'Hello?'

'It's me, my love. Reggie.'

'Oh, hello,' she replied, her voice cool. 'How is Sydney?'

'Going well.'

'That's good.' She paused, knowing that she was expected to show interest, but she was still smarting from his mother's words.

'Is there something wrong? You don't sound like your usual self.'

'I've just spoken to your mother.'

'Ah, that's the problem. Mavis still not being friendly? I will speak to her.

CHAPTER THIRTY-FIVE

Be patient, my love.'

'She says that you talked to her today.'

There was silence. 'Dusty and I haven't stopped since we arrived here. I haven't rung anybody. Not you. Not Mother. Not *The Argus*.'

'Really? That's strange. Do you think your mother is being–'

'Difficult. Indeed, I do.'

'You know that she won't accept me as your fiancée.'

'Give her time. She will come around.'

'I don't think so.' Ruby sighed, her anger dissipating away. 'Now, tell me all about Sydney. And then, I'll tell you about Madame Esmeralda and the Ten of Swords.'

Reggie couldn't control his curiosity. 'I don't have long, unfortunately. What's this about Madame Esmeralda?'

He listened intently as Ruby gave him an account of her visit to the Eastern Arcade.

'Well done. It's significant that the tarot card was missing from the pack.'

'Have you made any important discoveries in Sydney?'

'We've been filling in some background on Jasper Howard, but the next few days will be the key. I'm seeing Lottie O'Leary, alias Odette, at the jail. We have interviews lined up with some of Howard's victims. I'll tell you all about it when I see you back in Melbourne.'

'I'll look forward to it. Give my love to Dusty,' said Ruby. 'I miss you, Reggie.'

'And I miss you, too. I know it's a lot to ask, but could you telephone Mother one more time? Perhaps tomorrow? Just to check that she's alright? Trunk calls are so expensive.'

Ruby reluctantly agreed. She stepped away from the telephone and shook her head. Winning Mavis over was not going to be easy, no matter what Reggie said.

She started to wash the dishes, then sighed heavily. She had let another opportunity slip to express her concerns over Mrs da Costa's health. The telephone call confirmed that there was something wrong with her: her listlessness and inability to concentrate, her forgetfulness, and most worryingly, that she was now slurring her words. She hesitated to admit it, but was there a chance that Mavis da Costa had a drinking problem?

Chapter Thirty-Six

Sydney Harbour looked a picture, its waters glinting in the November sunshine, as Dusty and Reggie stood on the deck of the ferry taking them to Double Bay, on the south side of the harbour. Behind them, at Dawes Point, and on the northern side, at Milson's Point, work was being done in preparation for the construction of the Sydney Harbour Bridge.

'Not much to see yet,' observed Dusty. 'I read that it's going to cost more than five million pounds.'

Reggie nodded. 'They say it will be 1930 before the spans meet. It's a huge project: six lanes of roadway, four railway lines, and two footpaths.'

At Dawes Point, preliminary work on the huge concrete piers faced with granite was underway, as well as the building of a great retaining wall, its southern extremity adjacent to the Mining Museum building and extending some 300 feet towards the harbour. Electric and steam cranes and a mass of scaffolding had been delivered to the site. On the other side the work was going slowly, with only a large plot of dirt to show in the way of construction.

'Imagine what a difference it will make to the city?' said Reggie. 'It will be so much easier to travel from one side of Sydney to the other and up the north coast of New South Wales. No waiting for ferries to take you to the other side.'

'What's our destination this morning?' asked Dusty, watching as the ferry crested the waves. 'I thought we were going to the Women's Reformatory.'

'That's tomorrow. We're due to meet Mr Randall Wigg today. He lost everything in one of Howard's get-rich-quick schemes.'

'Is his name mentioned in one of those letters?'

'Not in this case. One of my former mates at *The Argus* gave me his name. He says that the spectacular rise and fall of Wigg made headlines in Sydney. Wigg's apparently happy to spill the beans on Howard to anyone who'll listen. He's still angry two years on.'

The ferry glided past Fort Denison, known to the locals as 'Pinchgut', a small sandstone fortification situated on a tiny island in the harbour. Further along, the ferry pulled into Darling Point Wharf, allowing passengers to get on and off, then rounded the coastline and stopped at the Double Bay Wharf.

The gangplank was lowered, and the reporters joined a small group of people getting off. Reggie nodded in the direction of Bay Street.

'He lives up there, at the top of the hill.'

Half a mile up lived Randall Wigg, the state of his house the outward sign of a dire change in financial circumstances. A modest weatherboard, it had not seen the stroke of a paintbrush for some years. The corrugated iron roof was rusting, and the branches of a large gum tree, in serious need of lopping, bent perilously over it. Roses grew wild in the small front garden, through which curved an uneven brick path, the weeds breaking through the gaps. One of the front windows had a broken pane of glass covered with a piece of cardboard.

'He was a millionaire?' asked Dusty, staring at the dilapidated house.

'Hard to believe, I know. He lived in Vaucluse, one of the poshest suburbs of Sydney. The best of everything. Apparently, he took a few of his friends and family down with him into bankruptcy, and he's been *persona non grata* ever since. It doesn't help that he was not a particularly nice gent to start with. Very ambitious. Only friendly with those who could benefit him.'

Dusty intoned, 'Wigg Withers as Wealth Wanes.'

Reggie chuckled, then pressed the button on the brass bell. There was no sound. He knocked loudly.

The door creaked open, and a man stood there, examining them. Wigg showed no signs of his former wealth, his clothing worn and stained. He was of medium height and, at some stage, had lost a significant amount of weight, given that his trousers were hitched up by a belt and his jacket hung on him. His face was sallow, and his teeth, when he grimaced, were stained yellow. Disconcertingly, Randall Wigg's eyes reminded Reggie of his mother's: big, blue, and innocent.

'Who are you?' he demanded.

'Reggie da Costa from the Melbourne *Argus* and this is my colleague, Dusty Rhodes.'

'He's *Dusty Rhodes*? Is this a joke?'

Reggie ignored him. 'We're investigating the murder of Jasper Howard. We believe that he was operating as a confidence man in Sydney a couple of years ago. He went under a variety of names, including Jasper Waters and Redmond Waters, amongst others.'

Wigg scowled. 'Murdered? He's dead?'

'He is.'

'Scum. Got what he deserved.' He stepped aside. 'You'd better come in.'

He showed them into a small sitting room, smelling of damp, and settled himself into an armchair, pulling a blanket over his legs. Reggie sat at the dining table while Dusty took the remaining armchair, the springs of which twanged as he sat.

Reggie looked around. Above the fireplace was a painting of yellow chrysanthemums in a dark green vase, while on the mantelpiece sat a clock in a mahogany case, the only decorations in a sparsely furnished room. The carpet was threadbare. A dark stain was working its way down the wall, the leak causing the wallpaper to peel away from the cornice. A sheet had been pulled across the window, in lieu of curtains. How the mighty have fallen, he thought.

They sat in silence. When it became clear that Mr Wigg was not about to offer refreshments, Reggie took out his notebook and began the interview.

'What name did Jasper Howard go by, Mr Wigg?'

The man blinked. 'Redmond Waters. Vice President of The Atlantic Investment Company, or so he said.'

'Did he say where he came from?'

'London. He told me that the company was interested in acquiring a tract of land in Northern Queensland. Rainforest; undeveloped. He claimed that the Atlantic Investment Company was interested in developing the land for housing. Queensland was booming, he said, and demand was outstripping supply.'

'Did he offer any proof for his claims?'

'Indeed, he did,' Wigg snarled. 'Letters from the Queensland Government encouraging investment in this "new venture" as they called it. A government guarantee that they would participate in the building of homes. Maps and plans, itemised financial statements of proposed costs, and projected earnings for those who put their money into the scheme.'

'Well-documented.'

'That's right. Convincingly so.' He shook his head. 'It was only later that I heard about the "Swampland in Florida" fraud. If only I'd read about it earlier. In that case, the new owners found that the land they'd purchased was under water and worthless. In my case, the rainforest was unusable, as I was to discover, when I made my own enquiries after Redmond Waters disappeared. There was never any plan to develop it.'

'Did anyone else fall for the scheme?' asked Dusty.

Wigg sighed heavily. 'I talked some of my associates into putting their money in, but I was far and away the biggest backer.'

'How much did you lose?'

He blinked. 'Over £350,000 of my own money and £45,000 of my father-in-law's. Or should I say my *former* father-in-law.' Wigg went quiet.

Reggie took out the photograph of Jasper Howard with Dulcie Smith. 'Is this Redmond Waters?'

Wigg nodded slowly. 'That's the bastard. I recognise her, too, from some of the dinners at the time. Didn't speak to her though.'

'How did you meet him?'

'It was July 1923. The official ceremony to mark the "turning of the first sod" for the construction of the Sydney Harbour Bridge. By that stage, he'd become accepted into the top tier of Sydney society. A smooth, elegant Englishman with astute business acumen. That's the way he presented himself. The ladies liked him, too. Afterwards, he was among the distinguished guests who attended the celebration banquet hosted by the

Premier of New South Wales. That's where we started talking.

'It appeared unplanned, not predetermined at all. I asked him what he was doing in New South Wales, and he mentioned in passing that he was pursuing a business opportunity on behalf of his company. Naturally, I took the bait, and it went from there. Before I knew it, I'd agreed to go in with him and his company. All the documentation that he provided proved it was a sure thing.

'Now, when I look back on it, I have to question what he was doing in New South Wales if the proposed development was in Queensland, over 1500 miles away. And I should have visited the site. I would have realised that the land was worthless. Rainforest, for goodness' sake. Impregnable, uninhabitable, hot, and steamy.'

'What did you do after Waters disappeared?'

'I contacted the police. They couldn't find him. There was no sign that he'd ever entered the country. I hired a private detective. His hotel room had been vacated. He left behind a trail of unpaid bills and worthless cheques. It was clear that he was a swindler, and that he'd gone.'

'You lost everything?' asked Dusty, glancing around the room.

'Everything. My associates lost their money, and they blamed me. My father-in-law would have nothing to do with me. My wife left me. My business was ruined. The life that I'd known was over. I used up what I had left to buy this place. Lovely, isn't it?' Wigg laughed bleakly.

He studied them. 'How did he die?'

'He was stabbed ten times.'

'I wish I'd done it. I wish that I'd seen him dead.' He stood up, the interview over. 'I'm tired, gentlemen. I'd appreciate it if you'd see yourselves out.'

Chapter Thirty-Seven

There was one more interview scheduled for the day, with Miss Mae Ann Horsley who lived at the Australia Hotel in Castlereagh Street. Reggie had tracked her down using the letters that she had sent to Jasper Howard, and through his contact at *The Sydney Morning Herald*.

Miss Horsley was a reclusive, rich old lady who was renowned for her philanthropic works, supporting worthy causes and investing in schemes to benefit the community. Aged in her late seventies, she had crossed paths with Jasper at the opening of a new wing at one of Sydney's public hospitals, where they had struck up a conversation. According to Reggie's colleague, it was rumoured that Miss Horsley had lost over ten thousand pounds through her association with the confidence man.

The Australia Hotel was an impressive building. Reggie and Dusty, the latter wearing his new cream suit, climbed the highly polished steps of the imposing entrance, with its red Doric columns, and crossed to the reception desk in the lobby.

'Miss Horsley is expecting you,' the clerk informed them. 'I'll get someone to take you up.'

They followed the bellboy up a magnificent multi-coloured staircase, quarried from Carrara marble, to the first floor.

'This is a beautiful hotel,' remarked Dusty.

The bellboy stopped and smiled. 'Indeed, it is, sir. Downstairs is the Winter Garden, which is famous for its morning and afternoon teas, light luncheons, and theatre suppers. We also have the Emerald Room, which has a twenty-foot-high ceiling, Italian chandeliers, and a white marble fountain.

The Australia Hotel is the best hotel in the city.'

A look passed between the two reporters. The lad sounded like he was reciting from a script.

'Miss Horsley lives in Madame Sarah Bernhardt's suite on the second floor,' he continued. 'She was the actress, you know.' Reggie raised an eyebrow. He did know. 'She stayed here in 1891. Her salon was filled with flowers. They say that she had one hundred pieces of luggage.'

'Indeed,' remarked Reggie.

'And she had pets. A St Bernard, a pug, a native bear, and cages containing possums and parrots.'

'How remarkable. Does Miss Horsley have a menagerie, too?'

The bellboy shook his head. 'One cat. Miss Horsley prefers a quiet life.'

He knocked on the door. A voice said, 'Come,' and they entered the suite.

'Mr da Costa and Mr Rhodes to see you, Miss Horsley.'

She nodded, and he left, a shilling in his hand.

The lady came towards them, her hand extended. They shook hands and seated themselves on the Louis XIV chairs.

Reggie took a couple of moments to study Miss Horsley, given that he knew almost nothing about her.

She was a tall, fragile-looking lady with thinning white hair pulled back into a bun. Watery green eyes were almost hidden beneath heavy eyelids, her nose was hooked and narrow, her lips were thin around a generous wide mouth. She wore a black dress, devoid of decoration, apart from a pince-nez that hung from a pale grey ribbon. As she sat stroking a large, striped tabby cat, Reggie's eyes were drawn to her knuckles, swollen and deformed.

'How can I help you, Mr da Costa?' she asked. 'You've come a long way for what purpose?'

Despite her age, Reggie sensed that the woman's faculties had not faded. Her voice was strong and self-assured. Her body might be showing the passing of the years, but her mind was sharp.

'I am investigating a murder, Miss Horsley. I believe that you were associated with the victim.'

'His name?'

'Jasper Howard. Also known as Redmond Waters.'

A shadow passed across her face. She paused before answering. 'I knew Redmond. To my everlasting regret.' She looked from Reggie to Dusty. 'How did he die?'

'He was stabbed to death in The Hotel Windsor. His killer has not been found.'

She made the sign of the cross. 'God forgive him.'

'Can you tell me anything about Mr Waters?'

She raised her eyebrows and grunted. 'I've tried to forget that name. It seems as if I'm destined to relive a sorry episode in my life. You're from *The Argus*, I believe?'

Reggie nodded.

'How did you hear about me?'

'Some letters you wrote were in possession of the murdered man.'

Miss Horsley blanched. 'My letters. He kept them?'

'He did.'

'And you obviously have read them.' It was a statement, not a question. 'What do you want to know?'

Reggie was surprised by her directness. There was no sense that she wanted to avoid difficult questions.

'I do know that he purported to represent the Drury Lane Theatre. I do know that he asked you to help fund the refurbishment of the building. And I do know that you gave him money towards it.'

'Twelve thousand pounds.'

'I believe that you became close.'

Miss Horsley's eyes narrowed. 'I'd rather not discuss it. I'm not the same woman now.'

Reggie had made a misstep. He could sense her withdrawing. As he was tossing around how to undo the damage, Dusty broke the silence.

'Redmond Waters thrived on building trust. He charmed people. We know that many others were taken in by him. I spoke to a woman only a month ago who lost her house and all her money to him.

'Rather than ask for the sordid details of what he did to you, we are more interested in whether Mr Waters revealed something to you, something small, in confidence, that might help us in our investigation.'

Reggie nodded approvingly at his apprentice.

'Thank you for your kindness,' she said. The old lady had recovered her equilibrium, her eyes on Dusty as she gave him a sad smile. 'I've always prided myself on my ability to detect those who only wanted me for my money, but I failed dismally when it came to Redmond. It makes me feel slightly better to know that there were others who were taken in.' She stroked the cat on her lap as she gathered her thoughts. 'You asked me if there was anything he said that could help you. There was something. It struck me as odd at the time. We were talking about our childhoods. I told him that I was born near Long Bay Penitentiary, within sight of the walls, and he said that he knew it well. And yet he was English. I asked him when he'd been there, and he said that he'd come out to Australia six years before.

'When I thought about it later, I realised that it would have been about 1917. Would he have come out here for a visit during the Great War? I doubted that. Of course, by that stage, he was gone, and I never had the chance to ask him.'

'You're right, of course, Miss Horsley,' said Reggie. 'Redmond Waters was not English. Born and bred in Sydney. And his lies and deception meant that he left a string of victims behind him after his death.'

She nodded slowly. 'Is that all I can do for you, gentlemen?'

Reggie took her letters out of his jacket pocket and laid them on the arm of the chair. 'You've been very helpful, Miss Horsley. Burn these, and all evidence of your encounter with Redmond Waters goes up in flames.'

'Thank you, Mr da Costa. If only it were that easy.' The cat on her lap purred loudly, its contentment at odds with the demeanour of its mistress.

Chapter Thirty-Eight

I t took an hour the next morning in the archives of *The Sydney Morning Herald* to unearth the article Reggie and Dusty were seeking.

'Here it is!' cried Dusty, waving a newspaper at his boss. 'It was at the bottom of page six, not front-page news at all.'

LONG BAY PENITENTIARY
MAN ESCAPES

Jasper Waterson (aged 29 years), formerly of Darlinghurst, escaped from Long Bay Penitentiary this afternoon. He was serving a one-year sentence on a charge of fraud.

The manner of his escape is unknown. Police believe that Waterson, who was dressed in prison uniform, somehow eluded the guards, and made his escape with the assistance of accomplices who supplied him with civilian clothes. The fact that a sedan motorcar, with the blinds drawn, was seen travelling swiftly towards the city from the direction of the jail is considered to have a significant connection.

Armed warders and police searched the scrublands in the Long Bay and La Perouse districts without success.

[The Sydney Morning Herald **August 12, 1917]**

After reading the article, Dusty and Reggie fell silent. They had finally tracked down the man they knew as Jasper Howard, discovering that he was no more than a felon on the run. It was an important development in the investigation.

'He learned how to change his appearance and identity to avoid being re-captured,' observed Reggie. 'He moved to South Australia, then Victoria, with plans to head back to New South Wales.' He tapped the newspaper report. 'The police would have given up looking for him long ago.'

'What a life,' said Dusty. 'Always looking over your shoulder. What do we do now, Reggie?'

'We use this in our interview with Lottie O'Leary.' He checked his watch. 'We're due there at half-past eleven.'

* * *

Close to the rugged coastline south of Sydney was the State Reformatory for Women, an imposing building composed of sandstone, with an enormous gothic arched entrance flanked by two crenelated towers. Within the walls was a central glassed circular conservatory, set in a spacious quadrangle around which four large halls radiated as diverging wings, each containing a row of single cells.

Reggie and Dusty were shown to an interview room by a female warder wearing the regulation uniform of a printed blue dress.

'She looks more like a nurse than a warder,' commented Dusty after she left them.

'But did you see the exercise yards?' replied Reggie. 'They look like cages. This place is supposed to be the latest in humane incarceration, but it makes you wonder what our next interviewee thinks of it.'

As he finished speaking, Lottie O'Leary was escorted into the room. She took her place in the chair opposite and smiled at the two men.

Although she was dressed in prison uniform, a pastel-coloured shapeless affair, there was no hiding her charms. The tilt of her head, the knowing look on her face, the captivating nature of her smile. Her hair had been pulled back into a tight bun, only accentuating her beautiful blue eyes and full lips.

'Hello, darling,' she said, appraising Reggie. 'You're a reporter from *The Argus*, I'm told.' She turned her gaze on Dusty. 'You're a young one. I could fall for you if you had a proper haircut and spiffed yourself up a bit, *mon cheri*.'

Dusty blushed and ran his fingers through his wild thatch of fair hair.

'What can I do for you, gentlemen?' she asked.

'I'm Reggie da Costa, and this is Dusty Rhodes. We're interested in an accomplice of yours: Jasper Waterson.'

The smile left her face. 'Jasper. I heard about him. Such a pity.'

'We found a photograph of you amongst his personal possessions.' Reggie showed her the photograph that they had found in Jasper's suitcase.

'They were the good times,' she commented. She sighed when she saw the inscription on the back, then handed it back to Reggie.

'Can you tell us about Jasper?' asked Reggie.

'Why not? He's dead now.' She pulled a face. 'Where do I begin? I suppose it's when I first met him.' She looked up at the high barred window. 'It was the first of June, 1923. I was at the Conservatorium Hall for a charity concert. The Sistine Soloists were making their last appearance before sailing back to Italy. I noticed Jasper in the lobby at the interval. He was hard to miss. Very handsome. Impeccable grooming. Rather like you, Mr da Costa.'

Reggie smoothed his Ronald Colman moustache. 'Please, call me Reggie.'

Lottie looked at him coyly. 'If you insist, *Reggie*.' She paused briefly, then continued. 'I sidled up to him, pretending to be interested in a poster that was behind him. We started talking. He was going by the name Redmond Waters. I did my Odette performance. You know, French accent. The Marchioness de Montignac. Cousin of famed French actress, Renée Adorée. That sort of thing. I was taken aback when he laughed out loud. No one's laughed at me before.

'He leaned down and whispered in my ear, "We are one and the same, my dear Odette, if that's your real name. I'm no more Redmond Waters than you are a marchioness. Let me order a bottle of the best French champagne

196

and make a toast to our continued success in this business."

'I laughed, thinking it a great joke. Later, we drank wine, made love, and exchanged our stories, knowing that we could trust one another to keep our secrets. And afterwards, when we crossed paths, which was frequently, he'd give me a sly smile.'

Reggie raised an eyebrow, surprised by the ease with which she described their relationship.

'Did you keep in touch after he left Sydney?' asked Dusty.

Lottie threw the full force of her gaze on him. 'Jasper wrote recently. He wanted to know if I would assume the role of *femme fatale* in a partnership with him.' She gave Dusty a wink. 'That's seducing men before I blackmail them for adultery.' She turned her gaze back on Reggie. 'I hadn't made up my mind, to be honest. I think that Jasper wanted to renew our relationship, whereas I like my freedom. He wrote that he wanted to be rid of one of his colleagues. Moving to Sydney would give him that opportunity.'

'Was that Dulcie Smith?'

Lottie threw her head back and laughed. 'His sister?'

'Dulcie was his sister?' Reggie couldn't conceal his surprise.

'Didn't you know?'

'No. I thought she was an accomplice, but not related. Did you know that Dulcie's dead, too?'

Lottie shook her head, a look of undisguised shock on her face. 'Dulcie's dead? What happened?'

'She was murdered. Ten stab wounds to the body, this time at the Menzies Hotel. The Ten of Swords in her hand.'

'Tarot? Is Essie involved?'

'Essie?'

'Madame Esmeralda. She's a tarot card reader and fortune-teller. They met in Adelaide. She followed Jasper to Melbourne. According to him, her obsession with him was getting tedious. She's the one he wanted to let go.'

'Perhaps this gave her a reason to kill him,' commented Reggie.

'You're the investigator, not me. But love is the other side of hate. Essie was useful for a while, bringing women into Jasper's orbit. She'd give them a reading and tell them that they'd meet a handsome English stranger, and *voilà*, there was Jasper. Cutting Essie loose would present a problem, he told me.'

'Interesting,' commented Reggie.

'Where did Jasper come from?' asked Dusty.

'It's obvious, isn't it? The poor part of Sydney. Nobody works that hard to make money unless they've never had it. From what he told me, he and Dulcie lived in Surry Hills when they were very young.'

Reggie nodded. 'The notorious slums of Robin Hood Lane.'

Lottie looked wistful. 'That's right. Sly-grog, cocaine, and prostitutes. Jasper said that they shared their house with three other families. All he wanted from an early age was to escape.'

'He went to prison in 1917. Long Bay Penitentiary.'

She shook her head. 'I don't know about that. He probably didn't want to admit to me that he'd been caught.' She shifted in her chair, smoothing down her dress. 'You think that Jasper was killed by one of his victims?'

Reggie nodded. 'There's a few to choose from. He convinced some to invest in his shady schemes. He acquired goods under false pretences. He wrote dodgy cheques. He blackmailed vulnerable women. We know all that. Now, what can you tell us about Dulcie?'

Lottie shrugged. 'Not very bright. Pretty though. She looked up to her brother and did what she was told. Played the part of the outraged wife or extracted money from gullible men. She wasn't suited to that kind of life. I think she always wanted a nice house, a husband, and a few kids. Not going from one town to the next. Which I'll have to do once I get out of here.' She glanced at the female warder, who was watching the clock. 'Most of the people in our game have to move a lot. Alter their appearance and their name. It only needs one sucker to go to the authorities, or ask too many questions, to make our house of cards fall over. A big city like Sydney works for a while; you can lose yourself in it, but eventually, you will come into contact with someone who you've duped in the past. Or someone who calls your bluff.' She laughed. 'I should know the pitfalls. Look where I am now.'

The warder stepped forward. 'That's enough now. Time to go back to your cell.'

Lottie reluctantly got to her feet. 'You know that they sentenced me last week? I'm going to be in this hellhole for ten months.'

'Stand up straight, O'Leary,' ordered the warder. 'Shoulders back.'

Lottie rolled her eyes. 'Goodbye, boys. It's exercise time now, followed by a cold bath. And yet another afternoon of needlework, sweeping, and doing laundry. Fancy me, the Marchioness de Montignac, having to get my hands dirty? I swear I'll die of boredom. Thanks for breaking up the monotony.' She winked at Dusty. 'Good to meet you, handsome. Don't break too many hearts.'

Chapter Thirty-Nine

Back in Melbourne, Ruby was relaxing after a long week at work. Sales of furniture had increased as Christmas approached, the coming of the festive season making customers aware that entertaining friends and family required new dining settings and lounge suites. The invoices were coming in thick and fast, and Ruby was almost snowed under with paperwork.

Sunday stretched out in front of her, promising to be a welcome respite from work. It was lunchtime, so she fixed herself a meal of baked pork chops and vegetables.

Once the dishes were washed, she walked up the hallway and stopped in front of the telephone. It was one o'clock. She stood contemplating what she should do. Mavis had sounded strange when she had spoken to her on the telephone on Friday evening, and twice on Saturday, she'd tried to ring her, and twice there had been no reply. Was it really her responsibility to ensure that Mavis was alright while Reggie was away? But she had promised him, and she didn't like to break a promise, even if Mrs da Costa didn't like her.

She picked up the receiver and asked the operator to connect her with Mavis's number. The telephone began to ring. Ruby was on the verge of hanging up when Reggie's mother answered.

'Hello, who's there?' Her voice sounded odd; the words slurred.

'It's Ruby Rhodes, Mrs da Costa.'

'Who?'

'Reggie's friend, Ruby.'

'Can't understand you. Reggie. Is that Reggie?'

Ruby stared at the telephone, unsure what to say or do. She tried to explain again, speaking slowly, but the woman had hung up the telephone.

Ruby sighed. What was she going to do? Reggie's mother didn't sound like her normal self; her speaking voice, usually strong and clear. Today, it seemed that Mrs da Costa had, she hated to admit, imbibed a bit too much wine. She took a deep breath and rang the number again. This time the telephone rang out, the operator informing her that Mrs da Costa was not answering and to try again later.

It crossed her mind to ring Reggie at The Hero, but he was unlikely to be there, most probably interviewing witnesses or dining out, knowing him. And what could he do from Sydney anyway?

She had no choice. It was only a ten-minute drive to Mavis's place, and she could take Dusty's Australian Six. And, if Reggie's mother was unpleasant, she'd leave and not go back!

* * *

Mavis da Costa lived in a modest, red brick house in Firebell Lane. It was a narrow building, with a small parlour at the front of the house and a dining room and two bedrooms off a side hallway. The kitchen was in the lean-to built across the back of the house. Outside, in the brick courtyard, was a toilet and a small washhouse. A brick garage extended the full width of the block, opening onto the alley at the back.

Ruby knocked on the front door, but there was no answer. She knocked again. It crossed her mind to enquire of the neighbours whether they had seen Reggie's mother go out, but the 'To Let' sign on one side, and the fact that the other property had boarded-up windows were not encouraging. She tried the front door, but it was locked.

The window facing out into Firebell Lane was open, a gentle breeze wafting through the curtains. Ruby put her head through the opening and called out, 'Mrs da Costa, are you there? Mrs da Costa, it's Ruby Rhodes.'

She listened, but there was only silence. She scratched her head, unsure of what she should do. Once more, she called out, 'Mrs da Costa, it's Ruby. Are you home?'

She looked around. The street was empty. 'Here I go,' she muttered, taking a deep breath. 'I hope someone doesn't think I'm breaking in.'

She crawled through the open window, landing on the floor of the sitting room. She got to her feet, her ears straining for the sound of footsteps or a nervous 'Who's there?' from the lady in question. But all was quiet. As before, the room was a confection of fussy florals, with an overstuffed couch and armchair occupying most of the space. But whereas everything had been clean and tidy when she had visited in the past, this time, there were dirty glasses on the table and magazines strewn around the floor.

The dining room was no better. Unwashed cups and saucers, a plate with a half-eaten sausage on it, and some withered flowers in a vase were on the table.

Ruby ventured into the hallway and stopped at the door to the main bedroom.

'Mrs da Costa. Are you there?'

She hesitated, then turned the door handle and looked in. The room was in darkness and smelled stale, but as her eyes adjusted to the gloom, she could make out the figure of someone lying on the bed.

'Mrs da Costa?'

The shape didn't move. Ruby hesitated, aware that she was intruding on Mrs da Costa's privacy, but her instincts told her that something was terribly wrong. She approached the bed tentatively, stepping over cast-off clothing and shoes. Mavis was fully dressed and lying on her back on top of the bedclothes, her eyes shut.

'Mrs da Costa. It's Ruby.'

She bent down close to her face. The woman's breathing sounded laboured, uneven. She shook her gently. 'Wake up. Wake up.'

What is going on, she thought? She opened the curtains and turned on the light. Mrs da Costa was almost unrecognisable. Her curls were lank and greasy; her cheeks shrunken and her face an ashen pallor. Where once she had shown an obsessive concern with her appearance, today her dress was creased and stained, the skirt pulled up to show a most unladylike amount of bare leg.

'What's happened to you?' she asked, pulling a blanket up over the woman's body. It crossed Ruby's mind that Mavis was drunk, or had had a turn, or a heart attack.

She glanced at the bedside table and noticed an empty bottle of syrup.

'"Dr Wishbone's Restorative Syrup,"' she read out loud. '"Cures stomach ailments and insomnia."' It was the same brand of medicine that she had seen at Madame Esmeralda's. She sniffed the bottle and caught the unmistakable odour of alcohol. She pulled open the drawer. There were six more bottles inside, four empty and two full.

Whatever Mrs da Costa had taken had rendered her unconscious. The telephone was in the parlour.

'Can you connect me to the ambulance service, please?' she asked the operator.

'Putting you through,' the woman replied.

A voice came on the line. 'Ambulance. How can I help you?'

'There's an unconscious woman at 13 Firebell Lane, Richmond. I need an ambulance urgently.'

'I'm sorry, miss. All our ambulances are busy right now. There'll be an hour's wait.'

'But it's an emergency!'

'I'm sorry, but I can't help you. Can you get someone to drive the lady to the hospital?'

Flustered and anxious, Ruby hung up the telephone. With no neighbours or ambulance available, the task to save Mavis had fallen squarely on her own shoulders. Time was of the essence.

Back in the bedroom, Ruby took Mavis's arms and pulled her up into a sitting position, then tried to swing her legs around so that they hung over the edge of the bed.

'If I can get you to stand up, we might be able to make it to the car,' she said to the unconscious woman, whose head was resting heavily on Ruby's shoulder.

Ruby grunted and shoved and heaved, but to no avail. Reggie's mother was a dead weight. There was no way that Ruby could get her on her feet, much less walk her out to the motorcar parked in Firebell Lane.

Exhausted, she lowered Mavis back onto the bed.

'What am I going to do?' she cried in desperation. 'Reggie's not here, and there's no one who can help me, unless–'

She ran back to the telephone. 'Could you put me through to Mr Striker, please? Number J2666.'

A deep, sonorous voice answered. 'Horace Striker speaking.'

'Thank goodness you're there. Horace, it's Ruby.'

'This is a pleasure, Miss Ruby.'

'I need your help.'

His tone changed, all business-like now. 'What's wrong?'

'It's Reggie's mother. She's in a bad way. I rang for an ambulance, but there's none available. Reggie and Dusty are in Sydney. I have a motorcar, but I can't lift her. I can't get her out of the house. Can you help me? I've no one else to turn to.'

'Where are you?'

Ruby gave him the address.

'Burke and Hare will be there very soon. After you hang up the telephone, unlock the front door and then sit with her. And Ruby–'

'Yes?'

'Once the boys have taken her to hospital, you should ring Reggie. He'll want to know.'

While she waited for the footfall in the hallway, announcing the arrival of Burke and Hare, Ruby sat with Mavis, holding her hand and whispering words of encouragement. Minutes later she breathed a sigh of relief.

'Miss Ruby,' said Hare, standing in the doorway, his bloodless face and red hair stark in the harsh light of the room. 'We'll take Mrs da Costa to The Melbourne Hospital. Mr Striker says that you should pack a bag for her and meet us there. You have a car?'

'I do. I found this medicine next to her bed.' Ruby handed him the bottle of syrup. 'Could you show it to the doctor, please? It smells of alcohol.'

'Of course.' He smiled at her reassuringly. 'She'll be alright. We'll see to it.'

Horace's two bodyguards picked up Mavis and carried her out of the house.

'Thank Horace for me,' called Ruby as she watched them lay Reggie's mother along the backseat of the Daimler.

Hare touched his forehead in response and climbed into the passenger seat, while Burke gunned the engine. They took off at a fast pace down Firebell Lane.

The Daimler disappeared around the corner. Back in the house Ruby packed a bag for Mavis: some toiletries, a couple of nighties and her dressing gown and slippers, and a change of clothes. Then she went into the parlour and picked up the telephone.

'Could you put me through to The Hero of Waterloo Hotel at Millers Point in Sydney, please?'

She gave the operator the number.

The telephone began to ring.

Chapter Forty

Earlier that day, Reggie had decided that there should be a bit of rest and relaxation during their time in Sydney, given that they would be catching the train home on Thursday. While Dusty went off to see the sights of the Harbour City, Reggie renewed his friendship with one of his former colleagues from *The Argus*, Warren T Warren, who was now a reporter with *The Sydney Morning Herald*.

Warren, known to his colleagues as 'Rabbit,' was a gangly man, about six feet six inches tall, who spent most of his life ducking under doorways. Amongst his newspaper colleagues, Rabbit was renowned for his prodigious appetite, although where he put it remained a mystery, apart from his huge feet.

Rabbit was a political reporter whose main aim was to expose corruption both in government and in the police force. And he had found plenty to report on in New South Wales compared to his time in Victoria. Melbourne represented the 'Establishment,' with its exclusive clubs, old money, and ingrained respect for social status, while Sydney, in contrast, was wilder and more bohemian, a city where risky business rewarded opportunists and the unscrupulous. Like Melbourne, Sydney's criminal gangs specialised in cocaine, illegal liquor, prostitution, and gambling, but, in one respect, the Harbour City was far ahead of Melbourne, once police corruption was added into the mix.

Reggie and Rabbit found a table in one of the many cafés that overlooked Sydney Harbour and ordered their lunch and a bottle of wine.

'How's Sydney treating you?' asked Reggie.

'Lots to write about, luckily for me. I believe you visited Lottie O'Leary at Long Bay?'

'News travels fast. Good-looking woman, but you have to watch yourself.'

'You didn't see Tilly Devine while you were there, did you? She's been locked away for slashing a bloke with a razor blade. He needed 17 stitches. They reckon that she's been arrested 79 times for prostitution in the last four years. Lovely lady, that one.'

Reggie laughed.

'Talking about lovely ladies, have you found that elusive wife yet?' asked Rabbit.

'Surprisingly, I have. We're engaged.'

'Rich family?'

'No.'

'Social connections?'

'None.'

'The sort of woman who does what she's told?'

'Not Ruby.'

Rabbit was in shock. 'What's the attraction?'

Reggie stroked his moustache. 'If I told you what she went through to find her sister's killer, you'd never believe me. She's an amazing, brave woman. But the simple fact is that I like talking to her. Did I mention that she's beautiful?'

'Does Mavis like her?

Reggie frowned. 'Not yet, but she will. Once she gets to know her.'

Rabbit raised a glass. 'To the woman who captured Reggie da Costa's heart.'

They drank a toast and watched as the waiter placed their meals in front of them. Rabbit immediately started to demolish an enormous plate of Irish stew, served with extra dumplings.

'Mmmm,' was all he said, as he polished off a thick slice of bread.

Reggie took a bite of his curried sausages and smacked his lips in satisfaction. 'Delicious.'

He ate heartily for a few minutes, then put down his knife and fork. 'What do you have for me on Jasper Waterson?'

Rabbit spoke between mouthfuls. 'He was imprisoned for fraud. He claimed that he'd been injured at The Somme. Unfortunately, there were plenty of sympathetic women who fell for his story and gave him money to cover his medical and rehabilitation expenses. The problem is that he never served in the Great War.'

'Lottie O'Leary didn't know that he'd been in prison. Do you know how he escaped?'

'Unfortunately, no one really knows, but there's speculation that he had friends on the outside who spirited him away,' said Rabbit. 'I was able to locate someone who shared a cell with him in prison all those years ago. Waterson told this man that he would never be caught again. And he managed not to, until that night at The Windsor.

'He was an interesting man, according to his fellow prisoner. Jasper seemed to think that being a confidence man was his natural talent. He told his cellmate that there were certain rules that you had to follow to be successful. This bloke was so impressed that he wrote them down.' Rabbit took another piece of bread and dipped it in the gravy, eyeing it greedily before stuffing it in his mouth. 'You'll enjoy this, Reggie. I memorised it.

'Waterson said that the consummate confidence man should be a good listener, not a fast talker. He should never reveal his religion or political leanings until the target confirmed theirs, so that they would both have the same opinions. He should never look bored. He should never ask someone about their personal circumstances because, once he had their confidence, they would tell him anyway. He should be well-presented. He should never boast about himself or his achievements. And, you'll love this one: He should never drink too much alcohol, because a confidence man should always be in control of himself and the situation.'

Reggie threw his head back and laughed. 'That rules us out then.' He poured them both another glass. 'A toast. To the profession of confidence man. Arrogance before the fall. Hopefully they all end up dead or in prison.'

They clinked glasses and drank.

'When he escaped, there was talk that Waterson had gone to Adelaide, and now, you tell me that he moved on to Melbourne.'

'That's right,' said Reggie. 'In Melbourne he was a property investor known as Jasper Fitzalan Howard, distant cousin to the Duke of Norfolk. In Adelaide, Jasper Waters, art dealer. In Sydney, Redmond Waters, representative of The Atlantic Investment Company. He used a variety of names depending on what scheme he was hatching, with business cards to match. The fact is that one of his victims caught up with him at The Hotel Windsor. Whether it was someone from interstate or Melbourne, I need to find out. There's quite a list of suspects.'

Rabbit sat back, satiated for a minute or two, his plate wiped clean. He beckoned to the waiter. 'Another bottle of Bordeaux, thanks.' The man uncorked a fresh one and poured two glasses. Rabbit leaned forward. 'Go through these suspects for me, Reggie. I like hearing this stuff.'

Reggie finished his meal and pushed the plate to one side. 'Madame Esmeralda.'

'Who's she?'

'A fortune-teller. Apparently, she directed women his way. She was one of his associates, and she was obsessed with him. But he was keen to return to Sydney with his sister, Dulcie, and he thought it would be a convenient excuse to dump Madame Esmeralda. Whether she knew that or not, I don't know. But a tarot card was found on the bodies of Dulcie and Jasper, and the picture on it mirrored the nature of their deaths. Ten stab wounds and lots of blood sprayed around. There's also the fact that Madame Esmeralda has gone missing.'

Rabbit raised an eyebrow. 'Interesting. Who's next?'

'A nice little husband and wife duo, Councillor and Mrs Plumstead. He's a Victorian politician who seems to have strayed from the marital nest into the arms of Dulcie Waterson, Jasper's sister. It gets even more complicated. His wife was being blackmailed by Jasper, supposedly because she was having an affair with him. There appears to be little truth to that. But, on the other hand, there's not a lot of love between the Plumsteads from what I've observed.'

'Not a happy couple?'

'Without a doubt, but there's a truce in place, I suspect, until the killer is exposed. Then, there might be a very public clash in the courts. The divorce court, that is.'

'She knows about his dalliances?' asked Rabbit.

Reggie nodded. 'She does. So, I have to ask if Mrs Plumstead killed her blackmailer, given that she visited Jasper in his hotel room the night before his body was found and then, killed her husband's lover out of jealous spite.'

'But you think that's unlikely? Why?'

'She's classy. And beautiful.'

'What about the husband?'

Reggie chuckled. 'This is complicated, too. Councillor Plumstead was tricked into investing money in one of Howard's bogus schemes. Word is that he's financially strapped for cash now, so he had a powerful motive to kill Jasper. Supposedly, he didn't know about the blackmail attempt on his wife until *after* Jasper's body was found. But perhaps he did know about it, and that gave him an added incentive to kill Howard. Then, he discovered that Jasper's sister was none other than his girlfriend, Dulcie Smith. He was angry with her and felt betrayed, so he killed her, too. And there's also the fact that Plumstead was seen at The Menzies on the day of Dulcie's murder.

'However, there's one problem with that theory,' Reggie admitted. 'Plumstead had received an anonymous letter threatening to expose his adultery, and it may be connected to a group who are pressuring politicians to overturn Regulation 79.'

'What's Regulation 79?'

'It's a law to regulate the labelling of patent medicines, so that it's clear what the ingredients are. Obviously, the chemists, salesmen, and grocers who either manufacture or peddle this trash have a vested interest in getting the law repealed before it's introduced. There's word out on the streets that they have been digging up dirt on the politicians who support the new law. Apparently, they'll do anything to convince them to oppose it.'

'Even down to killing Plumstead's lover and pinning the crime on him?'

Reggie smiled. 'You have such a wonderfully devious mind, Rabbit.' He finished his glass and poured them both another.

'Who else is a suspect?'

'There's a member of the aristocracy who's lost a substantial sum of money on one of Waterson's get-rich-quick schemes. Sir Ambrose Beauchamp Kiddle.'

'What a mouthful.'

Reggie nodded. 'We know that he threatened to kill Waterson if he didn't get his money back.'

'So many suspects, all with motives. Is that it?'

'It could be plain old-fashioned robbery. The safe in Waterson's hotel room was empty. As you say, Jasper Waterson had accumulated many enemies over the years. He swindled people out of thousands of pounds with his dodgy deals. He blackmailed innocent, and not so innocent, wives and husbands, as did his sister. He stole automobiles and jewellery, and passed fake cheques. But finally, his past caught up with him.'

'Or his present?'

'Very true. It's hard to know. I feel in my bones that the answer lies here in Sydney.'

'These murders happened in hotel rooms. Surely a perpetrator covered in blood would be noticed?'

'Not if he or she came prepared. A premeditated crime in each case.'

'But unnoticed by the hotel staff? And these were superior hotels.'

'That bothers me, too. A murderer in plain sight.'

Rabbit cocked his head. 'You mentioned in your letter that you had some incriminating letters. Would you mind showing them to me? I might know something about the victims.'

Reggie took out his notebook. 'I'll show you the names, but not the letters. And you have to promise me that you won't reveal them.'

Rabbit smirked. 'Honour among thieves.'

'Have a look. Tell me what you think.'

Rabbit nodded. His eyes drifted down the list. He whistled and pointed at a couple of names. 'Thought so,' he muttered. He raised his eyes to Reggie's. 'If I were going to pursue anyone, it would be Mrs Augusta Relish. There were rumours and half-baked theories about her at the time. Nothing since.

Some of these people won't let you in the front door.' He beckoned to the waiter. 'Dessert, Reggie?'

'Better not.' He tapped his stomach. 'My waistline will suffer.' He put a pound note on the table. 'I have lots to do, so I'll go. Thanks, Rabbit. Enjoy the rest of the wine. It's been great to see you again. If you're ever down in Melbourne, look me up.'

They shook hands. 'I expect an invitation to the wedding,' Rabbit said. 'I can't wait to meet this woman who's tamed the da Costa beast.'

Reggie snorted. 'I am a lucky man.'

* * *

The senior crime reporter was feeling mellow by the time he returned to his room at The Hero of Waterloo, the result of too many glasses of wine over a most satisfactory lunch. There was no sign of Dusty, so Reggie decided that a little nap was in order.

He took off his shoes and hung up his suit jacket, loosened his tie and lay down on the bed. Soon sleep settled over him like a warm blanket and he drifted off, content.

It only seemed like seconds before he woke up. Someone was playing Paganini's *Caprice Number 24* on the piano. It was one of his mother's favourites. Nearly forty years before, on board the R.M.S. *Iberia* bound for England, Mario da Costa, an accomplished violinist, had played that piece to Mavis and won her heart. When they returned to Australia, married and expecting Reggie, their first and only child, Mavis went into raptures whenever Mario played it for her.

Rising from his bed, Reggie opened the door to his room and peered out into the corridor. The music seemed to be coming from downstairs. He put on his shoes and slowly descended the staircase, which led to the ground floor. The corridor was empty. He stood, hesitating, wondering why no one else had been drawn from their rooms in response to the music, then made his way along the hallway until he came to the stairs leading to the cellar. He paused on the top step, a strange feeling overwhelming him: curiosity yet a reticence to go further. The volume rose; the pianist's fingers skimming the keys; the melody swelling from the depths of the cellar.

Brushing aside his doubts, Reggie descended, treading carefully as he navigated the steep steps leading down into the cellar. He reached the bottom and took stock of the scene. The large flagstones of the floor, the sandstone walls, and the metal shackles glinting in the glow from the fire burning in the grate were his first impressions, but a more perplexing sight awaited him.

In front of the fireplace was a woman sitting in a wooden rocking chair. Her back was to him as she rocked back and forth, a shawl around her shoulders, her face turned towards the flames. The music swelled; the performance stirring and impassioned in execution. Reggie glanced around, looking for the piano, but it was not to be seen. Invisible fingers rippled across the ivories of an invisible instrument, reaching a crescendo. The thought struck him in his bewilderment: was this woman Thomas Kirkman's wife, who had been pushed down the stairs by her enraged husband? Was this the ghost that haunted The Hero?

He brushed aside such thoughts and stepped forward.

'Excuse me, madam. Where is the piano?'

The woman turned to face him. The music became discordant as heavy hands thumped the keys, jarring and harsh; the pianist's foot slammed down hard on the pedal, fortissimo. Reggie put his hands over his ears, trying to block out the pandemonium, while his eyes took in those well-loved features, that froth of white hair, those innocent blue eyes. His mother.

Someone was knocking loudly on the door. 'Mr da Costa! Telephone for you.'

Disorientated, Reggie sat up and realised that he was still in bed. He looked around the room, his head still ringing from the sounds of the piano. He was alone.

'Coming,' he called, putting on his shoes hastily.

As he followed the landlord down the hallway, he tried to calm himself, but nothing could shake the vision of his mother's face.

Chapter Forty-One

Ruby hung up the telephone, having passed on the news about Mavis's predicament to her son. It had taken her quite a while to convince Reggie that his mother was, by now, in the safe hands of the staff of The Melbourne Hospital, being cared for by the dedicated doctors and nurses who had treated her brother, Dusty, when he had been a patient there two years earlier.

'I'll be going there shortly,' she reassured him. 'Burke and Hare will look after her, I'm sure.'

'She was drunk?' He had sounded dumbfounded when she told him about Mavis's condition.

'No, she had taken some tonic.' She picked up the bottle and read what was on the label. '"Dr Wishbone's Restorative Syrup. Cures stomach ailments and insomnia." But it smells of alcohol, Reggie, and I think your mother might have taken a bit too much.'

She heard the intake of breath.

'I can't believe it. My mother taking patent medicines. Are you sure?'

'There's at least seven bottles in the house and another four in the rubbish bin outside.'

There was silence at the other end.

'Reggie?'

'I'm here. I'm thinking how I can get home fast. I've missed the overnight train to Melbourne and our return tickets are for this Thursday. I can't wait that long. What can I do?'

'You could fly. I've heard that there's a service between Sydney and

Melbourne.'

'Ruby, you're a genius. I never thought of that. But the money will have to come out of my pocket, rather than *The Argus*'s. I better go and organise this. Give Mother my love and tell her I'll be home as soon as I can.'

'I will.'

'And Ruby, I can't thank you enough for what you've done. Without you, my mother would have died.' There was silence, and then he laughed for the first time. 'I might be lucky and have a pilot from the Great War flying me home.'

Ruby said her farewells, then added, 'Make sure there's a parachute in case he shoots the propeller off.'

* * *

Ruby hung up the telephone and checked the kitchen for perishable foods, which she put in the outside rubbish bin, then collected the bag that she'd packed for Mavis. She closed the windows and locked the door behind her, then drove off in the Australian Six.

Arriving at The Melbourne Hospital, she parked the motorcar and entered the building, where the clerk at reception directed her to Ward 2C.

'You want Mrs da Costa?' asked the nurse on duty. 'She's with the doctor right now. If you wait, you can speak to him.'

Ruby took a chair in the corridor, watching the procession of doctors, nurses, and hospital staff go by, patients on trolleys or being pushed in wheelchairs, visitors carrying flowers, some looking anguished, bored, or relieved. Hospital was a difficult place to be, she knew from experience, because waiting seemed to take longer there than anywhere else.

It was around five o'clock when the doctor finally emerged from Mavis's room. 'Miss da Costa. Are you here about your mother?'

'I'm Ruby Rhodes. I'm engaged to Mrs da Costa's son. Reggie's in Sydney, so there's only me.'

'I see. Ordinarily, I'd only speak to the immediate family, but, given the circumstances, I'll make an exception. Mrs da Costa is resting. She's badly dehydrated and has a drip in her arm.'

'Did you see the syrup she's been taking?'

'Indeed, I did. You sent it with her, I'm assuming. I spoke briefly to the men who brought her in, but they seemed in a hurry to get out of here.'

'What was in the bottle?'

'Alcohol and morphine, from preliminary analysis. We'll know more shortly.'

Ruby raised her hand to her mouth. 'Morphine? That's horrible. Does she know?'

'Not yet. Mrs da Costa is conscious, but it will take some time before she registers how serious a state she's in.'

'How is she now?'

'She had to have her stomach pumped, so understandably, it will take her a while to recover. She should be here a few days. She's not been eating properly, and I'm afraid that she may need a period of time in rehabilitation. There are issues from ingesting large doses of alcohol and morphine.'

'Issues? Do you mean that she's addicted?'

'I wouldn't want to go that far, but we'll have to see how she is over the next few days.'

'Can I see her?'

'Not today. She needs to rest. I see that you've brought a bag for her. I'll get the nurse to take it to her. When will her son be back?'

'Late Monday, I should think.'

'Perfect. Mrs da Costa should be ready for visitors on Tuesday. Go home now. You look exhausted.'

Chapter Forty-Two

I t had taken an hour for Reggie to organise his trip home to Melbourne, but he was adamant that it was necessary to get back as quickly as he could, rather than wait around until Thursday for the train trip home to Melbourne. His arrangements were relatively complex. The first stage of the journey required a train trip from Sydney's Central railway station to Cootamundra. From there, he would catch the flight to Hay, change planes, and stop periodically for the aeroplane to re-fuel on the way down to Melbourne. It would be a long and exhausting journey, but Reggie was looking forward to it. The experience of flying and seeing outback Australia from above promised some new and interesting topics for conversation over dinner.

However, his train didn't depart until 10:50 p.m. that night, so he had about four hours up his sleeve before he left for Central Station at half-past eight.

As he laid out his clothes on the bed, there came a knock on the door.

'Maid service, Mr da Costa.'

Reggie didn't look up. 'Come in.'

The girl walked in, pushing a trolley. 'Can I turn down your bed, sir?'

'No, I'll be leaving tonight, so don't bother. No towels either, thank you.'

'I bring those in the morning, sir.'

Reggie glanced back at the door, lost in thought. The maid had gone. He finished folding his clothes carefully, ready to be packed, then went down the corridor to Dusty's room. Fortunately, his colleague had returned from his sightseeing expedition and, after being acquainted with the 'Mavis

Situation,' was ready to use whatever was left of the day to do one more interview before Reggie left.

'Who is this woman we're going to visit?' he asked.

'Her name is Mrs Augusta Relish. Rabbit insisted that we see her. I planned to visit her tomorrow, but that won't be possible now, what with my change in plans. She lives in Manly with her husband Archibald, a property investor. Unfortunately, I haven't had a chance to do any research on her so we'll have to take our chances that she'll cooperate.' He shook his head and grimaced. 'Unprepared is *not* the way I like to conduct interviews. However, we know from her letter that Jasper Waterson was blackmailing her over their affair.'

'Have you made an appointment to see her?'

'No time. Hopefully, we can bluff our way in and talk to her.'

Dusty and Reggie walked down to Circular Quay and caught a ferry to Manly. It was a long boat ride, in fairly choppy seas, dropping off and picking up passengers on the way up to North Harbour and on to the beautiful expanse of Manly beach, with its wharf and clocktower. The line of Norfolk Pines along the promenade made it particularly picturesque.

Reggie was pleased to see that Dusty was wearing his cream linen summer suit again, matched with a white shirt and the cream and green tie that he had lent him. Reggie had, despite the short notice, selected a suit in brown and cream check, with large pockets and three buttons on the jacket, teamed with a cream and gold striped tie. Neither of them would have seemed out of place in good society. Dusty had even brushed his hair.

The ticket seller at the wharf had been most helpful in giving them directions to Fairlight House, the former home of Henry Gilbert Smith, founder of Manly, and now the residence of Archibald and Augusta Relish. It was a classic Georgian design, two storeys high with verandahs at the front and to one side, along with a tower and portico.

The door was answered by a butler who showed them into a reception room at the front. Soon, they were joined by the master of the house himself, who didn't look pleased when he found out whom he was greeting in his house.

'*The Argus*. Crime reporters from *The Argus*. Why would I want to talk to you?' Relish was an unusual looking man, with a large forehead, squat nose like a boxer, and small irregular teeth. When he spoke, he whistled his s's.

'It's your wife that we'd like to speak to.'

'Augusta is gone. She packed her bags and left months ago. Where she is, I neither know nor care.'

Reggie smoothed his moustache. He had not foreseen this, and Rabbit was obviously unaware that the bird had flown the coop. Still, the husband might have some useful information that would help solve the case. Dilly-dallying around the reasons for Mrs Relish's departure wouldn't work; it was clear that he needed to take a firm line with this hostile witness before they were thrown out of the house.

'Your wife was being blackmailed by a man who was found murdered at The Hotel Windsor in Melbourne in August. I have in my possession a letter that she wrote to him.'

Relish leaned forward, menacingly. 'Where did you get this letter? And how do I know it's legitimate?'

'It was hidden in his suitcase, along with photographs, business cards, and other incriminating letters. I have it with me here.'

'What do you want?'

'What do you mean?'

'How much to make you go away?'

Reggie laughed. 'I don't want your money. You can have the letter. All I want is information.'

'Show me the letter first.'

Reggie handed it over and watched as Relish read the letter, his face darkening into a scowl. 'Whore.' He tore it up and put the pieces in his pocket.

'I've upheld my part of the bargain,' said Reggie. 'Now, tell me what you know.'

Relish scowled. 'There's not much to tell. We met him at a social event celebrating the turning of the first sod for the Harbour Bridge. After that, we saw him at dinner parties and the theatre. It appears that my faithless wife was attracted to Mr Waters. He was a distant cousin of the 14th Earl of

Westmorland. He told Augusta that he was on the board of the Drury Lane Theatre in London. All lies, it appears. Augusta liked to mix with theatrical folk, so she was intrigued by him.'

'Your wife became involved with him?'

'She did. I found out afterwards when I saw the diamond bracelet that I gave her in the pawnbroker's shop. She confessed. Said that Waters had blackmailed her and that she'd hocked it for £500.'

'She left you?'

'Only because she thought that Waters would go away with her, but he'd gone already. More fool her. He left behind a trail of broken promises, debts, and bad cheques. When she found out she was on her own and one of many who had been treated that way, she begged me to take her back. But it was the last straw. I'd had enough. Too many lies. Too many lovers. It was over. I cut her adrift.'

'Where is she now?'

'As I said, I don't know, and I don't care. Why do you want to know?'

'I'd like to talk to her.'

He shrugged. 'I don't know why.'

'Do you have a photograph of Mrs Relish?'

'I burned them long ago.' He called to the butler. 'James, show these gentlemen out.'

As they walked away from the house, Dusty noticed one of the maids heading towards the side entrance.

'Excuse me, miss,' he called after her.

She stopped and turned back. 'How can I help you, sir?'

'We are trying to contact Mrs Relish. Do you know who her close friends were?'

The young girl checked that no one was watching. 'Mrs Relish was friendly with Mrs Butt.'

'Where would we find her?'

'In the next street along, towards the wharf. Number 16.' She smiled at them and walked quickly down the side of the house.

Reggie nodded approvingly at Dusty. 'Good work. You're coming along very nicely.'

'Should we go there now?'

Reggie checked his watch. 'No time now. I have to finish packing, have some dinner, and get to the station.'

'We forget about this?'

'Indeed, no. You still have until Thursday. I want you back here in Manly interviewing Mrs Butt. Find out what she knows and try to get a photograph of the wife. I have a hunch, but it needs to be confirmed.'

'You know who the murderer is?'

'I think so, but we have work to do to prove it.' He lit a cigarette. 'This is important, Dusty. The whole case could hinge on your interview. And one other thing. Can you write up a report on the Australia Hotel? It's for Curtis Flange. Think gossip columns. The chandeliers, the Winter Garden, the marble, that sort of thing. Include Sarah Bernhardt. Don't forget her bears and the possums. And the hundred pieces of luggage. He'll love that.'

Dusty sniggered. 'Something along the lines of: "Bears, bags, and Bernhardt. Possums on parade."?'

Reggie chuckled. 'Very good. But before you go to Manly–'

'Yes?'

'Change your shirt. There's a stain on the front.'

Chapter Forty-Three

Ruby drove away from the hospital, emotionally and physically exhausted. She was sorry that she hadn't seen Reggie's mother in person, but what the doctor had told her would have to do. There was still the question of how Mavis had come into possession of this drug and what deleterious effect it might have on her health in the future. Dr Wishbone? She'd seen that name on the bottles and boxes of patent medicines at Madame Esmeralda's. Fancy becoming addicted to an insomnia drug? Ruby could only imagine how dispirited Reggie would feel after he'd spent hours researching and writing up his reports on the need to regulate patent medicines, only to find that his own mother had been taking them under his nose.

It was around a quarter to six when she turned into Bridge Road and headed towards Richmond. Although she was eager to get home, she decided to drive past Reggie's place in Swan Street. The truth was that she was missing him. Her life, before Reggie, had been uneventful, with each day as predictable as the last. Since the night of Horace Striker's costume party at The Stockade, when she saw Reggie dressed as an Egyptian pharaoh in dazzling gold and black, she knew that someone very special had come into her life, someone who would introduce her to new and exciting experiences outside her conventional existence.

With thoughts of her fiancé in her head, she stopped outside the grocer's shop and looked up at the window in the dwelling above. Reggie often stood there, he told her, watching life on the street below. Those people were the stuff of his stories, he said, sometimes the victims of crime, sometimes the perpetrators, with most being avid readers of his crime reports in *The Argus*.

She was about to pull out from the curb and head home when she saw a Hupmobile accelerate out of Coppin Street, turning in front of her. It was forest green, with white wall tyres and wire wheels, and appeared to be the same model as Reggie's automobile. She put the Australian Six into gear and did a U-turn, then took off after it, increasing her speed until she was close enough to read the registration plate. It was Reggie's motorcar, but who was driving it was a mystery. There was no chance that he would have allowed someone to borrow his automobile while he was away. He was nothing if not possessive of his pride and joy. The only possibility was that it had been stolen and the thief himself was behind the wheel.

What should she do? Contact the police or follow the motorcar? It took only seconds to make a decision: follow the thief rather than lose sight of the Hupmobile. She slowed down and settled in at a respectable distance behind it, remembering Reggie's first rule of tailing a suspect: do not make them suspicious. Fortunately, the driver was cruising along Swan Street at a law-abiding thirty miles per hour, heading west. At the intersection with Church Street, the Hupmobile did a left-hand turn and, further along, entered Balmain Street, with Ruby following. After passing the Rosella factory, the driver pulled into the curb in front of a large garage. Ruby coasted into the curb short of the garage and turned off the engine. She slunk down in her seat, watching. The driver got out, removed the padlock on a pair of wooden doors and opened them wide, then, drove the motorcar inside the garage.

The man emerged two minutes later and looked around before he locked the doors again. He glanced her way briefly and, reassured that all was well, walked away at a steady pace towards Church Street. Ruby made a mental note of the thief's appearance: early twenties, lean, olive-skinned, wearing baggy denim overalls over a khaki shirt, with a cloth cap on his head.

She waited five minutes watching for his return, until it was apparent that the theft of the Hupmobile and its delivery to the garage were the only plans for Reggie's motorcar that day. The Rosella factory stood silent next door, the workers having headed home. The street was empty.

Ruby crossed the road and entered the bluestone paved alley between the two buildings. A couple of windows had been cut into the corrugated iron wall, but the glass of the first one was covered by a thick film of dirt and grease. The second window further down promised a better view of the interior and appeared to have been replaced recently, judging by the cleanliness of the glass. Ruby dragged a wooden crate from the end of the alley and placed it under the window, then stood on it and looked through. The Hupmobile was parked next to a couple of other motorcars, one of which had been stripped down to its chassis, while the hood of the other lay on the ground, next to a bumper bar and a couple of mudguards. Along the back wall of the garage was a collection of car bodies and their parts, ranging from roofs to car doors, to running boards and headlights. On a table was the protective hood worn by a welder, along with his equipment.

But what took her eye was a motorcar that was parked over the pit used by mechanics to work on the underside of a vehicle. The front section of the automobile was painted green while the back was black. She stared hard at it wondering why it had been painted in two different colours, and then, it dawned on her.

'It's two different motorcars joined together, that's what it is. Fancy that?'

She stepped down and, after returning the crate to the end of the alley, crossed the road and got into Dusty's motorcar, gripping the steering wheel with both hands. The truth was that she had chanced upon the premises used for storing and reassembling stolen vehicles. Once they were reconstructed and painted, these automobiles would be unrecognisable to their original owners and could not be identified by the police. The motorcars would be sold off to unsuspecting buyers who were ignorant of their 'new' automobiles' origins. And soon, if not tomorrow, Reggie's beloved Hupmobile would meet the same fate. They had to be stopped!

Ruby started the car and headed for the Russell Street police headquarters, where she hoped to find Detective Sergeant Clary Blain, Reggie's friend and source of information on criminal matters. There was no time to be lost.

'Detective Sergeant Blain of the Criminal Investigation Branch, please,' she said to the desk sergeant fifteen minutes later.

He raised an eyebrow. 'And you are–?'

'Miss Rhodes. I'm a friend of Reggie da Costa.'

The policeman scowled. '*The Argus* reporter.'

'That's correct. And tell him that it's a matter of the greatest urgency.'

'One minute, miss.'

He reached for the telephone and spoke into the receiver, covering his mouth with his hand so that Ruby couldn't hear what he said. Whatever was the answer, there was no doubting the surprise in his voice when he told her that Detective Sergeant Blain would be right down.

Ruby had never met the policeman before so was taken aback by his appearance. In her mind, when Reggie spoke about Clary, she had envisaged a tidy, well-groomed person, with a discerning gaze and a mind as sharp as a tack. Instead, she was faced with a man whose large belly, rosy cheeks, and red-veined bulbous nose suggested a love of eating and drinking rather than chasing down criminals. In truth, she was disappointed.

However, once she shook his hand and explained the situation regarding Reggie's stolen motorcar, she was forced to put aside her preconceptions and admit that although the exterior might not be impressive, his response certainly was.

'Thank you for your information, Miss Rhodes. Rest assured that we will act in restoring Reggie's Hupmobile to him and ensure that these villains are put out of business immediately.'

He turned to the desk sergeant and issued instructions. 'First thing tomorrow, I want a squad assembled here at seven-thirty in the morning. Organise wireless patrol cars. Once they've been briefed, we'll head straight to Balmain Street, Richmond. Is that clear, sergeant?'

'It is, sir. I'll get that put in place immediately, sir.'

Blain turned back to Ruby. 'I've been wanting to put these villains behind bars for a while, Miss Rhodes. I can't thank you enough. We'll catch them red-handed, thanks to you. I can see that Reggie has chosen well.'

Ruby blushed. 'I appreciate that, Detective Sergeant Blain. And I wish you well tomorrow.'

Clary smiled. 'I'll bet a good bottle of Reggie's whisky that this mob of criminals will rue the day they stole his Hupmobile.'

Chapter Forty-Four

It was a weary Reggie who arrived late Sunday night at Central Station, ready for his trip home to Melbourne. He had packed his bag after his arrival back from Manly and had dressed in his olive-green tweed 'sports suit,' teaming it with a red and yellow striped tie and cream shirt. The first leg of the journey, a distance of some 230 miles, required that he take the 10:50 p.m. train to Albury as far as Cootamundra. In order to save some money for the flight, Reggie opted to travel second-class.

After storing his suitcase in the luggage van, Reggie boarded the train with only a small hold-all in his hand, containing the essentials for an overnight journey. He freshened up in the tiny bathroom at the end of the carriage, then settled into his compartment, pleased that he was alone. The countryside passed by, lit by the beams of a new moon. Lulled by the rocking of the train, he fell into a deep sleep.

Early the next morning, around half-past seven, the train pulled into Cootamundra railway station. Feeling rather stiff from sitting up all night, Reggie retrieved his baggage. As he was doing so, he was approached by a station assistant.

'Are you Mr da Costa?'

'I am.'

'There's an automobile waiting out the front to take you to the airport. Please be quick. There's only forty-five minutes till take-off.'

'So soon?' Reggie didn't like to admit it, but the prospect of missing a relaxed breakfast at the Cootamundra pub made him feel rather disgruntled. Most inconvenient!

Leaving behind civilisation in the form of the Victorian Italianate red brick station building with its prominent two storey, octagonal tower, the driver followed the dusty roads to the outskirts of the town, before depositing Reggie at the entrance to a large grassy field. And, sitting on the edge of the runway, was a De Havilland single-engine biplane capable of 240 horsepower, more powerful than his beloved Hupmobile in terms of engine capacity, but equally as impressive in appearance. His excitement grew despite the rumbling of his stomach.

Reggie climbed the ladder that was propped up next to the plane and went inside. The De Havilland carried four passengers in an enclosed glazed cabin between the wings, with the pilot to the rear in an open cockpit.

'This is different to my usual mode of travel,' Reggie remarked to his fellow passenger as he took the seat behind him.

'Don't be afraid,' his companion assured him. 'We'll be fine.'

Reggie gazed out of the window, experiencing a strange mixture of exhilaration and anxiety at the prospect of this flying machine's capacity to get off the ground. His attention was taken by the roar of the engine and the flurry of activity out on the tarmac. Behind him, the pilot checked the instrument panel and gave a thumbs-up sign to a member of the ground crew. The chocks were pulled away from the wheels, and the plane rumbled slowly down the runway. They reached the end, the aeroplane turning so that it was facing out towards the expanse of the airfield.

'Here we go!' cried Reggie, gripping the edges of his seat as the engine roared.

The aeroplane gathered pace, speeding down the runway, heading towards a bank of trees marking the end of the airfield. Just when it appeared that they would run out of space, Reggie was thrust back into his seat as the aeroplane lifted off.

'Your first flight?' bellowed his companion who had swivelled around and was observing the loss of colour from Reggie's cheeks.

'Yes,' replied Reggie. 'Loud, isn't it?'

'Not really. This is nothing compared to what it used to be like,' he yelled. 'In the past, you couldn't hold a conversation. It was cold, too.

No pressurisation, so you flew low. No insulation either in those days, only the racket of the metal sheets shaking in the wind.'

The aeroplane stopped climbing and levelled off, sitting above the clouds. The engine noise lessened, becoming a loud, monotonous drone.

Reggie pointed at the khaki jacket the man was wearing, ex-Royal Australian Air Force.

'You flew during the Great War?'

'I was a pilot. RAAF. Crashed, but survived. I was one of the lucky ones.'

'You've flown since?'

'That's right. I was a bit lost after the Armistice. Flying was in the blood. I decided to do what I knew. I managed to buy a Curtiss JN Jenny from the RAAF. Performed at country shows, barnstorming. Took passengers up. I'd bank, do spins and loop-the-loops and barrel rolls and dives.' His eyes were fixed on Reggie's face as he relived his exploits of derring-do. 'You'd see the crowd below you craning their necks for your next manoeuvre. I'd fly low till I could see the whites of their eyes. The passengers loved it. Wonderful it was.'

'Why did you stop?'

He shook his head. 'There was a near miss. It brought back the memories. I couldn't do it anymore. I walked away. Sold the plane to another barnstormer and bought a farm.'

'You like farming?'

'It's alright.' He turned back towards the front and stared out of the window, his interest in talking gone.

Reggie took the hint and looked out at the sea of clouds, the earth far below him. He tried to relax, taking his cue from the nonchalant demeanour of his companion, who didn't seem remotely concerned when the aircraft shuddered and rattled when it struck turbulence.

Less than three hours later, the De Havilland D.H.50 started to descend. A carpet of thick white woolly clouds gave way to wispy threads and blue sky. Flat, dry grasslands were replaced by clumps of gum trees, paddocks of wheat, and flocks of sheep. The occasional farmhouse and small dam dotted the landscape, whilst mile upon mile of fencing stretched as far as the eye could see. An idyllic setting for sure.

Looking down on the Australian outback, Reggie conjured up a different vision for himself. No longer the hard-nosed investigator, the city-dwelling crime reporter for *The Argus*, Reggie had become the archetypal frontiersman, the man of the land, rather like Tom Mix in *Lone Star Ranger*, riding off into the sunset with his true love, Ruby, perched in front of him on the saddle.

The aeroplane dipped and flew low over the outlying fields of the township of Hay. The vision faded. Reggie frowned; reality was intruding. Country life? Living in the outback? Riding horses? Chopping wood? What about the dust, the sweat, the flies, the lack of a good tailor, the distance from cinemas, restaurants, and clubs, and the horror of the Hupmobile navigating potholes in the unmade roads? How could he ever consider living in a place so far from civilisation? He shook his head. Not for him country life.

The aeroplane touched down and coasted to a stop on the runway, not far from a large hangar. The ladder was positioned against the side of the plane, the door was opened, and Reggie and his companion exited the aircraft.

Reggie tipped his hat to the other passenger. 'Are you going on to Melbourne?'

'No,' he replied. 'I'm taking the next plane to Adelaide. Off to see the parents. Enjoy your flight. You're an old hand now.'

The drive into town removed the last vestiges of Reggie's romantic vision of country life. The sun beat down from a cloudless sky, the shimmer of heat haze to the north, while to the south, the great, flat plain of Hay stretched for miles, disappearing into the horizon, with only the low-lying saltbush to break up the monotony.

The town itself offered some relief, with its impressive historic buildings, wide tree-lined main street, and verandahs fronting the shops and hotels. He was deposited at the Terminus Hotel, which proved to be a sanctuary from the flies and the oppressive heat. A good hearty meal compensated him for his lost breakfast, and a glass or two of beer refreshed his dry throat.

By one o'clock, he had boarded the flight to Melbourne, the last leg of the trip. Apart from some turbulence on take-off and a couple of refuelling stops, the journey was relatively uneventful, until a dust storm on the Echuca landing strip delayed the flight for three hours. It came as a relief to see the North Essendon Aerodrome appear beneath them.

Reggie stepped down from the aircraft and unfastened his tie. He was tired, his 'sports suit' was chafing him, and he wanted a shave and a bath. The unscheduled delay in Echuca had ruined his plans for an evening visit to his mother in hospital, which would have to wait till the next morning. Although the flight had been an adventure, and one which he would remember for a long time to come, a plane flight still had a way to go to live up to his idea of luxury travel. The Hupmobile was definitely a superior beast.

Chapter Forty-Five

I t was Wednesday, Dusty's last full day in Sydney. He felt the weight on his shoulders of the importance of this last interview, which would hopefully shine a light on who was responsible for the murders of Dulcie and Jasper Waterson. The previous day he had spoken to another of Reggie's contacts at *The Sydney Morning Herald*, gathering background information on Waterson's incarceration and his early life. Also, he had interviewed a man who had invested his money in a non-existent goldmine in Western Australia, on the advice of Redmond Waters. The Sydney trip had given Dusty a vivid picture of Jasper Waterson's evolution from disadvantaged child to petty crook and on to fully-fledged confidence man.

Over the first few days in Sydney, in close contact with his mentor, Dusty had learned a great deal. He closely observed Reggie's interviewing technique, how he skilfully elicited information and confidences from witnesses, and how he kept the interrogation on track, not allowing them to stray too far from the subject under discussion. And, crucially, how Reggie had known instinctively when to draw the interview to a close. As Reggie said, time was of the essence in a murder investigation.

As they had on Sunday, Dusty strolled down to Circular Quay and bought a ticket for the Manly ferry. Unlike the previous time, the waters of Sydney Harbour were like glass as the boat moved away from the wharf. Over to his right, he could see Mrs Macquarie's Chair, a piece of sandstone rock which had been cut in the shape of a bench by convicts back in 1810, so that the Governor's wife could enjoy sitting and watching ships arriving from Great Britain. Dusty had walked that way himself and had enjoyed the view that it gave of the entrance to the harbour.

Soon Manly beach came into view, its line of Norfolk Pines dominating the horizon. The ferry pulled in at the wharf, lines were secured, and soon the gangplank had been lowered. As he proceeded along the promenade, Dusty thought how enjoyable it would be to holiday along this stretch of beach, bathing in the sea and walking along the sand. He promised himself that one day he would return, when matters of crime were no longer occupying his attention.

He turned into the street before Fairlight House, and soon found the residence of Mrs Relish's close friend, pausing first at the front gate to check that his tie was straight. Although he lacked Reggie's obsession with appearances, he had no wish to disappoint his boss by not making a good impression on the witness.

Mrs Butt's house was not a patch on the scale and elegance of Fairlight House, but it looked to be a comfortable home with its well-tended garden. Built at the turn of the century, it was a single storeyed house built of red brick with a terracotta tiled roof and white trimmed windows. Two chairs were positioned on the front verandah so that their occupants would have a good view of the passing parade of residents and holidaymakers. Next to the front door was a brass plate engraved with the words 'Butt House.'

Dusty took a deep breath and knocked on the door. It was opened by a pleasant-faced woman in her mid-fifties, dressed in a subdued dark blue blouse with a matching skirt. Her grey hair was loosely pulled into a top knot, with tendrils of hair framing her face.

'Mrs Butt? My name is Dusty Rhodes. I'm a reporter with *The Argus* in Melbourne.'

'What do you want?' she asked.

'I was wondering if you might be so kind as to answer some questions regarding a friend of yours, Mrs Relish.'

She blinked. 'Augusta? Can I see some identification, please?'

He gave her his card and waited as she examined it.

'Please, come in.'

Dusty followed her through into a comfortable sitting room and sat on the nearest armchair, his hat on his lap. He glanced around the room, his eyes drawn to the family portrait above the mantelpiece of Mr and Mrs Butt and their five children.

'My husband died last year,' she said, staring up at the painting. 'He was a good man. I miss him. But I'm fortunate to have two sons and three daughters who visit regularly. This house is rarely quiet. The happy sounds of grandchildren.'

'You are fortunate,' commented Dusty, studying the woman. She exuded an air of quiet confidence.

'Why do you want to know about Augusta?' she asked.

'A man was murdered in Melbourne two and a half months ago. Jasper Waterson. He was a confidence man. He went under a variety of names, including Jasper Howard in Melbourne and Redmond Waters in Sydney. We believe that your friend was acquainted with him.'

'What does Augusta have to do with a murder investigation?'

'To be frank, we're not sure. We're following up leads and trying to get some background on the man.'

'What have you learned so far?'

Dusty was surprised by her directness and the ease with which she had turned the interview around so that he was the one being questioned.

'Waterson had a checkered history. We've learned that he was sent to Long Bay Jail for fraud eight years ago. When he escaped, he changed his name and resumed his criminal activities. He was a swindler and blackmailer. In Melbourne, he claimed to be a relative of the Duke of Norfolk. He called himself Jasper Howard. We found that he'd been in Adelaide and Sydney prior to that, so we came to New South Wales to see what we could learn about him. My boss, Reggie da Costa, was called back to Melbourne; otherwise, you would have had the pleasure of meeting one of the finest crime reporters in the State of Victoria.'

'That's glowing praise. You obviously admire him.'

'I'm fortunate to work with him. He's taught me so much.' Dusty cleared his throat. 'I'm getting side-tracked it seems.'

'Perhaps you'd like a cup of tea, Mr Rhodes?'

234

Dusty nodded. 'Thank you, Mrs Butt.'

She went out to the kitchen and soon returned. She poured the tea and offered him milk and sugar. Dusty waited while the woman took a seat near the fireplace.

'You want to know about Augusta? Well, I'll tell you.

'I'm a fair bit older than she, but we were both similar in that we enjoyed the theatre and liked visiting art galleries. Gussie was in her early twenties when she met Mr Relish and married him. They didn't have much in common, I'm afraid to say.'

'Not a love match?' commented Dusty.

'Indeed, no. Gussie was high-spirited whereas her husband was a dour man, not interested in any topic except business. She went her own way, and he went his, with the agreement on her side that she would never embarrass him or break her marriage vows. Gussie wanted children, but when it became apparent that it was not going to happen, she became quite moody and temperamental.

'Two years ago, she was living the high life as the wife of a wealthy property investor. Money didn't bring her happiness, but allowed her to meet talented and interesting people: singers, theatrical folk, artists, and writers. At times, she confided in me that she fantasised about leading another life: where her views and opinions were valued; where someone loved her for herself rather than the social class and connections she had brought to her marriage; where the possibility existed to express herself artistically. I tried to bring her back to earth, but she was a very determined woman.

'And then, she met an Englishman, Redmond Waters, a distant cousin of the 14th Earl of Westmorland.

'It was at a dinner party given by one of her husband's associates. Waters was seated next to her. They chatted about the latest stage productions and motion pictures. She found him to be well-informed about the Arts. He told her that he'd performed in plays at the Apollo and Drury Lane in London. Not as a lead actor, more minor roles.'

'So that she couldn't check playbills or old newspapers for his name,' suggested Dusty.

'How right you are. He was devious,' agreed Mrs Butt. 'He even went so far as to say that he had joined the British Army and fought at The Somme to impress her even more.

'I told her that she should be wary. It seemed like he was too good to be true. It made me suspicious.'

'She took no notice?'

'Unfortunately, no. It was all part of the plan to seduce her.

'By chance, they met up at various events over the next few weeks. At no stage did she consider that something more than serendipity was at work. Their conversations became more intense and personal. They seemed to agree on most subjects, and she found that his opinions mirrored her own. She found herself hoping that she would see him again, and when she did, she wanted to see him more. She was shocked to discover that she was falling in love with Redmond Waters.

'She confessed this to me and said that Waters was the man of her dreams. She'd even written him letters declaring her love for him. However, Gussie was nothing if not pragmatic. She thought that she could have an affair while holding on to the enviable position of being married to a wealthy man. In short, she wanted both. And that meant that she had a lot to lose. And she would pay a lot rather than see that taken from her.'

'What happened?'

'Her husband went away on business for a few days, so she decided to accompany Waters to a discreet hotel up the coast. In short, she threw caution to the wind. If I may be blunt, Mr Rhodes, she put herself in a compromising position.'

'And the trap was sprung.'

'Exactly. A woman pretending to be Redmond Waters' wife entered the hotel room, accompanied by a man who claimed to be her lawyer. There was a heated conversation. The wife threatened to name Gussie as the co-respondent in a divorce case, using her letters as evidence. Gussie protested. She told them that she couldn't afford to be publicly shamed and that her husband would leave her penniless. Not surprisingly, the lawyer suggested that the whole situation would disappear if she paid the wife a considerable sum of money. No one would know anything about it.

'When she told me this, I explained that she was being blackmailed, not only by the so-called wife and her lawyer, but by Redmond Waters, too. Gussie refused to accept it.

'She pawned a bracelet given to her by her husband on their wedding anniversary and handed over £500 to the lawyer, hopeful that the whole sorry episode would be forgotten.'

'But that wasn't the end of it?'

Mrs Butt shook her head. 'Mr Relish saw the bracelet in a pawnbroker's window. You can imagine the scene. She admitted her guilt, thinking her husband would forgive her. She was wrong. Her husband cut her adrift. Her family refused to know her.'

'What did she do?'

'She was still refusing to face reality. She was in love with Waters. She told me that she was going to follow Redmond wherever he went even if it meant moving to another city. But when she tried to contact him, he had gone. The manager of the hotel where he'd been staying told her that he had nothing to show for three months' accommodation and room service, except for a dud cheque.

'That's when she learned the truth. It hit her hard. Stories started to filter back to her. Rumours circulated of other women who had fallen for Waters' smooth tongue, who'd been blackmailed, too. It seemed that her beloved had been busy in other ways as well, his capacious pockets filled by gullible investors. His promises of profits from buying into get-rich-quick schemes were as thin as the cold night air over Sydney Harbour. Cheques bounced. The letter of introduction from the 14th Earl of Westmorland was found to be a forgery. Gussie had to face the awful truth that there was no Redmond Waters.

'In one fell swoop, she lost everything,' added Mrs Butt.

'Do you know where she is now?'

'I received one letter from her. She was staying in a cheap hotel outside the city. She wrote that she was going to flee New South Wales. She couldn't take the whispers anymore. But she never said where she was going, and I haven't heard from her since.'

'That's a terrible story, Mrs Butt,' said Dusty, running his fingers through his hair. 'She was the victim, not the perpetrator. She pays for the wrong done to her. She suffers for the immoral behaviour of the man she loved.'

Mrs Butt looked at him intently. 'You're very different, Mr Rhodes. Most men would blame her for what happened, but it was because she was desperately unhappy.'

Dusty stood and put on his hat. 'Thank you for talking to me, ma'am. One last thing. Would you happen to have a photograph of the lady?'

'There's one in the drawer.' She took out a bunch of photographs and thumbed through them. 'Here she is. You can keep it.' She shook her head. 'Poor Augusta. I wonder what happened to her.'

Chapter Forty-Six

It was the evening that Dr Hiram T Wishbone had waited for since his arrival on the shores of Port Phillip Bay in Melbourne. His Violet Ray Cure-All Miracle Machine was ready for its first public demonstration, to be held in the opulent drawing room of palatial Glenrothes. In attendance were Gladys and Oswald Onions, Edith McGillicutty and her husband, Cyrus, and, of course, Alfred and Mildred Bardsley Smith.

Prior to the arrival of the good doctor, the gentlemen were sampling some of Alfred's best whisky and enjoying it immensely, while the women were catching up on local gossip and news. Edith was showing off her new dimples, courtesy of Dr Wishbone's Delicate Dimpler. She was smiling at every opportunity, which was contrary to her usual facial expression, in an effort to show off the indentations in her cheeks. In truth, the assembled group found the appearance of happiness on Edith's face totally disconcerting, given that Edith had never looked happy in her life.

Gladys Onions adjusted her spectacles. 'They're dints, not dimples, Edith. The marks are still there when you're not smiling.'

'Don't be ridiculous, Gladys,' Edith replied, her thick eyebrows gathering like storm clouds above her dark button eyes. 'I've been wearing Dr Wishbone's device for over three weeks. The results cannot be questioned. Cyrus! Cyrus!' She called out to her husband, who was trying to ignore her. 'Cyrus! I do have dimples, don't I?' Her tone was severe, as unbending as the Delicate Dimpler.

He responded valiantly. 'Of course, my dear. Who am I to argue?'

'That's right. And you would be wise not to.' She turned back to Gladys.

'You see? You're wrong.'

Gladys's voice wavered. 'So sorry. I never meant to question you, Edith. It must have been a trick of the light.'

Edith was in a forgiving mood. 'And how is your indigestion?'

'Thank you for asking. I'm no longer using Dr William's Pink Pills for Pale People. I have a better alternative in Dr Wishbone's Liver Pills. So efficacious.'

'Where's Mavis this evening?' asked Edith. 'Isn't she coming?'

'You haven't heard?' replied Mildred. 'She's in hospital. Apparently, she's extremely unwell. Reggie has been sent for and is *flying* home from Sydney.'

'Flying? My goodness, me. What's wrong with her?'

'A stomach ailment, I believe. I've sent her flowers.'

The butler entered. 'Dr Wishbone is here.' He stepped aside to allow the doctor to pass.

Mr Bardsley Smith put aside his glass and, along with his wife, stepped forward to welcome their guest.

'Thank you, ladies and gentlemen,' replied Dr Wishbone, addressing the group. 'This is a great day, a great day for me! I have the honour of exhibiting the wonders of my miraculous Violet Ray Cure-All Machine, the likes of which the world has never seen.'

'We are honoured,' said Alfred Bardsley Smith, his massive bulk restrained by a silver and cream waistcoat beneath a black frock coat. He tugged at his waxed handlebar moustache. 'Your Electromagnetic Belt has helped me so much. My gout has eased, as well as the back pain I was experiencing. I am indebted to you, sir.'

'I thank you.'

Mr Bardsley Smith was feeling magnanimous, no doubt due to the large amount of whisky he had consumed. 'I would be most interested in investing in your device, as would my friends here. Please tell us what wonders this Violet Ray machine can do.'

Wishbone wiped his glasses with a large checked handkerchief and felt a warm glow pass through him. With Bardsley Smith backing him, the sky was the limit.

'My Violet Ray machine will cure a litany of ills, penetrating every cell in the body, its soothing rays finding the source of the discomfort and bringing immediate relief. My machine will cure hair loss, bumps of the humerus, asthma, blackheads, boils, pimples and bunions, dandruff, catarrh, chilblains, colds, constipation, hay fever, headaches, insomnia, lumbago, eye disease, obesity, pain, paralysis, piles, rheumatism, skin diseases, sprains, and high blood pressure.' He paused for breath.

'It's a miracle,' cried Gladys. 'Oswald, you must invest in it.'

Oswald Onions wasn't committing himself just yet. 'Let's see it demonstrated, my dear, before we decide.'

'Come, Dr Wishbone,' cried the host. 'Let us see this machine in action.'

The doctor scanned his audience. 'Do I have a volunteer?'

A hush fell on the group. Edith pushed her husband forward. 'Cyrus?'

'No, thank you,' he replied, seeking shelter behind his wife.

Bardsley Smith himself stepped forward. 'I'll do it. If the Electromagnetic Belt can cure me, then I am confident that Dr Wishbone's Violet Ray machine will be just as effective, too. It will prove to be yet another marvellous device in his catalogue.'

Wishbone adjusted his glasses, his gaze taking in Bardsley Smith's formidable frame. 'Is there some particular part of your body that needs attention?'

There was an intake of breath from the ladies present, but, fortunately, their concerns dissipated when Alfred replied: 'I have some arthritis in my left hand.'

The doctor threw back the lid of the highly polished oak case. The deep purple velour lining only enhanced the impressiveness of the contents: a set of glass tubes or electrodes in the form of a rake, a bulb, and a rod, respectively, an ozone generator, an electrical cord and plug, and a hand-held wand.

Wishbone removed the bulb-shaped tube and inserted it into the wand. He plugged the cord from the ozone generator into the electrical socket, but did not switch it on.

'Each of the tubes has a particular purpose,' he explained. 'In order to massage Mr Bardsley Smith's hand, I have chosen the bulb.'

While the doctor was addressing his audience, Alfred surreptitiously took a last swig of his glass of whisky and wiped his mouth with the back of his hand. He stepped forward and sat in a chair in the middle of the room, with Dr Wishbone to his left. The group gathered around, watching the demonstration expectantly.

'Do not be afraid, ladies and gentlemen,' Wishbone intoned, taking Bardsley Smith's arm. 'The appliance becomes a high voltage source of static electricity. Its discharge creates a lovely violet colour and a pleasant ozone smell. You will hear a sizzling noise and see sparks flow between the head of the bulb and Mr Bardsley Smith's hand, but it is completely harmless, I assure you. All he will feel is a gentle heat.' He paused for effect. 'I will now turn it on.'

He flicked the switch and placed the bulb in position above the patient's left hand. He turned the dial up. The glass tube started to glow, vivid violet rays swirling through the vacuum. Wishbone moved the device closer to Bardsley Smith's hand. There was a collective gasp from the audience as sparks flew from the head of the bulb to his skin.

'Do not be concerned, ladies and gentlemen; it is static electricity. It will warm the affected area and promote healing.'

Mrs Bardsley Smith was watching her husband closely and was disconcerted to see a look of pain flash across his face.

'What is it, my dear?' she asked.

Before he could answer, Dr Wishbone spoke. 'It is nothing, my dear lady; a slight electric shock, that's all. Completely harmless.' He tightened his grip on the patient's arm. 'Do not pull away, sir. All is well.'

Mr Bardsley Smith's face contorted. The smell of burning flesh filled the air.

Dr Wishbone looked concerned. 'You have not been partaking of alcohol, have you?'

The man gritted his teeth and nodded.

All eyes were on the hand in question. Sparks flew, and flames shot across the skin.

Gladys Onions screamed. Edith covered her eyes, afraid to look. Cyrus McGillicutty reacted immediately, taking matters into his own hands. He grabbed a vase of roses from the table and hurled the water at the patient, drenching him and saturating the Violet Ray Cure-All Miracle Machine. A gigantic crack rent the air as sparks flew. Smoke filled the room. Mr Bardsley Smith slumped forward in his chair.

Dr Wishbone looked aghast at the ruin of his miraculous device, dripping with water. The glass tube had shattered, the violet rays dissipating into the atmosphere.

'What have you done?' he cried. 'You've ruined it. My life's work destroyed.'

He looked from one face to the other, registering the expressions of shock and anger directed at him. Did no one understand that it wasn't his fault?

'It was the alcohol!' he cried as bedlam erupted. 'The alcohol on his hand caught fire.'

To no avail he pled his case, but not a soul was listening. Mrs Bardsley Smith was hysterical, Gladys Onions was screaming, and Edith McGillicutty's dimples were nowhere to be seen as she ran around calling for a doctor. Meanwhile Oswald and Cyrus had picked up the stricken patient and deposited him on the couch.

Cyrus glanced up and saw Wishbone wringing his hands in frustration. 'Get out before I call the coppers,' he said between gritted teeth. 'And take that infernal machine with you.'

The good doctor didn't need to be told twice. He picked up the shattered remains of his miraculous device and threw them into the case, then made a speedy exit through the front door.

* * *

By the time Dr Wishbone had parked his van outside the factory which housed his workshop, he was feeling bruised and battered mentally by the treatment he had received at the hands of the Bardsley Smith clique. This was yet another example of the ignorance that he had fought against all his life. It was not his fault that Bardsley Smith had been drinking heavily and had alcohol on the back of his hand. It was common knowledge that a high-frequency device would create an electrical current and catch on fire if it came into contact with alcohol. Any fool knew that. Why, only last week he had read it in one of the instruction manuals he had purloined.

He turned off the engine and was surprised to see Mr Higgs, the factory owner, waiting for him outside the entrance to the building.

'Dr Wishbone,' he said, approaching him, 'you've had some visitors. They have left a message for you.'

All the doctor wanted was a hefty dose of his medicinal calming tonic and a nap on his makeshift bed, but instead he was facing yet another situation, if the look on the man's face was any indication.

'Well, what is it? What's this message?'

Higgs pointed at the building. 'It's inside. See for yourself. The message is clear.'

Wishbone pushed open the door to his workroom and stopped dead. It looked like a hurricane had hit it. The shelves containing his bottles of medicinal syrups and tonics had been pushed over, with smashed glass and liquid pooling on the floor. Pink pills dotted the bench, some crushed beneath a hammer. Two Electromagnetic Belts had been slashed; the leather cut through to reveal the electrical wires within. Worryingly, there was the pungent smell of acid, which had eaten into assorted pieces of rubber and other materials that he used in the creation of his therapeutic devices.

He groaned as he picked up the beautiful oak box which would have housed the next Violet Ray machine. Someone had used a screwdriver to deface the surface. His chest heaved, his feelings and emotions bubbling up to the surface. He took out his handkerchief to wipe away a tear, then he realised that he was not alone. Mr Higgs was standing in the doorway behind him.

'Who did this?' Wishbone asked, his voice breaking.

'Two blokes in a Daimler. One with cold green eyes and red, cropped hair. The other bloke was stocky with black hair. They asked where you were. I couldn't tell them, luckily for you. When they came out of here the red-haired one came up to me real close and said that it would be better if I didn't call the police.'

'And did you?'

Higgs shook his head. 'You think I'm stupid, Dr Wishbone? Time you packed your bags.'

The good doctor looked at him forlornly and nodded. What with the debacle at the Bardsley Smith home and the destruction of his workshop by a couple of thugs, there appeared to be no future for him in Melbourne.

'Don't bother to clean up,' Higgs added. 'I'll wait for you outside.'

Dr Wishbone knelt down in front of the bench. At least he still had his nest egg locked away in the safe. Six hundred and fifty pounds at last count. He pushed aside the curtain and gulped. The safe door was open, the money gone. A lump formed in his throat. Everything he'd worked for was gone. All he had was the money in his wallet, a mere twenty-five pounds.

When he ventured outside, his suitcase in his hand, the factory owner was waiting. 'There's the little matter of rent. Five pounds six shillings, in fact.'

Wishbone stared at him, aghast.

'And Mr Clegg said that you owe him twelve pounds for the last batch of bottles.'

'But they're smashed on the floor!' he protested.

'That's not Mr Clegg's doing. Perhaps if you hadn't upset someone so badly, you'd still have them.' He held out his hand. 'That will be seventeen pounds and six shillings.'

'I'll have almost nothing left if I pay you. Have some sympathy, Mr Higgs. They took my money, too.' He looked at Higgs pathetically.

The factory owner thought for a moment. 'Give me the van. I can use it for work.'

'The van?'

Wishbone glanced over at his Ford Model T delivery van. 'But it's worth forty-five pounds,' he lamented.

'That's my best offer; otherwise, I'll take the cash.'

Reluctantly, Wishbone handed over the keys.

Higgs eyed the van. 'I'll give Clegg what you owe him, and then, we're all square.'

Dr Wishbone nodded and picked up his suitcase. There was nothing left to say. All his patent medicines, his miraculous devices, and his van were gone.

Chapter Forty-Seven

Mavis da Costa looked around her as she lay in bed at The Melbourne Hospital. The white walls of the room hurt her eyes, her throat was sore, her nose was running, her skin felt itchy, and she had a terrible headache. Added to that, there was a bag of fluid hanging on a hook, with a tube going into her arm. She closed her eyes and fell asleep.

Earlier that morning, she had a short and unsettling visit from the doctor. 'You were unconscious on arrival, Mrs da Costa,' he told her. 'Apparently, you overdosed on your medicine.'

She had looked at him wide-eyed and reacted angrily. 'Overdosed? How dare you? I don't take drugs, doctor.'

'Perhaps it was inadvertent, Mrs da Costa. However, your stomach had to be pumped, and you were badly dehydrated.'

She drew herself up in the bed and glared at him. 'I am a respectable woman. My best friend is Mildred Bardsley Smith and she lives at Glenrothes, in Brighton.' As she spoke, she could feel another headache developing. 'Where is Reggie? Where is my son?'

'We believe that he is arriving from Sydney this evening. No doubt he'll visit you as soon as possible.'

She shook her head in disbelief, making her head feel worse. 'Sydney? Reggie doesn't live in Sydney. I want to see the head doctor. I want to speak to someone–'

Her eyes closed, and she started to snore.

* * *

When she awoke, Reggie was sitting at her bedside. She reached out and touched his face.

'My dear boy. You're here.'

'I've been here most of the day, Mother. How are you?'

'I feel so strange. I seem to have some sort of sleeping sickness.'

'I came as soon as I could. I flew down from Sydney to see you.'

'Sydney? But you work in Melbourne.'

'I was investigating a murder, but I'm back now.'

Mavis gripped his hand and leaned in close. 'The doctors are mad. They're saying shocking things to me. You must speak to the man in charge.' She licked her lips. 'I'm thirsty.'

Reggie lifted a cup to her mouth. 'Drink this.'

'Get me out of here, sweet boy. I need to go home.'

'Listen carefully, Mother. I'm going to say it slowly.' He paused. 'You've become addicted to morphine.' She stared at him aghast. 'You have been taking a medicine–a syrup–that is supposed to help you sleep.'

'That's right. Dr Wishbone's Restorative Syrup.'

'Mother, it's full of morphine and alcohol.'

Mavis looked up at him and put her hand to her mouth. 'What?' She could feel the headache returning. 'No, no. Dr Wishbone doesn't sell drugs.'

Reggie leaned closer. 'He does. The trouble is that you had no idea what you were taking, and every sip made you want more. The doctor has been explaining it to me.' He stroked her hair. 'You were in a terrible condition when you got here.'

She lay back against the pillows and stared at the ceiling. What was he telling her? Dr Wishbone selling drugs? What would the Bardsley Smiths say?

Reggie's soothing voice broke into her thoughts. 'It will be alright, Mother. They will look after you here.' He kissed her on the forehead. 'Ruby's been waiting outside to see you. I'll bring her in.'

Mavis rallied. '*That* woman?'

Reggie looked her squarely in the eye. '*That* woman saved your life. She found you and had you brought to the hospital. And now, you're going to thank her.'

Mavis took a moment or so to take in what Reggie was saying. But one look at his face and the tone of his voice were enough to convince her that he was deadly serious, and there was no way she could refuse. She took a deep breath. 'Could you get me my dressing gown and hair brush, please?'

* * *

Five minutes later, Reggie re-entered the room, holding Ruby's hand.

'How are you, Mrs da Costa?' Ruby ventured, sitting next to the bed.

'Better, thank you.' She paused, collecting her thoughts. 'I don't understand any of this. Reggie tells me that you found me. I can't remember any of it.'

'Do you want me to tell you?'

'That would help, yes.'

'I tried to telephone you on Sunday, but you didn't answer.'

'What day is it today?'

'It's Tuesday evening.'

'Tuesday?'

'That's right. You've been here two days. As I was saying, I decided to drive around when you didn't answer and found you in bed. You were unconscious. I tried to rouse you, but I couldn't, so I rang for an ambulance.'

'And they brought me here.'

'Not quite. Let's just say that some of my friends helped me with that.'

Reggie broke in. 'Ruby gave the doctor the medicine that you've been taking. He had it analysed. There were significant amounts of alcohol and morphine in it.'

Mavis shook her head. 'I'm not a drug addict, I really am not,' she pleaded.

Ruby reached out and patted her hand. 'No one believes that.'

'I've been investigating patent medicines, Mother,' said Reggie, leaning down towards her. 'You've been taking one of the harmful ones.'

Mavis looked at him, her eyes filling with tears. 'I can't believe that. Dr Wishbone was a medical doctor, not one of those 'snake-oil salesmen' you wrote about.'

Reggie shook his head. 'Unfortunately, he is. He's a charlatan. He puts things in his medicines that shouldn't be there. Alcohol. Morphine. Cocaine. Tar. None of it is listed on the label.'

'You're not the only one who has suffered at his hands,' said Ruby. 'You haven't heard what happened at the Bardsley Smiths, have you?' Mavis shook her head, her eyes wide. 'Dr Wishbone almost electrocuted Mr Bardsley Smith with his Violet Ray machine. He's being treated for burns.'

'Oh, my goodness!' cried Mavis. She sat forward, her hand to her mouth. 'Will he be alright?'

'He will. The police have tracked down where Dr Wishbone was living. He seems to have disappeared without a trace.'

Mavis lay back against the pillows. 'There's so much to take in. I don't know where to start.'

Ruby took her hand. 'You've been through a lot, Mrs da Costa. You need to rest.'

'Reggie says that you saved me.'

'The doctors saved you, not me.'

Reggie shook his head. 'If Ruby hadn't found you–'

'Madame Esmeralda predicted it,' Mavis said, her froth of curls nodding with conviction. 'She told me that I would be in great danger. She said, "A woman will save you. It will be someone you least expect." And that was you.' Mavis's face was heavy with sadness as she stared at Ruby. 'I wish that I'd been kinder to you.'

Reggie hid his surprise at the mention of the fortune-teller's name. It seemed that his mother had placed her trust in more than one charlatan.

Mavis turned to her son. 'What will happen to me now?'

'You'll be here a little longer till you're feeling better,' he said. 'There's a nice place that you can go to after this. The hospital will arrange it. You can stay there for a few weeks, and they will help you get over your...problem.'

Mavis's innocent eyes widened. 'My...problem?'

CHAPTER FORTY-SEVEN

'Yes, Mother.'

The poor woman looked exhausted. She closed her eyes as a tear ran down her cheek.

'I'll see you tomorrow.' Reggie kissed her forehead. 'You need to rest. It's been a difficult time for you.'

As Reggie and Ruby stood to leave, hand in hand, they heard her whisper, 'My…problem.'

* * *

During the drive home, in Dusty's Australian Six, Reggie and Ruby were silent at first, contemplating the difficult road ahead for Mavis as she struggled to deal with her addiction.

'She'll take some time to recover,' said Ruby at last. 'She put a lot of faith in Dr Wishbone, and that's shaken her, knowing that the man who pretended to care about her health was not whom he claimed to be.'

'And to think that she knew Madame Esmeralda, too.'

'That was a shock,' agreed Ruby. 'Strange that she predicted your mother's close call with death.'

'Foretelling the future is like throwing a dart at a dartboard. Occasionally, you'll hit the bullseye.'

'I suppose so, but it's still quite a coincidence, isn't it? Speaking of coincidences, I'm amazed that I picked the right time to drive past your home. A few minutes before or after, and I would never have seen your Hupmobile.'

Reggie shuddered visibly. 'To think that it might have fallen victim to a welder's torch. I don't think I'll ever forget that conversation when you collected me from the airport.'

'You recovered when I assured you that Detective Sergeant Blain had rescued the Hupmobile from the clutches of the gang.'

'The thought of my forest green beauty converted into some run-of-the-mill automobile!' he cried, beads of perspiration breaking out on his brow. 'Perhaps painted a drab black. Perhaps joined to the back end of a Ford!'

251

He reached over and touched Ruby's hand as she drove.

'You saved my automobile and my mother. You're a wonderful woman.'

'Have you spoken to Detective Sergeant Blain?'

'I did, this morning. He needs the Hupmobile as evidence, he says, but he'll have it back to me by the weekend.'

Ruby glanced his way. 'In the meantime, why don't you borrow this one until Dusty comes back. I don't need it, and I'm sure that he won't mind. As long as you agree to take me out for dinner tomorrow night.'

Reggie chuckled. 'Of course.' He ran his eyes over the upholstery and the dashboard. 'It's a good car. I'd prefer that it was another colour than tan. That shade doesn't match any of my suits, but it will do. When I get the Hupmobile back, we'll drive to a jeweller and buy you that engagement ring.'

Ruby nearly let go of the steering wheel. 'Are you sure, Reggie? You really want to marry me?'

'More certain of that than anything else in my life.'

They fell silent as they travelled down Hoddle Street, heading for Richmond, both occupied with thoughts of a future together. The roads were empty, a light rain falling, reflecting the glow of the automobile's lights on the wet surface.

'Swan Street or Tanner Street?' asked Ruby. 'I could cook you something.'

'It's late and I'm exhausted. Could you drop me off at home, if you don't mind?'

She nodded and did the turn into Swan Street. 'When are you expecting Dusty back?'

'Friday, I think. I'll need to catch up with the Melbourne crime scene in the meantime and update my files on the Howard and Smith murders. I can't wait to see what Dusty has found out. Hopefully, the interviews went well.'

'You're closer to solving the murders?'

'I believe so. One final piece of evidence is all I need.' He stared out of the windscreen, his mind back in Sydney. 'It came to me in the hotel room of The Hero. It's funny how things fit together when you let your mind drift.

You're thinking about other things, and the answer comes to you out of the blue. Like a jigsaw puzzle when the last piece falls into place.'

'What's this piece of evidence that you're hoping for?'

'A photograph. I hope that Dusty was able to get it.'

'Who's in the picture?'

'What, you want to know who the murderer is?' He looked at her and smiled. 'There would be nothing that would give me greater pleasure than to reveal their identity, but I need to be sure.'

They pulled up outside the grocer's shop. Ruby cocked her head to one side. 'Nothing would give you greater pleasure?'

Reggie smirked. 'There is one little thing. Maybe one little kiss.'

Chapter Forty-Eight

Spring Street in Melbourne was home to two illustrious buildings: Parliament House adjoining the Treasury Gardens and The Hotel Windsor opposite, impressive with its two towers giving views across to Mount Macedon. It was the latter which drew Reggie da Costa and his young associate, Dusty Rhodes, the following Saturday morning, with the purpose of tying up the loose ends to the murders of Jasper Howard and Dulcie Smith. To celebrate the occasion, Reggie had donned his most recent acquisition: a smart navy and cream striped double-breasted suit, with a red and cream floral tie, topped off with a new cream fedora.

'You want to revisit the scene of Howard's murder?' asked Dusty, still in the dark as to the identity of the murderer.

'Indeed, I do,' replied Reggie. 'It's important to see where the murder took place, and how it was executed, if we are to expose the killer. At the time, I didn't recognise a vital piece of evidence when it was in front of me. It's a lesson for both of us. Don't let one small detail escape your attention. It was in Sydney that the penny dropped. If only I had seen it sooner.'

'Does that mean that the trip was a waste of time?'

'Not at all. We filled in the background to the Watersons which we could not have done if we'd stayed in Melbourne. And it's provided us with incontrovertible proof as to the identity of the murderer.'

'The photograph?'

Reggie nodded. 'The photograph.'

Dusty parked his automobile outside the entrance and accompanied his boss into the hotel lobby. The concierge stepped forward. 'Can I help you, sir?'

'I think not, Mr Grimes,' replied Reggie. 'We're here to solve a murder.'

He took the steps of the Grand Staircase two at a time, Dusty in hot pursuit, until he reached the second floor. They proceeded down the corridor until they reached Room 206.

'The scene of the crime,' observed Dusty.

Reggie turned the handle and pushed the door open. 'How fortunate,' he said. 'The room has been cleaned.'

He turned to Dusty. 'What do you notice?'

A voice came from behind them. 'Can I be of assistance, sir?' It was Rose, the maid. She took a good look at Reggie and smiled. 'It's you, sir, from the Coroner's Office. Are you back again about the murder?'

'That's right. This is my assistant, Mr Rhodes. I have a couple of questions for you, Rose, if you don't mind.'

'Not at all, sir.'

'Is Molly here, too?'

'She's in the next room. I'll get her.'

Rose soon returned, with Molly in tow.

'Mr Rhodes hasn't met you both before, so let me explain the situation to him.'

They stood meekly, listening to Reggie sketch the scene for his assistant.

'It was Saturday, the 29th of August, the day of the murder. Rose was doing the first floor while Molly cleaned this floor. Around five o'clock, Molly knocked on Howard's door. She was supposed to turn down the bed. She heard voices coming from inside. We assume that was Mrs Plumstead.

'Mr Howard told you not to bother. That's right, isn't it, Molly?'

'Yes, sir. They were arguing, sir.'

'You went away?'

'That's right.'

'Did you go back?'

'No sir, I didn't.'

'You didn't see Mr Howard at all that night?'

Molly shook her head.

'The next morning, around eleven o'clock, you knock on the door. It's locked. You call out, but there's no answer. You use your master key and go inside. It's dark. The curtains are drawn.'

'Mr Howard was an early riser,' said Molly. 'I thought that he'd gone out for the day.'

'But he hasn't. You switch on the light, and you see him, covered in blood. He's dead on the bed. Is that right?'

Molly nodded. She had gone pale. Her hands were shaking.

Reggie turned to Rose. 'You've made up the room this morning. Is that correct?'

'Yes, sir.'

'And you've left fresh towels on top of the chest of drawers?'

'That's what we do every morning.'

'Not at night?'

'No, sir.'

'If that's the case, why were there towels on top of the chest of drawers the morning that I inspected the room? The morning that Howard's body was found.'

Rose shook her head. 'That's strange. I don't know. Do you, Molly?'

Reggie leaned forward, pointing his finger at the maid. 'You know why, don't you, Molly?'

The maid let out a strangled cry.

'You've upset her, sir,' Rose protested. 'She wasn't herself after she found him. You're bringing it all back.'

'If she wasn't herself at that time, who was she?' asked Reggie. He pulled out the photograph and put it in front of Molly's face. 'Who was it, Gussie? Was it you who killed Mr Howard?'

It wasn't difficult to see the woman of two years ago despite the changes that her employment had wrought, now that she was no longer leading a pampered existence. Her curly hair had been cut short to fit beneath the maid's cap, her body thinner and more muscular, her hands coarse from manual labour, but the photograph was of her.

Tears gathered in Augusta Relish's eyes. 'It was me.'

Rose looked from one person to another, seeking answers. 'Are you saying...that *Molly* murdered Mr Howard?'

The concierge had finally caught up with Reggie. 'Excuse me, sir–'

'Good timing, Mr Grimes. I'd be obliged if you would telephone Detective Sergeant Clary Blain of the Criminal Investigation Branch and ask him to come here immediately. Tell him that we have the murderer of Jasper Howard and Dulcie Smith waiting for him.'

While they were waiting for the arrival of the police, Reggie indicated for Molly to sit down. He pulled a chair up next to her.

'You were used badly by Mr Howard, weren't you? He ruined your life. He broke up your marriage. Your family wanted nothing to do with you.'

'You know all about me?'

'I do. I've spoken to your former husband. My colleague here interviewed your friend, Mrs Butt. We know what happened from their point of view. Perhaps it's time for you to give your account.'

Augusta Relish wiped her eyes. 'Why not? It will be a relief to tell my story.' She took a deep breath, collecting her thoughts.

'When I was young, I dreamed of being an actress or an artist, but that came to a stop when Archibald proposed to me. He was much older than me, but he offered me a good life, and my parents were keen. I came from a wealthy family, which is all that mattered to him.

'I was very unhappy in my marriage. From the outside, it looked like I had it all, but I was lonely, and my husband was preoccupied with his business. He didn't love me, although I didn't know that at the time.

'I was on my own a lot, although I had a couple of close friends that I confided in. I went to exhibition openings, the theatre, mixed with an artistic crowd, and lived my life through them. Things became worse when I realised that there would be no children. I was locked into a loveless marriage with no way out.'

'And then, you met Jasper Howard,' said Reggie.

She pulled off her maid's cap and ran her hand through her hair. 'Redmond Waters, he called himself. A cousin of the 14th Earl of Westmorland.' She gave a hollow laugh. 'Tall, handsome, English. I fell for his stories. Even the one where he was awarded a medal for gallantry in the war.

'I didn't realise that he was a fake. He fed me bits and pieces; he seemed reluctant to praise himself; he was modest, even self-effacing. I found it refreshing after the arrogance and bragging my husband indulged in.'

'You fell in love.'

'That's right. I put myself in a compromising position, and I have no excuse for that. It was my fault. When that woman burst into the room, I truly believed that I had been found out. His so-called wife.'

'Dulcie Waterson, alias Dulcie Smith. She was his sister.'

Augusta looked surprised. 'I didn't know that. I paid the blackmail, but then, everything fell apart. My husband discovered the truth. The diamond bracelet in the pawnbroker's window. My family wanted nothing to do with me. Archibald wanted a divorce. I was ruined.'

'You left Sydney?'

'Only after I found out about Redmond. That he was a confidence man who had been blackmailing other women and swindling their husbands.'

'Why did you come to Melbourne?' asked Reggie.

'It's a big city. There would be plenty of work, and I could lose myself here. No one would know me.'

'You got a job as a maid at The Hotel Windsor?'

'Actually, no. I found work first as a waitress with a catering company. I discovered that I was not qualified to do anything, but that or cleaning.

'It was the night of the Mayoral Ball at the Exhibition Buildings. I was carrying a tray of hors d'oeuvres, offering them to the guests. It was his voice that I recognised first, his words oozing like honey from his tongue. That English accent, that deep manly register that I once found so attractive.' She sniffed. 'His hair was darker, surprisingly; he was a little heavier; he'd lost the beard. If it weren't for the voice, I never would have guessed. Two years had passed. Two years of degrading manual labour. Two years of loathing myself and the man who had done this to me. And there he was.'

'You weren't afraid that he'd recognise you?'

'I doubt that Redmond would have taken more than a fleeting look at the hired help. I came up beside him, almost daring him to recognise me, but his eyes slid down to the delicacies balanced on my tray. Anyway, he was engaged in his usual occupation: charming the ladies.

'I stood there. "Something to eat? Sir? Madam?" My voice nearly failed me.

'He took a devilled egg and popped it in his mouth and turned his back on me. And that was the extent of my interaction with the man I once loved.'

'How did you find out where he was staying?'

'I asked one of the other waitresses. She told me that he was Jasper Fitzalan Howard, cousin of the Duke of Norfolk. If I hadn't been so angry, I would have laughed out loud. She actually told me that he was out of my class. If only she knew! And then, she mentioned that he was staying at The Hotel Windsor.

'I walked back into the kitchen. It was as if my past had come crashing back, a past that I'd tried to put behind me. But this time, I had a name and address. Redmond Waters had become Jasper Howard. Residing at The Hotel Windsor. Revenge would be sweet, I thought.'

'You took a job at The Windsor, and you waited for an opportunity.'

'That's right. I had myself assigned to the second floor where he was staying. One evening, about a week later, I knocked on his door. I was ready. I'd hidden a knife amongst the cleaning products and towels on the trolley. I had a spare maid's uniform in a bag, ready to change into once I'd done it. But he told me to go away. I was disappointed, but I heard raised voices, and I knew he had a lady in there. When she'd gone, I knocked again, and he told me to come in. He was looking out the window. I put the towels on the chest of drawers. I took out the knife and stabbed him in the back. He turned around and stared at me in shock. I don't think that he'd comprehended what had happened.

'I think I said something to him like, "Hello Redmond, remember me?" I saw the look of recognition on his face, and strangely, he smiled at me. He raised his hands to fend me off, but I came at him and stabbed him again and again. He fell back against the bed, and I watched him die.'

'What about the tarot card?'

Augusta smirked. 'That was a nice touch. I was about to get changed when

I noticed it on the bedside table. A corpse lying face down with ten swords sticking out of its body. How appropriate. I stabbed him a couple more times for good measure, rolled him over onto his stomach, and put the card in his hand. I put my bloody clothing in the bag and wheeled the trolley out of there. Nobody was any the wiser.'

Reggie nodded. 'The visit of Mrs Plumstead worked in your favour, too. The police suspected her rather than the staff.'

'That's true.'

'And the empty safe?'

Augusta Relish looked at him defiantly. 'He owed me. It was open, so I took everything he had, just as he'd done to me.'

'With all that money, why didn't you quit?'

'I was planning to, once the police investigation was finished.'

Dusty was sitting in a corner, taking notes. 'What about Dulcie Smith? How did you know that she was at The Menzies?'

'Simple. When I started at The Windsor, I saw her in the corridor talking to Redmond. I recognised her. The outraged wife. When she left the morning after the murder, I was afraid that I'd lost my chance. I went down to the front entrance and asked the taxi driver if he'd taken anyone that morning. He said that he'd taken Miss Smith to The Menzies.'

'You murdered her, too?'

She turned to him, smirking. 'It's easy to dress up as a maid. I came in the staff entrance. No one takes any notice of you.'

'Why the tarot card again?'

'I thought it would put the police off the scent if I left the Ten of Swords on her body. No one would think it was me.'

Reggie nodded. 'No one takes any notice of the maid. That was the crucial clue to solving this crime. It came to me when I was in my hotel room in Sydney. The maid came in to change the towels. Not in the evening, but in the morning. Like Rose said before. I thought about the towels on the chest of drawers, and I realised that you'd been in there in the evening. In Room 206 at The Hotel Windsor. And Waterson wouldn't have suspected a thing. It was only the maid changing the towels.'

CHAPTER FORTY-EIGHT

'Don't you feel any sort of remorse for what you've done?' Dusty asked her.

Augusta pulled a face. 'I'm not sorry. Why should I be after what they did to me?'

She looked up as Detective Sergeant Clary Blain entered the room, a constable behind him. 'I'm ready now, sir. You can take me away. I don't care what you do to me. I'm content.'

Reggie and Dusty watched as she stood, erect and dignified, while the constable put handcuffs on her.

Clary Blain studied Reggie. 'No doubt you got the whole story.'

'No doubt, Clary.'

The detective took Augusta Relish's arm. 'You're under arrest for murder.' Then he turned back and nodded at Reggie. 'Thanks, mate. I'll see you at The Duke, Monday, at four o'clock. The first one's on me.'

Chapter Forty-Nine

LIES AND DECEPTION
THE DEATH OF A CONFIDENCE MAN

By REGGIE DA COSTA, Senior Crime Reporter

Truth is stranger than fiction.

Never in the annals of crime has such a strange story of love, lust, murder, and revenge come across the crime desk of this Melbourne newspaper. It all began with the murder of Jasper Fitzalan Howard, the cousin of the Duke of Norfolk, a cultured English gentleman with letters of introduction to the elegant drawing rooms of Melbourne society, where he was welcomed with open arms. But good people were deceived and fell victim to the web of lies and deception that he wove. Women fell for his charms only to be blackmailed; trusting investors were swindled out of thousands of pounds; gullible salesmen were defrauded.

Mr Howard was none other than Jasper Waterson, an escaped convict from the slums of Sydney, who partnered with his sister, Dulcie, to become accepted amongst society's elite. Using fake identities and the money acquired through their criminal activities, the Watersons deceived and bamboozled their innocent victims, leaving a trail of broken hearts and broken marriages, dud cheques, empty bank accounts, and trusting souls who will never trust again.

A woman bent on revenge!

Two years ago in Sydney, Waterson chose the wrong woman to blackmail when he met Mrs Augusta Relish, the wife of a wealthy businessman. In August this year, she took her revenge on the man who ruined her. Employed as a maid at The Hotel Windsor, she bluffed her way into Room 206 where Jasper Waterson was staying. Clutching a knife, she stabbed him ten times, leaving him bloodied and dying, then made her escape. In a bizarre twist, the manner of his death resembled the appearance of the tarot card that he clutched in his hand: the Ten of Swords, which portrays a corpse lying face down with ten swords protruding from its body.

Shortly after, Mrs Relish murdered Jasper Waterson's sister and partner-in-crime, Dulcie Smith, at the Menzies Hotel.

The police were baffled. Multiple suspects were questioned and released.

Ultimately, it was the investigation carried out by *The Argus*'s crime reporters, Reggie da Costa and Dusty Rhodes, that provided the true identities of the dead man and woman, as well as the final clue as to the killer.

Mrs Relish has now been charged with murder and will plead guilty. However, it has been reported that she will plead for clemency on the grounds that Jasper Waterson ruined her marriage and exposed her to public humiliation, leaving her destitute.

Waterson's victims can rest easy in the knowledge that this predator will never again ruin lives, destroy reputations, or take advantage of people's trust.

This case is now closed.

[*The Argus* November 16, 1925]

Epilogue

Dr Hiram T Wishbone stood on the deck of the Union Line steamer *Manuka* as the ship braved the tempestuous and swirling waters of The Rip, leaving behind the city of Melbourne and Port Phillip Bay. To his left was the quarantine station and military fortifications of Point Nepean, whilst on the other side of The Heads was the seaside town of Point Lonsdale, with its elegant lighthouse. The wind was howling as he held onto his hat, the lone passenger prepared to brave the elements to bid farewell to Australia.

The good doctor was feeling mellow as he considered that yet another country was lost to him. He had hoped to make his fortune in Victoria, but the change in laws had closed that door, as well as the unfortunate incidents relating to the Bardsley Smiths and their Brighton coterie. It was a sad fact, he thought, that Australians, and also the English, were sadly out of step with the technological advances possible in the twentieth century. They tended to be critical of innovation and loath to forgive the small stumble or misstep that was part and parcel of developing a life-changing medical device or potion.

Wishbone had considered going home but had ruled that option out. A return to the United States of America would require that he sleep with one eye open to avoid detection by the authorities, who were seeking to arrest him on outstanding warrants. He could conceivably change his identity, but the fact was that he'd grown rather attached to his 'Dr Hiram T Wishbone' persona.

He needed a new country where he could begin again. And the strong wind blowing off Bass Strait put him in mind of a new device. 'Oxygenised air,' he would call it. A cure for catarrh, scrofula, consumption, and respiratory tract infections. Why not lung disease, too?

'The world is my oyster,' he said, raising his arms to embrace the future.

The ship blew its horn. Dr Hiram T Wishbone looked up at the sky as seagulls looped overhead. A new beginning and a new country awaited him, one that would surely appreciate his talents and embrace his remedies: the Land of the Long White Cloud. New Zealand.

A Note from the Author

I have retained Australian spelling, punctuation and word usage, where possible.

Acknowledgements

Writers Victoria has been instrumental in my development as a writer. Dr Kate Ryan's editing skills helped me polish the manuscript and prepare it for publication. Thanks also to Angela, my designer daughter, for creating the location map. Talented girl!

Researching the historical and social background to this book has been aided by the National Library of Australia's research portal, *Trove*, using their digitised newspapers from the past. In particular, I drew on reports in *The Argus* about the confidence men and women who preyed on the innocent and unwary.

My sincere thanks must go to the Dames of Detection—Verena Rose and Shawn Reilly Simmons—of Level Best Books, for their continued faith in me as an author. I also wish to acknowledge the part that Harriette Sackler, formerly my primary editor, had in giving me the opportunity to be a published author. I have enjoyed the support and advice offered by my 'Level Besties'.

My love and gratitude go to my two children, Trevor and Angela, and their partners, Lauren and Sam, for their support and encouragement. My grandchildren, Ellie and Maddie, give added joy to my life. Thanks also to my friends and those members of my family who have shown a keen interest in my writing, as well as my golfing buddies at the Victoria Golf Club.

Kate Becker, from Thesaurus Booksellers, Brighton, has accompanied me to many of my author events. Thanks, Kate! The support of Cheryl and Andrew, of Beaumaris Books, has been most appreciated also.

Finally, where would I be without Bob, my beloved husband, who has encouraged me throughout my writing career, reading and re-reading my manuscripts and offering advice and encouragement. Thanks, sweetheart.

About the Author

Laraine Stephens lives in Beaumaris, a bayside suburb of Melbourne, Australia. With an Arts degree from the University of Melbourne, a Diploma of Education and a Graduate Diploma in Librarianship, she worked in secondary schools as a Head of Library. On retirement, Laraine turned her hand to the craft of crime writing.

SOCIAL MEDIA HANDLES:
   Laraine Stephens | Facebook

AUTHOR WEBSITE:
   https://larainestephens.com

Also by Laraine Stephens

The Death Mask Murders: A Reggie da Costa Mystery

Deadly Intent: A Reggie da Costa Mystery

A Deadly Game: A Reggie da Costa Mystery